Nomad's Land

Susan Kathleen

deus ex machina
Chicago, IL

Outskirts Press, Inc.
Denver, Colorado

Outskirts Press
http://www.outskirtspress.com

ISBN-10: 1-59800-818-8
ISBN-13: 978-1-59800-818-0

Library of Congress Control Number: 2006931323

For Blue Penn and NFN

Rah-Rah & Z-Z

Acknowledgements

Words cannot begin to express the buckets of thanks I owe to members of the higher education community who have come in and out of my eccentric life. For introducing me to African-American Feminist Literature and Zora Neale Hurston was Professor Maire Mullins. Doctor Gus Kolich lead the march of believers in not only my writing, but myself. Others have attempted to teach me Chaucer, Hawthorne, Yeats and Joyce, and each hold a special place in the file cabinet of literature in my mind.

At Outskirts, Krista, my artist representative, was calm and collected throughout the process which led me to believe she either enjoyed the book or was an expert when dealing with neurotic insomniacs. For this and for holding my mouse, I thank you. Arlene, my editor and Joyce, the guru of the music business are also top notch in my eyes.

A few businesses have silently aided in the tedious journey, such as Carmex, Neutrogena, Swedish Fish, *The Enquirer* and *World Weekly News* and *The Onion* newspapers, Bath and Body Works, Oriental Trading Company, Alpha Books and their *Idiot's Guide* to everything, Tobasco, Volkswagen, HBO, Old Navy, Claussen Pickles, Mandalay Bay in Las Vegas, and

Palermo's Pizza. The hippie incense-turned-perfume, Nag Champa, and the store that sells it, Patchouli Garden in Park Falls, Wisconsin, is a supporter and always went out of their way to keep the shelf filled with my favorite products.

Computer master, Tony, went above and beyond. Without him, none of this would exist—my computer really DID die—the kind of death you only whisper about around a campfire. If you are reading this right now, thank him.

A lifesaver in my countdown to death, literally, is Dr. Vlad Badescu. He knows why and I thank the world for doctor-patient confidentiality.

Bettina, Catherine, Coleen, Laura, MaryAnne, Tina, Elvis, Fritz, and EJ all deserve a gold medal for putting up with my need for *constant positive feedback* and willingness to read and reread chapter after chapter.

Raise a glass to my fifth grade teacher who tore apart my first attempt at a short story—she ruined me for life. Accolades also go to my high school counselor who suggested I attend trade school in lieu of college, and highest honors to the numerous undergraduate professors who did not appreciate my creative flair in assignments or Blue Books. They somehow managed to overlook a term paper-selling business I ran out of my dorm room. To this day, my handcrafted papers continue to spread at many universities on various subjects and enlighten future generations who decided they didn't want to bother with homework. Good for you!

Magicians Penn Jillette & Teller gave my mind a jump-start when I hit a dead end. Although this novel is dedicated to you, I still want to give thanks—especially to Teller, for your amazing underwater abilities to make a submarine and writers block disappear before my very weary eyes. (Penn, the ear thing is bullshit). Thank you for reminding me of the First Ammendment, and every "cuss" word is dedicated to you. Most important, thank you for unlocking my mind. Where exactly do you hide *that* key?

One of the most prolific artists of the late 20th century, Tony Fitzpatrick, deserves a lifetime of thanks for the cover art. The guy called me a nut, read a few sample chapters and then handpicked the piece and shared it with this budding writer.

My pessimist, deadbeat brother and best girlfriend, Neil, warrants a kick in the ass. But if it wasn't for his drivel about my exaggerated talent, insistence to continue and groans about his meaningless existence and need for my success to support him, I would still be sitting on the couch watching Lifetime Television Network. So, thanks, I guess.

A special thanks goes to my team Wisconsin: Grandpa, Margie, Jane, John, Candace, Katie, Molly, Brit and Chels. They were excited for me and believed in what I was doing.

Carl played an important part in the process by ignoring my off-the-wall habits. He always carries a pen and paper for surprise attack brainstorms. He also doesn't seem to mind cooking and cleaning, which is great for me, "the wife." But most important, he loves me. He believed in me when I didn't—I still don't. Also, thanks for keeping an eye on my babies, Dogaloo and Munchie, the smartest and smelliest dogs in the hemisphere. It was their tail-wagging, leg-kicking, parading and cold wet noses that got me through some rough nights. Each deserves an extra dash of flavor in their dinner.

Finally, thanks needs to be given to the woman who has given me a continuous stream of love, understanding and wake-up calls: my mother. I know this is as far as she will read of this book and I thank her for pushing me farther than I thought I could go. I have put her on a non-stop bus ride to hell and back more than a few times. She understood my dramas—how she puts up with me is anyone's guess. The finish line is here and I would never have made it without you.

So, without further eloquence, let the "nascent writing career" begin...

Susan Kathleen
October 2006

*I'm just sitting here watching the wheels go round and round;
I really love to watch them roll.*

Watching the Wheels
—John Lennon

ZVP 731

So many cars; so many door handles. But never a way out.

A woman's place is in the home; barefoot and pregnant; in the kitchen cookin' vittles or TV Dinners; tendin' to the kids. Her car is practical. She rarely wonders about the highway mileage or various oil changes—car maintenance is one of the few tasks in life reserved for men. No, the *good* woman was put on this earth to question nothing more than the color of the carpeting against his Lay-Z-Boy (a leftover from god-knows when) that he will possess until his death which will inevitably occur in his sleep on this very chair; adjust the mirrors, and make sure the vehicle can fit a baby seat(s), the groceries and an occasional soccer team. Welcome to the 1990s frame of mind.

What, then, does a guy drive? Since it is discussed in the close confines of locker rooms and designed solely to attract stray pussy, it is surprisingly common knowledge among women. Guys like to drive fast, spin their wheels and play thunderous tunes. They envision that the world outside their garage is waiting for them to excel. The car must be smashingly sporty, exotically expensive and, most importantly, the guy-mobile requires make-out seats and a well-kept backseat— should he be that fortunate. The trunk carries nothing but a

1

spare tire, speakers and perhaps a dead body if you run with the right crowd.

It's not a man's world; it's a guy's.

She had not planned on coming back to the cold city ever again. She never intended to return empty-handed and alone. But death happens and sometimes it's dealt in deuces. And sometimes you have to go home to reinvent yourself. Back to what you know and to what is familiar so that you can create someone unconventional. Sometimes the worst is best in the end. She needed to get a new identity—perhaps donated to her by the witness relocation dudes. Or maybe a first-class makeover was all she needed. To truly get by in this world, you follow the rules set by Jackie O: assume the timeless-yet-vacant stare and shoulders broad while exuding poise, grace, and style. Then toss on a pair sunglasses to hide the fine lines and possible stray tear; dress in your finest, tailor-made, tasteful outfit and the sun will shine in your direction—a picture perfect Chicago afternoon as the casket rolls past your place in local history. Yea, it's all about getting a makeover and a stiff drink.

Only the regulars were in Justin's on Monday nights. They sat in the expected stools in the established order and eagerly awaited the scenes from the upcoming *Melrose Place*. Mick, the actor-by-day-bartender-by-night was adding a new flavor to the already impressive list of beers, stouts and ales available in this Wrigleyville sports bar. Televisions were in every corner and the walls adorned with jerseys, banners, flags and autographed bras that hung like trophies. Unlike many of the other drinking establishments in the area, the clientele was mostly straight, white, artsy twentysomethings trying to meet the future. These floppy disks scraped themselves together night after night and complained about "the man" (who was now a mythical creature from no specific ethnic group or gender, set out to ruin the career of every man and woman of every color, race and sexual orientation) who had used them up and discarded their dapper bodies onto El tracks only to return a few hours later for another day chained to a cube in the corporate grind.

However, on this particular Monday, the lip service was not entirely devoted to Heather Locklear and her fabulous mini business suits. Tales of the past weekend's drunken antics and other venomous tales were spun in this womb-like arena as well. "E got lucky, Y got into a fight, Z puked in the back seat of *another* taxi after taking home *another* nameless dude who, of course, had great hair—didja hear that S and H hooked up? Who saw that coming? I guess they started in the beer garden and finished in the alley before heading over to Nookie's for some waffles—maple syrup and rough sex, awesome combination. Q went to the company happy hour on Friday and wasn't at work today while J bitched that no one called to invite him out. Though it wasn't that bad, J ended up doing laundry at the Launder-Bar and then renting videos the following night. It was no big deal, really. I don't mind. Man, remember the time N was drinking at the Launder-Bar and got so fucked-up he forgot his clean clothes? That place will do it to you, man. But that cute Romanian babe who works there folded them up for him and everything—she even put them in one of those special laundry bags she sews and sells. Half of those boxers and T-shirts were gone the next day when he arose from his hangover. They make a killer Bloody Mary on Sunday mornings, spicy as all hell. Yea! They put pickle juice and celery salt and a ton of strange great shit in 'em. You've got to have a Bloody Mary and watch football at the Launder-Bar on Sundays—that's the life. Da Bears."

Over raspberry ale and after the toast to the never-forgotten and well-loved Ditka, someone mentioned that an unusual classic yellow Volkswagen had been seen parked in front of the girl's empty brownstone. Tongues began flapping with gossip. "Could it be who I think it is? I heard she went to Mexico with Danny and bought a Bug—what did the license plate say? Did it have Vegas plates? Hello, *Nevada* plates? Nice education, Mr. State School, or were you the proud graduate of our community college? Does our little boy even have an associate's degree? Danny, smuggling heroin and Beetles into these United States, he's the man. If I could have gotten her an old Bug I would have—she loved them. The papers said it was cocaine and they never proved anything— she wasn't even there, he got the car for her as a surprise. Doing coke, what's up with that? She's smarter than that. No she wasn't, where have you been? Where's that Danny? *He* was the partier, funny as all funk, he must have gotten her into some kind of trouble. My cousin in Vegas said she was pregnant and living the high life with him in like the Elvis penthouse at the MGM. The MGM wasn't even around when Elvis was alive, moron! He played places like the Flamingo. The MGM, isn't that like where Carrot Top is? Danny wouldn't open a door for Carrot Top. Prop comic, what a joke. No, Danny Doyle would work where the best buffets were— my money is on Caesar's and that's a classy enough place for Cat with the couture shops and glamorous shows and golden glitz. She was way better than him, he totally let himself go weighing over four hundred pounds, always covered in sweat and being the slob that he is and she's like—what's that word? Urethra? Ethereal, she's that. She had no right being with him—he had no right being with her! Who was he—some freakin' stand-up comedian? Last time I checked, she was educated, giving up her cushy job and that great pad and wham! Out of the blue, she runs off to live in Vegas. Don't you get it? That's what she liked about him—he didn't put expectations on her about weight and his family didn't give a crap about manners and being proper and going to country clubs for tea and wearing little white gloves and touching up her hair color every two weeks. He liked it when she wore jeans and a T-shirt more then her little skirts and super-high heels that seemed a requirement for some guys, guys at this table. And the biggest thing that Danny did that no one else ever did—for those of you who still jerk off to images of her in the shower—he made her laugh. He could be the hunchback of Notre-freaking-Dame on parole for killing his mother with a Barbie doll and a super-long prison record for child rape, but if you could make that girl laugh, she was in your pocket."

"Speak of the goddamn devil."

Every mouth dropped and each eye turned towards the door to see the young woman walk in. Her bright smile lit the smoky bar and she waved to Mick, who was knee-deep in bitter banter. Seeing her after such a long absence allowed their tongues to fill with Tobasco tidbits of flames. The whispers turned tawdry as they watched her pull a fifty from her Versace wallet and point at a far-off corner booth.

"Do you see that ass? She must have gained twenty pounds! Hey, she *was* pregnant and women tend to gain weight when they're knocked up. She wasn't knocked-up—it was Danny's kid. If you're *not* married and you're pregnant that means you are knocked up. What about that cash Danny took from her when he first went off to Vegas? Remember when she went to visit him and he disappeared with her souvenir money? I bet it went for one of his lost weekends of hookers and drugs and pizzas and shit! Remember those? Stupid, you're not supposed to remember those! Who the hell does she think she is coming in here like she owns the place and dropping that kind of coin? I bet *she* dumped *him* and his baggage—you know fat guys have tiny dicks and she obviously got fed up and frustrated. Maybe *he* left *her*. I bet he got bored with her nagging and queen-bee attitude and he got all well-known and it was *he* who dumped *her* flabby ass— come on, the guy has hosted *Saturday Night Live*, and no offense to Cat, but he was a star and could get better than her any day. Oh, now you think there is someone out there who is better than Cat? Yea, he's off with some showgirl or porn star or something. G was positive he was cheating, but she thinks

5

everyone is cheating. Rose told me all about some stripper she met when she was visiting who was sleeping in their extra bedroom—can you believe a hotel suite would have extra bedrooms—she said there were like five bathrooms and it was two stories high! For the record, I think Danny loved her with all his heart and I think she's as beautiful today as she's ever been. Excuse me? You obviously don't remember how she dumped you. Fax machine? *At work?*"

The jealous talk diminished as she neared the table. Her hair was long and shiny; her skin was glowing and clear.

"You just missed *Melrose*," J smiled, fondly remembering the times they had spent together in the past. Instant memories of sunset walks along the lake and nights of take-out Chinese food eaten on his condo floor interrupted his vision. He was blinded by memories, *his* memories, breathtaking memories of her.

"I did?" She ran her fingers through her endlessness mass of hair and looked at a nearby flickering television. She didn't care about some soap opera or the lives that were lead on the small screen anymore. "What day is today?"

"Monday. *Melrose* Monday. The place hasn't been the same without you."

"Monday? Already? Man, times flies." She smiled politely while her eyes searched for an explanation in the ceiling fans before walking away into a new world that began to revolve around her corner booth.

The group's curiosity was aroused by the girl's sudden emergence from the road they had never dared to travel. They were painfully resentful and unforgiving when pondering the myriad of opportunities she was handed—in their eyes—on a platinum platter. The vindictive accusations whirled from inebriated lips like bees buzzing, circling a hive in late August, waiting for the next golden arrival from behind Door Number Two. Talk is cheap, but gossip is priceless. It wasn't since the Superbowl party when the first four drinks (in honor of Brett

Farve—Justin, the owner, was a Wisconsin transplant) were free was the banter this candid. The comatose Monday evening drinkers became magically revived by the guest appearance the girl had decided to make. No sir, not a single person could recall a time when the chatter had been so alive and animated when a sporting event (or Aaron Spelling) was not involved.

"Attitude babe is back in town, that's for sure. She is the size of a house! And those mirror-cracking baggy pants—was that corduroy? Hello, last season. What's the deal with that? I guess the freshman fifteen finally caught up with her. Good for her, little bitch. Try the farmhouse fifty. Oh, I cannot believe The Gap doesn't make a maternity muumuu for the little junkie. Gucci housedresses missing from the runway this year? No Chanel sweats in her future? At least now we've got a new supplier for pot. You think she still sells? She never sold, you're thinking of W."

While the broads traditionally noticed the outer layer of bad and ugly, the guys admired the good. She had been too thin before, almost emaciated and skeletal. High-priced and dazzling clothes had draped her body as if she were a runway model with a lethal eating disorder. Now she appeared before them healthy, curvy, mentally complete—almost serene. The glimmer in her green eyes revealed a lack of care for their penniless talk. It was the words men silently spoke to one another, only words that could no longer confine her wandering soul.

"Who does she think she is coming in here and buying *us* drinks? Like we can't afford to buy our own drinks? *We* have jobs—when was the last time she kept a job for more than a month? I heard she still did the crossword puzzles while in Vegas—she faxed them in every day. I really don't care for the way she blew us off. She should have at least said something besides that usual pothead garble. Maybe—*just maybe*—we had been worried about her. She *has* been gone for god knows how long; maybe we give a tiny shit. You gave a shit, right? The only thing you missed was her checkbook and willingness to loan you money without question. Money you never paid back, I might remind you. Fuck her. We don't need to know how badly she's screwing up her life chasing druggies all over the country."

Mick emptied the used shot glasses from the table and cleared his throat while taking off his beer-wet apron. He took a long look at the sorry people he considered friends and sighed, "Come on, guys. The girl is like a sister to me and all that crap is just that. Crap."

"Oh, sorry, mister kiss-ass. Please, accept our sincerest apologizes for not being let into her inner circle like you. You know she only likes you because you're black—you even out her—and I apologize for stealing from the Reverend Jesse Jackson—federation of diversity. Jackass, Jackson is the Rainbow Coalition. You think she liked Mick because he's black? I always thought it was because he was a fixer-upper, like Danny. *She* was the fixer-upper. No one has more baggage than that one. I don't think she's as chubby as you say. I think she's got a little shape to her, for once. I like it. Maybe Danny beefed her up a bit in his own idiotic way. Danny was far from being an idiot; the only thing idiot about him was his constant prattle about her. Prattle? Where'd you come up with that one? Tell me you're taking that LSAT class again? Wasn't she going to go to law school? She was always in school for one thing or another—what was that all about? She was always in school because she was always dating her teacher. Listen for one minute, guys. All I am saying is that she could have spared two seconds of her time to chat. It's not like we're those bottom-feeding fat fish, waiting for algae and leftover spillage from the more eye-catching fish in the tank. We *were* all pals. We all swam in the same school."

"Let me get this straight—you're all pissed that she didn't dish dirt with you about her *mid*-mid-life adventure?" Mick laughed and continued with a line he momentarily regretted. Momentarily. "You're just a bunch of resentful, narrow-minded assholes. Grow up."

"Hey, faggot, what are you, her lady-in-waiting? If you're not interested in her tall tales, why did you tell Marcy to make up a bowl of chili and watch the bar while you took a break? Sure, Mick, we can just sit our pretty little selves right here and wait for you to get the story in its entirety. You know she trusts you. And don't hand us anymore of that *narrow-minded* train wreck bullshit—you're as fascinated as we are. You do what you do best, empathize with the ladies, and get back here pronto. I personally volunteer to wait tables if you guarantee a front page headline."

"Your assistance as barkeep is greatly appreciated, believe me." He shot a dirty look at them while his mind traveled to the mysteries surrounding the corner booth. Hunger for her laughter filled his heart as he anticipated the kaleidoscopic dialogue that would soon follow when he joined her. "Both she and Danny were not only good friends, but they were always there for me and I have no agenda, unlike some people. Order from Marcy."

Mick's pace to the kitchen was relaxed. There was no way he would ever admit to the leeches that they were remotely correct in their analysis of the situation. Bottom line, she *was* his dear friend and confidant. They had spent years sharing and appreciating the fortune of genuine love and respect that grew from bona fide friendship. So what if he had planned on joining her at the table and feeding her some of the world famous Justin's chili—it *was* her favorite and she looked a bit worn out from her positively entertaining travels. The welcome mat of cheese and sour cream that topped the heaping bowl of beans, meat, onions and tomatoes brought more than a smile to her anxious face. She looked at home in that candle lit booth with a book cradled between her hands, bare feet balancing on a nearby chair, her lustrous sandy blonde hair sheltering her overall-clad shoulders.

"Hey, bra, what's happening?" Her warm smile immediately ushered him into her cloistered cavern. She jumped to her feet and hugged the first familiar, friendly face she had seen since returning. "Is that chili I'm smellin'? Fucking A! I've been dreaming about the stuff since I left this place. This is honestly the only thing I missed about this god-awful town. Well, the chili and you."

"I'm sure you did." He kissed her cheek and prepared for her foul-yet-educated speech pattern. The warm hippie scent of Nag Champa drifted from her neck and filled his mind with tender memories of days on North Avenue beach playing volleyball, running from the Southport El station in the soothing silence of winter after yet another endless day of brainless work and ghastly auditions, "So, Miss Catrin Moran, where do I begin to ask who, what, where, when, why? How have you been?"

"Not too shabby, man. Is Rose around?" A smidgen of fiery amber beans dropped from her mouth to her chin which now appeared to be almost double—Cat had a double chin? A wave of laughter came from the table of glassy-eyed, loose-lipped interlopers and Mick shook his head. "I have got to drink this road trip out of my body. Do you think you can get carpal tunnel in your feet? I have been on the road for forever and a day and that Bug has no respect for my old dogs, and learning stick-shift isn't the easiest thing in the world, either. But man, let me tell you, the thing is awesome for the soul." She managed to force an unmistakably counterfeit laugh and forged smile. Behind this somber facade was a sad little girl crying out, not for acceptance, but a confessional.

Or was she?

"You look exquisite—still turning heads, I bet!" He flicked a lone piece of cheese off her overall strap. "These have got to be some of those head-turning duds that are the rage in Vegas. A little bird told us you were living it up in Sin

City. Rose had some great stories and, well, Q's brother flew out for a bachelor party and saw Danny's show."

"Q, Q, Q. How the hell's that little tramp doing? Still trying to change back the queens? Who's she been spreading herpes to since I left? Is she still the reigning queen of Lunt Avenue? Those meatheads, I bet they were begging you to come over and retrieve some verbal souvenirs. Yep, those are the parasites I know and love. Except for stories and memories, I didn't bring anything exciting back to old Chi-town except this old body and my Volkswagen." She frowned and reconsidered; the car was far from vacant. The shells of dreams and unconditional love cluttered the tiny automobile as well as empty cans of hope, plastic bottles of family, and airtight containers of a future. "I take that back. There's a couple of Twinkies in the back and plenty of beef jerky wrappers under the passenger seat. Danny used to eat them like mad and I developed a taste for them myself."

"Come on, you know how the gang is. They care about you and wonder where you've been." He saw new golden specks in her bright green eyes as they rolled in her perfect facade. "OK, it *is* Monday night—*and* you've been gone so long they're expecting a whale of a tale—excuse the *Moby Dick* reference, Professor."

Cat fed on the chili and withheld speech for sake of nutrition. An underage pinball player directly behind their booth was dulling the backwoods sound of Hank Williams Jr. on a far off set, musically announcing to get ready for some football. She covered the empty bowl with her napkin completely so that no part of the remaining meal was in view. Mick knew this was a sign to immediately move the bowl to a neighboring table, as far out of her sight as possible before she did it herself.

"Thanks, man. You know how I feel about plates of former food."

"It's good to see your OCD hasn't disappeared." Mick

pulled a snowy-white wet-nap from his breast pocket and tossed it in her direction. She ripped it open and ran the lemony fresh mini-napkin over her perfectly groomed hands, stopping only for a speck of bean between her fingers. Once again, a small roar came from the callous consumers which caused a grimace from Cat.

"I guess they've got home court advantage," she signed and folded the wet-nap. "And if my daily planner was as empty as theirs, I'd be making up jealous talk just as quick as my mouth could blurt it out. And *you*, you're the ringleader; letting them in here every night like circus clowns popping out of a tiny car, each with a personality more shocking than the one before. This place is an old-time carnival that lets the freaks proudly flaunt their personal freakiness on a regular basis—you should charge admission for the straights. At that table alone, you have the symptoms of every basic mental disorder. I wish I had known before what I know now about people. More than what I learned in Psych 101. I probably wouldn't have had to blow the teacher to get that grade. I'm kidding! I never blew anyone for a grade! I just slept with them!"

"Come on, I *have* to work here. Paying rent is the only reason I put up with this bullshit—I have no choice. Or have you forgotten the woes of the working class? All they are doing is spreading childish chitchat and I provide a room large enough for the combined ego. You know as soon as Justin comes in, he throws them all out. He says they should be in Palos Rehab or some detox center, not here, and I agree."

"As long as they drop pocket change to the bell-ringing Santa in front of Watertower at Christmas and buy Girl Scout cookies, they think the pearly gates will open a tad quicker when their time arrives. Being good and doing good are not the same. All is always well in Boystown as long as there's a yearly parade, in their eyes." She laughed and sipped on the bubbling beer, "Speaking of that higher power, does Justin still think Jesus is coming and will stop here first to find out which one of them stole the autographed Jordan jersey?"

"Not no more," he laughed. "I told him P swiped it during the playoffs."

"All those freaking two-faced yuppies do is sit around and pass Supreme Court rulings and they're a great bunch to throw stones. Off the wall *Jerry Springer Show* audience in the making, if you ask me. All that cheering and laughing at us mirrors the show's human trash on parade; tossing shoes, throwing chairs and throwing punches, but on a higher level. They're the ultimate citizens knowing right from wrong. Should you even be sitting with me, bra? They'll burn a cross in your yard if you don't make a statement soon."

"And what should I tell them? Shit about you and Danny? How Danny supposedly ran off to Vegas and is now with someone who's not you and, more importantly, blew off with all your cash?" He frowned before the words left his mouth. "Where *is* Danny? And what's with the maternity clothes? Those *are* maternity, right? Where are all your belly shirts? Hip huggers? Where are the Manolo's? No Prada on your arm? No Cartier hanging from your lobes? Inquiring minds want to know."

"Inquiring minds? Screw them! They don't have minds!" She gulped her shot. "I don't want to waste my precious breath on a bunch of people who have no vision, no goals, no life experience. You, my friend, can tell them whatever you like, because once the story leaves my lips, it becomes public domain, but unlike those old Christmas movies they play over and over, I won't be repeating, retelling or recapping each holiday season or even on the ten o'clock news—nor will I answer questions. Wait for the book or movie or video game."

"That's not what I'm saying. You know I'll tell them only what you want them to know." He looked at her with a smirk, "Of course, *you'll* only tell *me* what you want me to know."

"Well, for one thing, I *know* imaginations have already

gotten the best of them and even if you tell the goons the truth verbatim, it'll still get shaken and stirred and served with an olive. A martini sounds good. Not the martini, just the olive. Do you think I could get Marcy to bring me some olives?" She gazed beyond the table out the window in awe at the endless string of cars pausing and proceeding on the corner of Southport and Roscoe Avenues. She hadn't remembered a stop sign being on the corner before the Red Tomato, but neither was the Caribou Coffee, Jamba Juice or Starbucks— things had changed, but not improved. "I know how they think, I *was* one of them. But I got up one morning and realized that life isn't about a Taco Bell that stays open after a Cubs night game and that love is nowhere to be found in a bar during happy hour. Or any hour for that matter."

"The hook has a fresh worm so they think it's OK to drop their lines in the water as long as they have a fishing license." Both smiled at Mick's misfired philosophy bullet. "Usually they're wrong in the tales they tell, but they think if someone else said it first, they can continue passing it on. Occasionally, they may rearrange the facts and perhaps dirty up a person's rep—which is only temporary. But every now and then, they're right and people's feelings still get disregarded. It's the Zen of gossip."

"Hello, Mike Brady, speak English for me." She smiled, completely confused by his lecture. "Mickey, if they really wanted to know where I've been and what—or who—I've been doing for the past god knows how long, they should come on over. Be a man and pull up a stool. Drinks are on me, as long as it stops their primitive and ludicrous fairy-tales."

They sat silently across from each other in the shadowy booth. Mick was dying to live vicariously through her, but feared his craving would be mistaken. He saw a certain aura of calmness around her; an almost tranquil pelt of peace cradled her. For the first time, he thought she felt one with herself, her appearance and her surroundings. She gave the impression she wanted to feel like an intruder, but she knew all lights pointed in her direction and center stage was hers. When the silence was no longer bearable, Mick cleared his throat and Cat began to tell her tale as a castaway on the ship of Danny Doyle.

"If they're moaning about my money and my love life and my weight—and I know that scalawag D is—tell them they have no reason to worry about me, not that they are. You can tell them I have money in the bank if you think it's their business and to be honest with you, I don't think my bank account *is* any of their business. Danny didn't blow any of my cash, and no, he didn't leave me for someone else—like J wishes." Her eyelids closed softly and she sighed. "He gave me the sun, the moon, the stars, and his heart. He would set them straight if he were here—he would never let that group of resentful dolts say an unkind word about me. They'd be afraid to open their daft holes in front of him. But he isn't."

This was the million-dollar-question he had been dying to ask since he saw the polished canary yellow Volkswagen with the vanity plate "KITTEN" parked days ago and he knew her return to the watering hole was eminent. "Where is he?"

"He's gone. *Finito*. *Muerto*. Dead." She watched his mouth drop and eyes widen in dread. She was used to this look; she had originated "the look" herself the night she found him lying dead on their bathroom floor. "Do you really think I would come back to this shitty city if he were alive? There's nothing in that dreadful desert now that he isn't around to give it meaning. There's even too much sin for *me* in Vegas. Hooking, gambling, drinking—"

"Hold on a minute here—I am totally lost. Start at the beginning." He didn't want to miss a single word. "Slow down, you're totally speaking in tongues. Did you just tell me Danny Doyle is dead? Are you kidding?"

"It's not as exciting as you might think—just promise me to listen and believe what I say. You know me well enough to know I would never lie to you, especially about my Danny.

Unless you see the label, Equal tastes just like regular sugar. But I wouldn't slip you Equal without a warning label. No mickey for my Mick." She scanned the room and waved at Marcy behind the bar for another shot. "You sure they don't need you serving drinks?"

"Mondays are slow. Marcy can handle it."

"More important, have you got a good seat? Is your butt comfortable? 'Cause you're in for a bumpy ride."

AMF 572

In every American neighborhood, there was a junk car. It was always prominently placed in the most visitor-visible driveway in an old-car coma. The occasional weekend was spent with miscellaneous individuals (most local guys & men, dads & sons, brothers & passers by) bending under the hood, kicking the tires or polishing the paint. The body was a classic. Never a chip or a speck of dust marred its façade. Every now and again (a good number of Saturday afternoons in the summer), the lucky owner would rev it up and slowly drive it through Joe Neighborhood, the fleeting envy of all. After the triumphant outing, the beast would spend the remaining sunny days and nights under a tarp of shame, silently begging to be taken out on the town again, but the owner was left feeling unable to again master the monster machinery, preferring to look back fondly at the old days and remember when.

That was the dusty, cast-aside trophy Catrin's life had become.

At first, just like the old car, some guy would use his time-honored, traditional lines on her; trying to work his magic like a gear-head aligning the wheels or pulling the engine. After the help of knowledgeable friends, insightful advice from elders and hours paging through the owners manual, the sophisticated sedan could be coaxed into coast at any pace he desired, stopping anywhere the driver pleased to show off his showroom model wishing only the sticker price was still attached so all could grasp his out-of-pocket expenses. She was the ultimate pawn, the fluffiest stuffed prize from the top shelf, and without a suitor trying to win her from that carnival shelf, she sat collecting dust.

"Jesus, the more I think about it, my life thus far has been fifty-percent soap opera and fifty-percent *Oprah* and I'm not sure I'm even good enough for *The* Oprah." She half-smiled at Mick and gulped another shot of Bushmills. "I've got so much to tell you—I just don't know where to start.

"You know that whole deal about my parents, right? *Everyone* knew that whole deal about my parents except me. All that shit about the lovey-dovey high school sweethearts getting hitched in college, my dear old dad cheating on M, M leaving dad, Cat never meeting dad who died in a car accident only to discover he didn't, M finding herself by dating women and finally settling down with that nice Aunt Jillie of mine?"

"You're right, this is like a soap opera, but everybody's families are screwed up. You don't have the corner on that market, sister." Mick smiled and put his hand over hers on the Formica table. She whisked it out of his reach and waved for another beer. It was then that he noticed a mammoth pink diamond on her ring finger. Left hand ring finger.

"That's when the shit went down, man, when Aunt Jillie moved in and tried to turn me into a mini man-hater." She lit a cigarette and stared blankly into the wood paneling at her immediate right. Her eyes saw through the wall, across the street, past the dry cleaners and the squatting Japanese woman inside, beyond the walls of the Vegetarian-Buddhist-Vietnamese restaurant that still didn't have a liquor license; past another nameless coffee house and finally to her car, that beautiful, wonderful car whose locks would never again be fucked by an anonymous key. She, just like the car, must drive forward with a map that had yet to be drawn, her own map. For the first time, the lines and boundaries were yet to be determined. "I had plenty of positive masculine role models all right. They had breasts, but they were usually more manly than anyone with a penis I can think of."

"That's right. I remember when you came to parent-teacher conferences with your mom and your Auntie Jillie."

"I thought all kids did! I mean, we grew up in the era of *Three's Company* and *Bosom Buddies* and *Soap*—I thought single-sex households and cross dressers were normal. We watched *My Two Dads*! But then again, I didn't realize sex was even happening!" Giggles erupted. "Remember that big birthday party I had when I was ten? The one with the pony and the jumping jack?"

"Yea! There were clowns making balloon animals and then that big show in the basement with Liza Minelli and Barbara Streisand and Judy Garland and we all sang songs and danced! Good times."

"Honey, how many kids had birthday parties with drag queens? With my luck, the clown was Gacy."

"Hey, I remember that day as one of the best—it was awesome! I even remember we all got little bags of toys to take home that had dress-up clothes like tiara's and lipstick and glitter and a tool belt—my mom was all freaked out because she thought I got a girl's bag by accident."

"Oh no," she devilishly chimed in, remembering the mayhem behind the gift bags. "It was pretty much an asexual or unisex mixture in every bag—remember the plastic handcuffs?"

"I never got handcuffs! What a gyp!"

"Well, you know Jillie, always trying to get the mind working—she told me it was a personal choice that every woman has to make at one time or another—I was like, eight. I never had a proper sit-down about a menstrual cycle, but I do, for some reason, know the lines from 'The Rocky Horror Picture Show' by heart. On the previous subject, I later discovered the handcuffs to be more nuisance than delight, but the gals thought it was a nice touch."

"They were pleasant, big-boned ladies, if I may say." He joked. "And you may have learned about your period from our missing third of the triangle, Rose, but I bet there was never a shortage of feminine products."

"Very funny. I see your acting classes have yet to cover comedy. Don't quit your day job, Belushi." Her smile apologized immediately for her careless joke. Mick had been taking acting classes of some sort since the teen years and Cat was far from dissuading him at this point. "Do you know how it feels going over to a friend's house and seeing family pictures or having kids ask, 'What does your daddy do??' I had no fucking clue!"

"I believe I once told you my dad could beat up your aunt."

"Perfect example. There was no Melissa Etheridge when I was growing up. No Ellen DeGeneres. Lesbians weren't hip like they are today, and to make matters worse, I liked boys. I *really* liked boys."

"What's wrong with that?" He swallowed the small glass of whiskey, "There was a time when even I thought boys were the way to go."

"Mickey, can you even conceive of the idea of learning about the birds and bees from two non-shaving, men-hating dykes? To them, making love to a man was comparable to cocktails and a ride home from Teddy Kennedy—or any Kennedy for that matter." She rolled her eyes and gazed at the beer-wet table, which she instinctively wiped dry with her napkin. "They didn't teach me that there could be love or pleasure with a boy—boys were about a lack of choice. Women made love and guys fucked. When you were with a man, you were merely a wet hole to lay back and close your soul with your eyes and let some anonymous penis enjoy the ride. Excuse the bluntness of my conversation, but you should be comfortable with my fish wife vulgarity after all these years."

"No offense taken, but there's no way—they couldn't possibly view straight sex as that sinister!"

"Oh, totally," she half-joked, and sipped the beer, knowing he had no idea what had really gone on all those years in their Lakeview walk-up. "*And* they had the pictures to prove it. All I saw was fear and force—and this was years before you guys explained what was really going on at my house."

"You know, I have always offered to help you change your opinions of the male species." Mick laughed nervously knowing Cat was an award he would never place on his mantle. On second thought, he did not want to have her as a trophy, but as a friend.

"Keep it in your pants." Her ignored cigarette dwindled and burned out in the ashtray. "But come on, after my first few sex trips, I saw their point of view. I mean, I saw where they were coming from and I now know they were only trying to protect me and convince me to make decisions unlike M's, but I don't know. They would constantly remind me how *he* went to college and *she* worked day and night to pay my dad's med school bills and where did that get *her*? Boo hoo, alone and broke with a newborn. In high school, they went on and on telling the same story of the years she spent letting him get smart so that she could be dumped for someone with blonde hair and perky tits. And Jillie's key to my heterosexual marriage was to find someone who was older and settled into a career, preferably balding—someone who couldn't get chicks based on looks. I was supposed to seek out a man who owned, not rented. And an older bald guy is someone who nobody wanted and then he *couldn't* cheat because in the end, they all cheat."

In her mind, Catrin Moran knew exactly when the first day of the rest of her womanhood began; it was the moment she entered Introduction to Middle English at her elite, private, anonymous Midwest University that seemed to burst with butch. Not so surprisingly, it was a member of Aunt Jillie's circle who coached water polo who encouraged them to send their off-the-charts-SAT-scoring, wild-eyed girl who refused to wear a bra to the institution a few hundred miles away from the Windy City. It wasn't long after Cat paid a visit to the Middle English teacher early in the semester that the rumors began to fly. She went in for notes and came out with trouble brewing. To her, he was an older (thirties as compared to her eighteen) professor who flirted nonchalantly and smelled phenomenal. The young Doctor L was a recently divorced gentleman in good standing in the community, but when word got back to the homestead that he also preferred to be standing when he took her on the desk in his office, all hell broke loose. In her wholesome eyes, he was the first man to make love to her with her consent. She had tried unsuccessfully to disregard the two boys in high school who had restrained her and allowed themselves to get off while tears burned down her pubescent cheeks. Just like Jillie had said, they cared about her tightness, not her tenderness.

"Doc," as Cat called him, was compassionate and sincere and simply a fling. Neither believed this was anything more than a passing fancy, a lonely afternoon, and an exceptional screw. However, M and Jillie would not hear of Cat's reputation diminishing, grades suffering or mind wandering—something had to be done.

The young Catrin refused. Along with the assured "A," the good doctor aided more than in merely the discovery of superior sex. He encouraged her personality to emerge and demanded that she begin to make her own decisions. He forced her to choose on everything from entrée to major; to learn from her own mistakes and not the mistakes forced upon her by others. Most importantly, he made her promise never to let any silly guys use her for what he and she were doing; *their* lovemaking was a learning experience, precious and understood. *They* were the exact opposite of a drunken frat boy on a Friday night who would not have the sexual aptitude or appreciation for her pleasure the way he did.

"He was really interested in me, you know—in a sick Catholic school kind of way, of course." She lit another cigarette and continued to chat as she strolled behind the bar, seized a bottle of Bushmill's and a napkin filled with olives. The eye of each barfly was on her every move and she took full advantage of their fascination. "Hey, J, no hard feelings about that fax thing, eh?"

"Not at all." He was flattered that she remembered his name. Again, his mind went blank and his heart skipped a beat. "Do you and Danny want to get together now that you are back in town? *Maybe* a movie or dinner?"

"I'll see if I can't dig him up and ask him."

"Hey, I saw him on *The Tonight Show* a few months ago—he was great! What else is he up to?" J's mind raced with possible motives for offing the young comedian and up-and-coming movie star who had no right to steal the girl of his dreams. Catrin had been promised to him almost at birth. Good old Jillie and M had made sure of that, but a desire to live on the edge would often lead his Cat to stray. Hopefully, that edge had crumbled and she was back in Chicago to stay.

"Oh you know Danny, always looking for the pot of gold at the end of the rainbow." She thought for a moment before shoving three olives into her mouth and sitting back down with Mick. "Maybe he was just looking for the pot—it's hard to tell. And yes, I stopped smoking when I was pregnant. But, back to the story, Mumsy freaked out and pulled me out of St. Norb's and threw me into Northwestern between semesters. I would love to say the rest is history, but as always with the life of the Kitten, it gets more complicated. It would also make M happy to hear I never got involved with another teacher, but that's also not the case."

"Ah yes, the Wolf," he howled and laughed. "Another 'A' I am assuming?"

"Of course, but before him was J and those sun-drenched and snow-covered days of undergraduate studies on the lake."

The cool fall air in Evanston smelled like burning leaves. Cat was lying on a blanket trying to read some sort of Nathaniel Hawthorne for a literature class, but was unable to stop her mind from wandering and eyes gazing at Sheridan Road that separated her from the campus about a mile away. The empty pavement tolerated every set of wheels. Some wheels were attached to a visiting Mercedes, a day-tripping Honda or a traveling Pontiac. Locals sped by in American classics like Ford trucks or Jeeps or Chevy's. Every car—whether fast or slow—had a destination. North, south, east and west, the blacks, blues and reds traveled, never appearing to need a map.

She was done studying, but dreaded returning to her room where her mother would be arriving shortly in her sky-blue Volvo. It was time for their weekly interrogation known as brunch. Cat's present would be broken down class-by-class over scrambled eggs and her future discussed over a second and third Mimosa. How were her grades? Did she meet any new friends? Are there any boys in the picture? Any girls?

The incense-smelling hallway felt shorter than usual that day and Cat was stunned to see a male figure looming outside her dorm room door, hands in his khaki pockets, shuffling his feet. M emerged and opened her arms to kiss the daughter, who had realized the preppy-dressed gatecrasher was no stranger in the hall just happening to be standing outside her room, it was J.

"Catrin! Come here!"

"Hi M." She loosely hugged the woman Cat suspected was playing matchmaker.

"You remember J. He's going to join us today. I hope you don't mind—of course, you don't mind. You two are old friends."

"That we are" She smiled at J who stood smugly at M's

side, adoring every minute of Cat's mortification. He knew that she knew that this whole debacle was as much his scheme as it was her mother's. She imagined their covert phone calls and chuckles shared over chamomile tea while devising their fiendish plan to marry off her only child. J was the picture-perfect catch for Cat; M and many others were convinced of this. It wasn't just because of his old-money-family and their escalating business that J would go into and eventually inherit, but value was added by their lakefront property in Lake Forest, home on Ocean Boulevard in Palm Beach, and a timeshare in Telluride iced the cake. He was more eye-catching than someone whom Cat would typically pick for herself, and this caused some alarm in her M (don't forget that the good-looking ones cheat), but J vowed he would never betray or cause the girl in question a moment's distress. He was enamored of Cat and had been since junior high when she taught him how to bait a hook on a field trip to a trout farm. "Good to see you again, J."

"It's terrific seeing you." He kissed her cheek. "I trust you don't mind my surprise visit."

"Of course, she doesn't!" M grasped her daughter and walked arm-in-arm down the hallway toward the exit leading to the parking lot. "J mentioned that he could use some assistance with his Italian and I told him you would be more than happy to spend some time with him going over verbs. You *do* have a minute or two for him between classes, don't you?"

"Of course, *mora dhuit*!" She glanced at J who had no idea she had just wished him a good morning. He was at their heels. "I'm really good in a subject I've never taken. Try again, Mother."

"French? Spanish? Russian?"

"Gaelic," J beamed. "Cat studies Irish."

"Someone's done his homework. *Is luí casta ě.*" Cat had accused him of lying, but no one understood so she glared at the trespasser who delighted in making her already dreadful brunch worse. "You must be studying it on your own, I've never seen you at the language lab and there are only a few of us in the program."

"Actually, I'm going to Ireland this summer, after graduation," he cooed while opening the door for M and daughter. "I'm planning on spending time in the West, where they still speak the language."

"*Is Arastatail ceart,*" she said, proclaiming him a genius. Her Irish was still slow, but he was not interested in Ireland or Gaelic or anything foreign. He was interested in her.

"What are your plans after graduation, Catrin? It's right around the corner, you know," M eagerly inquired as they opened the car doors. "I told you Jillie and I closed on that house in Hinsdale. We're going to be suburbanites—isn't that exciting? We're even talking about getting a dog! We were thinking about a big dog, like a lab or a terrier—"

And that was it. Conversation over. Case closed.

The trivial dialogue continued through the afternoon without a pencil—this talk was in ink and there was no erasing the lines Mama Moran had drawn in the proverbial sand. From that day on, Cat was going to be spending time with J, teaching him an ancient and dying language, thwarting his advances and slowly but surely driving herself insane to shut her mother's mouth.

Notes turned into phone calls. Phone calls turned into lunches. Lunches into afternoons. Afternoons turned into evenings. Evenings turned into dinner. Dinner slowly turned into movies. Movies burst into sex. Cat no longer considered J the nerdy boy from science class or the uninvited insect M had set her up with. J had unexpectedly vaulted into manhood with thick brown hair and dreamy hazel eyes and a body Cat could not stop touching. He had matured into a tall and muscular gentleman with arms that were permanently around her shoulders or waist. His hands were never far from her face or hair, always stroking and caressing her skin, sniffing her sandy brown hair that smelled of her homemade patchouli-scented shampoo.   As seniors they attended usually disregarded dances and parties, football games and campus concerts.   Cat was invited to his family's mansion for Christmas and Easter, which is when J's family proposed a joint graduation party for the two inseparable and blossoming flowers.

As graduation swiftly advanced, so did the prospects of the two who were considered a serious item by friends, families and classmates—all of whom wondered what would happen when the final school bell rang early in May.

Just as he had said—staying true to his initial lie—J was off to Ireland to shear sheep and speak a language he barely grasped, but what would become of Cat?   She was now significantly skilled and a graduate of a first-rate institution with a good head on her shoulders. J's father arranged for an interview with a friend at the *Chicago Tribune* while his mother introduced her to the ladies' group at their country club, signing Cat up for charity events and fundraisers beginning in mid-August with a late summer tea honoring local women in politics. Aunt Jillie and M insisted she fly to Ireland with J, to just jump on his coat strings and jet off to another land, a romantic land, and be with the man they coerced her to love and cherish, but none of this was in Cat's playbook. She was young and ambivalent—far from being independent and able to make such significant decisions about her immediate future wholly on the cue from two suburban spinsters who couldn't decide between a black lab or German shepherd. Cat still desired the shelter of college and the protection of dorm life and decided to stay on for summer classes that would eventually lead to graduate school in the Fall. She would linger on campus, wait for J to return, study the African-American literature she had begun to love, and sporadically help out M and her adaptation to the suburbs. Her fixed plan was to find her own apartment that was close enough to Evanston sometime before September. Evanston, the seemingly tiny college suburb, was the only location she had ever thought of as home.

"But when did you move in with J? I don't remember you having a place in Evanston." Mick questioned, curious about the timing of the events that led her to this point in her life.

"J's place ended up being the apartment I found that Fall. It was the one I was so proud to call my own, my very own first place, and no amount of Irish lassies he screwed would get in my way."

"Wait a minute. J cheated on you in Ireland?"

"In Ireland, in England, in Chicago—the man is a walking condom ad. And why shouldn't he be? Look at him—I'd do him right now. But back in those days, I was a different person; I was a little girl who couldn't give him the devotion he needed and wanted. The cheating never bothered me. *I* bothered me. And poor J was just along for the ride."

Cat-a-lata-ding-dong,
Yo!

Congrats on graduating! I would love to be there and see you in your cap and gown—thank the dykes for inviting me to the big shindig—but Dallas has lassoed me and I'm like a calf at a rodeo—more like the greased pig at the state fair. You can take the girl out of the Midwest, but not the Midwest out of the girl. I don't even have the money (or a phone) to call you, but I thought a letter and a nice stolen "reserved for" parking sign from the Texas Stadium for Troy Aikman (enclosed) would suffice. For the time being, remember that I am here and you are loved..

What's up with you and J having a joint party (and I don't mean pot!)? Are you guys getting along or is M just hoping you will? And what's with him going to Ireland? I thought you were the one who always wanted to find your roots and figure out where that name of yours came from? Isn't he Jewish?

Anyhoo, I'm supposed to be coming home for my mom's birthday—we'll catch up then.

Miss you!
Write soon.
Rose

WFV 463

There are maps that come with directions—stuffed inside birthday party or wedding invitations—sometimes attached to letters. Crumpled, stained and found under the passenger seat is usually another map with no single destination; just a state filled with lines and dots and meaningless words that outline communities and define parishes. Since Cat's itinerary was filled with emptiness and fueled by longings, she had to ask for help at the first service station. Would cohabitation end her feelings of desertion? Could sharing a phone number suddenly ensure her happiness and embrace her like the cashmere blanket of serenity she had been searching for? Might she rise to greet the sun every morning with passion for life in her heart, curl in her hair, song on her lips and bluebirds on her balcony? How could the simple addition of a dresser in an apartment eliminate her intense longing and need for inner harmony?

Days before her title was transferred over to the scrumptious space J called home, Cat was beleaguered with questions. What in hell was she doing? Where was she going (aside from a plush condo on Michigan Avenue)? Was she running from something bad into something worse? She spent hours wandering up and down the safe blocks of the Belmont and Clark area looking into the pierced faces and past steamy store windows for the answers to her life and ended up with nothing but a receipt for pink Doc Martens and a lemongrass-scented candle. Since Rose had run after that shit-head and moved to Dallas, she had no one to confide in, no one to ask for help, no one to borrow a shoulder—no one to even call. And Mick? Mick worshiped J and wished he could spend an evening in her sandals being wined and dined by one of *Chicago Magazine's* most eligible bachelors. Sure, she supposed the queasy feelings in her belly would eventually fester into love and that was somewhat comforting. But was that enough?

The magnificent housewarming party was more majestic than she could ever imagine. The whole gang from Justin's was there; family members she forgot existed; other people who lived in the building—there must have been a flashing sign on the street advertising the free food and an unlimited liquor supply. To further publicize and crystallize the event, J invited a gang of miscellaneous co-workers and former classmates to his—err, *their* place for the open house and feeding frenzy of gourmet delicacies catered by some swank *it* place, where none of their gang could get a reservation, let alone a table. Decorative raw flops of meat and fish eggs adorned the Crate & Barrel and Ikea showroom J called home, while Cat hid in the kitchen with a heavy silver-plated bowl of Pringles and a bottle of Sam Adams. Everything was white and sanitary; it was a space empty of emotion, lacking a heart, absent a soul. For some reason, she hadn't noticed this lifeless sophistication while she was merely a sleepover guest a few nights earlier. She felt like the only sweater left on the shelf after a Field's Super Sunday sale and wondered what she was getting herself into. This was not a home; it was a hospital suite. Any decor was solid in color, and the color usually black or chrome. But somehow, Cat had liked it enough to agree to move in. In fact, she had liked *him* enough to move in. Maybe she could spruce up the place; use that old "woman's touch" thing people had talked about to liven up the thousands of dead square feet that were now, in theory, half hers.

Theories always look better on paper.

After a few weeks of counterfeit bliss, she decided to ask M for the advice she had expected that this great "love" she had for J would erase. Before she got into the car for the lengthy trip to the suburbs, Cat knew that this was the worst possible plan, but it seemed M's current situation was comparable to a married couple as they had been together for over fifteen years; the woman must know something. There was bound to be some miniscule woman's secret of life that had been eluding her that would be shared. A valuable lesson would be learned. Everything would suddenly become clearer. She and her mother would even bond.

M let the dog out as soon as Cat pulled into the recently paved driveway. She was wearing a pair of Capri pants and striped T-shirt. Both M and the dog were thrilled to see the city dweller had found her way to their new spread in Hinsdale. While Cat noticed M's hair had been cut short and recently highlighted, M silently wondered why it was that her only child had made such a long journey on a radiant and cloudless Saturday afternoon—in J's Mercedes, no less. The two sat in the immaculate kitchen and sipped green tea with a drop of honey. M stared at her daughter with a wide smile and began to laugh.

"You can't move in, if that's what you're going to ask. We've already decided the extra room is going to be for books and—"

"It's not that, Jesus!" Cat was again nine years old. She slouched in the chair and felt too weak to hold the cup of tea. "I just wanted to get some advice from you about this man and woman thing."

"Advice? About men and women? From *me*? You're not

pregnant, are you?" Her mother grabbed a cigarette and reached for the lighter. "If I have told you once, I have told you a million times that boys like J will not get suckered in by those knocked-up tactics. Getting pregnant wouldn't work on a boy like J in high school, Cat. Even this ridiculous graduate school thing is way—"

"No, I am not pregnant, Mother." Cat felt anger instead of fear. Why did her mother insist on belittling her? Why couldn't she stop with the never-ending bowls of puppy chow and finally feed her grown daughter adult dog food? She *was* an adult and she was more than ready to take on adult issues, fears and even conversations. "Thanks for the concern."

"Are you two fighting about something? What have you done to upset him?"

"He's not upset with me, not at all. He's J. He's perfectly mannered and makes sure there are groceries and that I wake up and get ready for class on time. I don't know. I guess I thought that I loved him or that I *would* love him and I don't," she explained; then questioned, "Am I doing something wrong? *You're* happy. Tell me what I need to do and I'll do it."

"For starters, stop being ridiculous. I'd like to know who filled your generation's head with these grandiose notions of love at first sight and everlasting, unconditional happiness because they were wrong—*way* wrong. You have always thought love was about someone standing up and smiling when you walked into the room or your heart fluttering when you heard a name mentioned. That's not love, not by any definition of the word. It's just not."

"It's not?"

"Of course, it's not. Love is the result of hard work and years of togetherness. Love is what comes with sacrifice and tough times. Love is the ability to laugh at the end of a long day when you have a crying baby in a dirty diaper while the phone is ringing off the hook with bill collectors and your electricity has just been turned off for the third time in four months. Catrin, if you're too lost in your dream world to realize J is what's right for you, then wake up and smell the Starbucks. Stop losing sleep about what you *think* love is about and start thinking about making him happy."

"Making J happy?"

"Yes, make J happy. This isn't the most important thing, mind you, but he has got money—money that he doesn't seem to mind spending on you. You and your hippie ways have somehow managed to win over his family, you're living rent-free in a fabulous high-rise in downtown Chicago, and the last time I checked, it was his hard-earned money going for tuition—tuition for a useless degree because you have this infantile urge to stay in school. *That*, my dear, is love. Do you get the picture, or do I need to spell it out in more down-to-earth terms?"

"Yes, but—"

"But nothing. Does he physically hurt you?"

"No."

"Does he listen to you?"

"Usually."

"Do you ever go to bed hungry?"

"No."

"Then, my dear, *you* are happy. You've got it better than ninety-nine percent of the girls out there—married or otherwise. How would you like to be Rose, living out of a suitcase in an unfamiliar city because your *supposedly* better half felt like running away from his problems? Or Q, she's another winner, a girl so forlorn with dating that she places ads in *The Reader* pleading with men to take her to dinner? No, little dreamer, you have got nothing to complain about. Be happy and show it."

"But doesn't he deserve better? Doesn't he deserve someone who—"

"Better than you? I didn't raise you to think you were

worthless. Erase that thought from your mind at once. You, my dear, are a beautiful, gifted young woman. You are talented and can carry on a conversation about almost anything and come across as intelligent. Sure, you could stand to lose a few pounds, but you are a catch and J knows it. You go back to that apartment and bake him a cake, wear a nice sundress, fix him dinner, and it won't kill you to curl your hair the way he likes every now and again."

It was this astonishing and unexpected anti-feminist lecture that caused Cat to cry. The confused part of her became irate, which turned to sadness powerful enough to evoke tears. Once they began, there was no stopping. Cat sat in the high-backed oak chair sobbing uncontrollably, stopping only when their stinky pooch jumped on her lap and began licking the salty droplets from her cheeks, leaving long strands of dog hair on her shorts. M grabbed a washrag and shooed the dog away before rubbing the streaks and cracks in Cat's previously flawless Clinique foundation.

"But that's not right! None of this can be true! You can't expect me to believe this shit! Being all June Cleaver and making cakes and wearing pearls and acting like a happy housewife is fifty years ago! It's not about my hair and a dress! It can't be! I don't believe this is coming from *you* of all people!"

"What? You think I don't know? I was around the block while it was still under construction and the same rules apply. Women may have changed since I was dating, but men haven't." She took a sip of her cool tea and gave the dog a cookie. "If you didn't want to hear what I had to say, then you shouldn't have asked."

"I just don't think I'm what J wants."

"You are everything he wants and he will become everything you want. Remember how you hated college at first and thought you didn't fit in? This is the same thing. You used to write me letters and talk about sitting in your god-awful dorm in Wisconsin and watch those cars on the highway driving past and cry. You *knew,* somehow you *knew,* that every single person in every single car was happy and coasting through life. Everyone in the world was happy except you. Well, princess, it isn't that grand in the real world, is it? You're in one of those cars now and you don't know where you're headed, do you? Why don't you imagine your balcony as a new view of the world and sit on one of those leather lounge chairs, watch the sailboats on Lake Michigan going by and imagine *that* life? Because that life can be yours and it doesn't get much better than that."

Thankfully, Jillie returned from the store with a car filled with flowers for the garden they were planning to create. Jillie always had a separate place in Cat's heart; over the years it had been her who had enforced curfew, kept an eye on Cat's schoolwork and decided what was best in her life when choosing a sport to play, class to take or school to attend. Even though she was the one with the career—she was a lawyer—she never missed a parent-teacher meeting, band recital or dance class Cat needed to be driven to or picked up from. If there was ever a problem, it was Jillie she cried to and that was fine with M. Cat always thought this was odd because she wasn't even related to her, but she filled the shoes of both mom and dad. Jillie didn't look like the stereotypical lesbian; she was tall and thin and knew the world of the fashion and beauty industry that she taught the impressionable Cat. She had always wanted a child and Cat became her own.

Cat spent another hour at the house composing herself, meditating on her future and watching the content couple plant and weed in the yard from their glass house. No matter how much of a mistake it was to have asked, Cat knew her mother's words would permanently tattoo themselves in her mind.

In black ink.

That night, she put on a sundress. Cat took M's medicine and curled her hair after making a cake that she served to J as he attentively watched a program about Hitler on the History Channel. He turned from the television and took a look at his roommate who was holding a plate of angle food cake with a heaping pile of fresh strawberries, his favorite.

"What's this? Did we have dinner plans?"

"No, I just thought I would make you a little something special." Her smile felt mandatory even though she was genuinely pleased to see him take that first bite and not gag.

"I never knew you to be a cake baker." He put down the plate and began to stand up. "You look great. Are you going out somewhere? That dress looks—"

"Where are you going?"

"To the kitchen to get some milk."

Cat jumped to her feet and pushed him back into place. "I'll get it. You just sit yourself down and relax." She ran to the kitchen and poured him a glass before returning to his side on the couch.

"I don't know what your mother said to you this afternoon, but I like it." He smiled and cleaned the plate, cake and all. He sat back in his comfy seat, put his arm around Cat and began to surf the channels without another word. Occasionally, he would look in her direction, play with a curl between his fingers and smile, but for the most part, she was invisible.

That is, until they went to bed for a romp; *du lag marcaíocht.*

Sex with J wasn't the worst thing she could think of and knew J was actually trying to please her, but it just didn't happen. Since her rape, Cat had been negative about intercourse and if her thoughts were awful, she let her mind wander to someplace better until the ride came to an end. The art of faking an occasional orgasm was a talent of many, and she did not see the harm of continuing on the tradition.

The next morning, Cat awoke to find an empty house and a note reminding her that he would be in Houston on business until Thursday, take out the garbage. She immediately forgot about her writing class at the University of Chicago, plans with friends, obligations, everything.

M had been right, but very wrong. It wasn't about a dress or a cake or curled hair. There was, without a doubt, something missing from their love nest—love. Cat decided that love existed, but it was something that just happened or it didn't. For her and J, it didn't and probably never would. He was a good guy, just not *the* guy. But her mother was right; she was comfortable and didn't mind living this lie of a life as long as the "L" word didn't come up in conversation.

Cat settled on the floor in front of the television and remained there for what felt like a week. An unseasonably cool July breeze came off the lake and covered her body in waves with every strained breath she reminded herself to take. On the street, cars were going by at the usual stop and go pace; she could hear mufflers, engines and horns. She didn't have the energy to move. She didn't want to move. Everything that she assumed was her life was a lie. J was gone and would never again be back in the same soft lighting. She went to the bathroom, ordered food she never ate and answered the phone for no one. A cocoon of self-hatred and pity enclosed her unwashed frame and no one was to blame except herself for believing in the dream of Prince Charming who wanted nothing more than an occasional fuck and cake with strawberries. She longed—even fantasized—about the buffalo chicken strips she had ordered from Leona's or the Rueben's that came from Snicker's. She could smell their zesty blend of seasonings and knew they were everything the menu had said. Unlike a guy, buffalo chicken strips were defined correctly— there was no surprise when they arrived steaming at your table or warm at your door. Food was reliable, dependable. Thirty minutes or less of foreplay for the phone order, getting the paper plates and the actual eating was the act, while the wet naps were the afterglow. No wet spot on the bed or towel to clean up the mess. And that was just availability—what about comfort? What was better after a bad day of work than macaroni and cheese or mashed potatoes? Who could turn down a slice of cheesecake for a celebration? Filling, tasty and lively conversation versus sulking, pouting and drunk—this was the choice in front of Cat.

She knew now that boys did not create, foster or flourish love—it could not be found anywhere near their presence. Cat's delusion quickly faded into the horizon with every setting sun, so she smiled politely and continued her lie of happiness that she was now accustomed to expose.

She took another bite.

Yo!

Howdy from Texas! Sorry it's been so long since my last letter, but we moved again—the new address is on the envelope, but only pencil it in your book. I'm sure we'll be heading for the Midwest as soon as K loses this job. Yes, you heard correct, he lost his shirt-folding position. He has gone from fixing cars at Amoco to Gap worker to busboy (present) at a sushi joint. We are flat broke and living with his gay brother (don't tell anyone!), the manager of a hip pizza place in Addison, a suburb of Dallas. Gee, I wonder who got him the busboy gig? Did I mention that I am the hostess at the same place? We are one big happy family of restaurateurs.

How is your job? Are you working or still in school? I remember you saying you were going to take more classes, but you've got to get a real job at some point, chickie. P called and was telling me all about his job at his dad's insurance company and that sounds like crap. I may not have the college education you guys have (and that's not my fault so don't get me started), but I would never be able to sit in an office for 8 hours a day listening to people selling some sort of shit. I couldn't sell anything to anyone, so in a sense I'm lucky. I'll never have to.

When are you coming to visit? You would love it down here—the guys all have cute hick accents and sexy cowboy hats and every single (and I mean single) one of them has a gun rack on their pick-up. The sun is always shining which makes me forget about our situation and the mess my life is in. I never imagined that I would leave everything and everyone I know and love to live in a completely outlandish place in a different time zone and spend my nights taking people to their tables for dinner. But I love K and know I'm doing the right thing. As soon as that job comes through in Chicago for him, we're back.

In a heartbeat, sister.

Hey, I heard you're living with J? Tell me this isn't true!

How the fuck did that happen? I'm out of the picture for two months and the next thing you know my best friend is living in sin with her complete opposite. I never even knew you liked him! Remember in high school when he asked you to the Sweetheart Dance and you laughed so hard you spit orange soda all over the cafeteria? His uniform jacket had a bright stain for months! Has he changed much? How is he in bed? I always thought he was kind of cute, in a khaki sort of way. But if you're living with him, he must have moved up and became a blue or green—remember my color-coding of men? I find I am using it more than ever in Dallas, just to confuse K.

Anyhoo, keep Chicago in one piece for me—I will be back. Oh, and send me that recipe for that Mexican chicken you made for us before we left—K loves it and keeps asking me to make it for him. If only we could afford chicken. Just kidding—not!

Write soon!
Rose

5318 AA

Long before the passing lane was open, Cat noticed that her better half had stopped taking the time to go to the passenger side and unlock the car door for her—he wasn't even unlocking it before his. J just clicked the remote for the driver's door and got inside. At some point after that, he would, at times, lean over the seat and push her door open. This happened only when he was securely behind the wheel. The other times, he would just unlock her door from his side. Without knowing it, J's ill-mannered use of the newly purchased remote-entry thingy had subconsciously installed a dead bolt on the car door of entry that was Cat's soul.

It was also around this time that J started to make some noise when Cat didn't prepare for the take-out dinners by setting the table, getting napkins and silverware in place or remembering what his favorites were at the various restaurants from which they frequently ordered. In the past, J had said he found it "sweet" or "cute" when she used the plastic utensils delivered, as they always melted or broke. She recalled his dreamy gaze as she fumbled her way through sticky Pad Thai with chopsticks she could never master or when pizza dripped mozzarella or red sauce on her chin. They even had a routine whenever her sandwich from Eat-A-Pita would drip a drop on whatever shirt she happened to be wearing that usually ended up in intercourse.

No more.

"I work all day and if I can unearth the take-out menus in the junk drawer that was supposedly cleaned out last week, decide on a place, order the food and then pay for it, the least you can do is set the table. I have never dated someone as thankless as you when it comes to the basic functions of life. Do you think S gave me this much grief about setting a freaking table? I don't think so—she was too happy that I was dropping some coin for her belly to bitch about place settings."

"*Thankless*? I'm about as thankless and unappreciative as, as—whatever. If you're in the kitchen spending all this time finding menus and deciding the type of food you want to eat and thinking about eating, why don't you just make some real food?"

"*Real* food? That's where you come in, my darling." His words were ripping scratches into the flesh surrounding her heart that was already on its last beat. And then he dropped the bomb. "I know she's a dyke, but didn't your mother teach you *anything*? Did you miss the day in school where they taught the girls how to cook dinner and do laundry? You are nothing but a spoiled princess and I made you that way."

Game over.

Cat knew she could no longer get away with baking the occasional strawberry cake or putting a curl in her hair before the seventh-inning stretch. M had been right. This meal-making crap and house-cleaning shit was going to be the deal-breaker in J's eyes, and since neither was taught to budge, the subject was mute. No matter the price or amount of gifts (gold, silver, diamonds, rubies, etc.) and acceptable companionship he provided on the rare occasions he was in town, she knew the game would be ending without overtime and her team had lost. He wanted—and deserved—the domesticity that accompanied home field advantage. He wanted to play house. She wanted convenience with room and board. Cat desperately had to locate the escape hatch or find a parachute and jump off J's private jet of urban living that she had grown accustomed to living.

After a few nights of ignoring the subject, J called out for her. She was knee-deep in her studies on the sofa and walked into the kitchen with attitude in hand. She had been absorbed in an unsettling novel written by a soldier after his hellish Vietnam experience which could actually have prepared her for the upcoming onslaught of testosterone, but it didn't. There J stood in the kitchen, proud as a new father looking from a recently installed dishwasher to her. Cat smiled at the enormous machine, knowing its function in the world, in general, but not caring—as she would never be using the gargantuan metal box. Aside from childhood chores, she was never and *would* never be a slave to housework and believed it was everyone for themselves when it came to cleaning up a joint.

"This is the answer to all of our problems." He beamed and placed his arm around her. "Now we can use real dishes—glasses even—when we order out and you don't have to worry about washing them in the sink. Isn't this great? It's the top of the line model."

"Yea, but how do the dishes get from the table to the machine to the cabinet?" She asked coyly, knowing full well she would forget to run the thing or empty the clean dishes or disregard the entire process altogether. "Or we could just take the plates out when we eat and put them right back in as soon as dinner is over. I am assuming this is a *we* process, correct?"

"I was kind of thinking that you could empty it out when you get back from school, before I get home. That way, when I get home, *we* could order the food together and you would set the table, like a traditional family, and *we* could sit down to dinner every night without a fight."

"*Traditional family?* There is nothing traditional or family about this whole set-up."

"Well, we could be." He took a velvet box from his pocket and handed it to her.

"What's this?" She opened the box to find a long gold chain and an antique locket with her initials engraved. She was taken aback, but comfortable with his gift giving when he felt guilty, or at times when things needed smoothing over, but still dismayed at the fact that J wanted his milk free. Not that she wanted to get married; it would just make swallowing the pill from houseguest to housewife a little easier. "A necklace. It's beautiful."

"Not half as beautiful as you." He moved behind her to close the clasp and seal the deal. "Now what do you say we order some Ben Pao and waste some time before I go pick it up?"

"Waste some time? By setting the table? I know, why don't we read the instructional manual together? We could learn how to use it together, like a team. A *traditional* team."

"I had something else in mind, smart aleck." His kiss told her that reading was not his intention and her clothes were not an option. It was now time to give thanks for his considerate gesture, whether it was the dishwasher or the necklace. At least she could imagine the sweet taste and smell of her cashew chicken during their brief sexual encounter and that image alone would cause her to sigh and moan in moments of boredom.

"Something else? Like what?" She cooed warmly in his ear. Cat unbuttoned his shirt and rubbed his chest, knowing her place in this game and taking it from the kitchen to the playing field that had gotten her this far. "You want to make a woman out of me in front of the new dishwasher? It's still a baby."

"You know I'm leaving town tomorrow for a couple days and that would give you the time to get used to it," he whispered while pulling off her jeans. "I've got to finish up that deal in Seattle for my brother, but do you think that maybe you could try it out for me? Just give it a chance? Maybe?"

"Maybe."

"I could look into a self-cleaning oven when I get back."

"I love it when you talk dirty to me."

A few days later, Cat was worried that she hadn't had a dry run on the appliance—the safety seals and price tag were still attached and J was scheduled to return the next morning. She simply sat and stared at the beast. Every ounce of her despised the idea of scraping leftover pieces of something or another from his macabre black plates into a garbage can and then placing them gently into a machine meant for sanitation. What in god's name was wrong with paper plates and plastic forks? In her eyes, that was the American way.

There had to be an easier answer, a better answer, a reasonable answer.

The summer sun shone in from the balcony and mirrored the chrome giant to create bright images on the walls like a disco ball at Studio 54. Afternoon turned into early evening and the bright light became a dull orange glow from the setting sun. Dishes needed to be done and Cat required detergent. A trip to Potash on State for incidentals was now the only name on her dance card.

Cat always looked forward to a trip to the market. She imagined the grocery store a noble adventure that was not at all homemaker-related. There were things to smell and touch, new products to stumble upon, old favorites with which to reacquaint. She loved to stroll through the produce section while telling herself to eat more green leafy things. The aisles of snacks reminded her there was always something new and unhealthy to be grateful for and begging for a trial run in her kitchen cabinet. She adored smelling the shampoos and soaps, imagining that a fresher, cleaner, happier Cat would materialize with just the right blend of cocoa butter and jojoba.

All the doors of life opened up, for a price, at the grocery store.

While checking calories in bacon bits, Cat heard a soft voice humming along with the Kenny Loggins song that was playing in the store. More amused by the devil-may-care of the store singing than interested in the singer, she smiled to herself and continued the search for the perfect salad toppings. As the humming turned to singing and got louder, she needed to see who was the fan of canned music and faded artist. The face belonging to the somewhat musical sound was a familiar sight: a well-dressed, good-looking man in his fifties who currently taught African-American Feminist Lit, was strolling down the salad dressing aisle, himself with a half-crooked smile. He was lanky, well over six feet tall, still in his gray suit with a loosened tie and had a buzzing cell phone and a head of lettuce in his basket. He glanced down the aisle and saw his amused and bemused student studying the newest addition to the Paul Newman family of dressings.

"Catrin? Catrin Moran? At a grocery store?"

"Professor Wolf, what a surprise."

She immediately noticed his almond-colored eyes that twinkled behind his tiny-framed glasses and an evening shadow was making an appearance on his face. Cat had always thought of him as striking in class, his mountains of wisdom creating an aura of mysteriousness, but now, in front of the croutons and in a human setting, he was downright godlike. His shaggy brown hair was every inch the spitting image of Jackson Browne—even looking like it needed a thorough washing. He must have had a long day in the graduate school grind.

"Oh, just call me Wolf. Everyone else does. I don't even remember my first name anymore," he joked, smiling at his own brilliant wit. "How are you? Doing a little late-night shopping, I see."

"Yea, I needed to get a few things for the old homestead. How about you? Had an urge for salad or is there a sale on cucumbers?"

"It seems salad is the only thing I can make these days with all the undergraduate papers that need grading and my lack of cooking abilities." He glanced at his basket, ignored his still-ringing phone and looked into her eyes. "How are things with you? Classes going OK?"

"Yea, great—listen, I should let you go. You've got that phone thing happening and I'm sure a hungry tummy. I'll see you tomorrow." She didn't *want* to walk away, but she wanted to look as if she was in control by appearing independent, confident and unavailable to the man who she just noticed didn't wear a wedding ring. Had he ever? Why did she care?

"Catrin—"

"Please, call me Cat."

"*Cat*, are you genuinely busy right now? This may sound out of left field, but how about we grab some real food—I don't know, how about a sandwich? I know this great place right around the corner. We could talk about your paper."

"What paper?" She was intrigued—was he hitting on her?

"I'll think of one." He smiled and dropped his basket to the ground after taking out his phone. "I couldn't possibly handle another volley of vegetables this week."

"*Volley* of vegetables? Is that proper usage?"

"It's too late to know. How about it?"

It was love at first sight.

Just as he had said, there was a little bar around the corner that served food and he ordered promptly. Cat initially felt uncomfortable, but not uptight. Doctor—err, Wolf made her feel not at ease, but like the crown jewel someone had unexpectedly placed at the center of this learned man's attention. They discussed the English department and swapped gossip each had heard while nibbling on nachos; so-and-so was dating someone and you-know-who had to drop a class for fear of failing and what's-his-name needs to retire. Over the main course, they talked about the class they shared, Cat's expectations and the anticipated final outcome. Never once did the absolutely insane notion of a hook-up leave her mind.

"So I'm guessing that you're single."

"Actually," she wanted to lie, but was unable, "I'm living with someone."

"That leads me to believe that you wouldn't be interested in having a drink sometime," he added casually between bites of his corned beef on rye. He grazed on the rye gently and never once let a stray piece of his messy corned beef fall from his mouth to the basket the meal was served in.

"I didn't say that," she flirted. Concentrating on her composure took energy from her desire to look sexy eating a turkey club; there were bits of lettuce and tomato dropping from the bun and landing all over her area that she quickly wiped with the gingham napkin provided. "I'm far from married, if that's what you mean. We're more like roommates and I was under the impression that students couldn't date professors, that is, if a date is what you had in mind."

"You're a graduate student, Cat. The rules have changed."

"I've never been a big fan of rules." She wanted to sound daring. Part of her wanted to leap from the barstool and kiss his tasty ruby lips. The other part of her demanded she remain calm, sipping her iced tea and glancing frequently past his movie star face into the brick wall beyond the beams of light that shot from his eye sockets. "If you want to have a drink, then let's have a drink. No better time than the present."

They ordered drinks with dessert. Cat forgot all about the dishwasher and its angry dirty plates that were caked with leftover pizza and ravioli. She wanted to talk, she wanted to learn, and most importantly, she wanted to live.

Wolf had tales of traveling the world, studying at the finest schools and experiencing life to a degree she had only dreamed about. Each sip of wine brought another story of greatness, another belly of laughter, another moment of closeness. It was his boyish charm and years of mileage that intrigued her; each line around his eyes was a set of encyclopedias that she was determined to read from beginning to end. She didn't want to be his student; she wanted to be his concubine, his secret mistress. Why her? Why now? Why secret?

"Tell me, do you have a job outside of school, or are you independently wealthy?"

"I'd have to say the guy I live with is the bread winner. He sort of supports my lifestyle." She shrugged and placed her napkin over the basket of leftover fries. "He just bought me a dishwasher."

"A dishwasher? Cat, please, you were not bred for captivity. Your brain wasn't meant to be someone's live-in. A good friend of mine runs an ad agency in the city and they are always looking for fresh minds. I could give him a call if you like—I bet you would fit right in. Then you could find your own place and be your own woman." He smiled and delicately placed his hand on her knee anticipating a positive response. "I've been watching you all semester—last year as well. One thing I can tell you is that your work is not only more advanced than the other students', but there's some sort of fire inside of you. It's a fire that I can't describe and can't help but be attracted to, Cat. I guess I'm also a sucker for that beautiful face of yours."

"Me?" Her voice squeaked like a teenager. "I can see my comments in class as being a little off the beaten path, but I never thought—"

"Don't think, just enjoy." He finished his wine and looked at her. Each second that passed was a lifetime of lustful thoughts. "Well, Potash is now closed and you, my dear, are unable to buy your dishwashing fluid. There is a Jewel on Division that's open twenty-four hours and I'm going in that direction if you need a lift."

"No, I've got my car." It was J's car, but who was listening? God? No, god had sent this man to her wrapped in a bow. "I guess I'll see you in class."

"Think about what I said, Cat. You are worth more alive

than you are dead and right now your petals are wilting." He kissed her cheek and they physically went their separate ways.

Floating on a cloud, but lost in a fog, Cat stopped at 7-11 on State for detergent without hesitation. Thinking of nothing and no one but Wolf, she failed to notice that she was hand-washing the dishes and then putting them each in their cabinet home. She suddenly had a purpose, a found prince, and the possibility of happiness, thanks to salad dressing in aisle 8 of the local grocer and the now revered *Caddyshack* theme song.

The next morning, J crawled into bed while Cat was still dreaming of her possible knight in shining armor. The smell of cigars and the stale airport air caused her to roll over and wiggle under the covers. His arms encircled her, drawing her lifeless body to his, pulling her close for a kiss. She drifted in and out of her state of deep sleep for the next few minutes as it became clear that J was there and had tickets for the ride.

"Cat, are you asleep?" he whispered in her ear.

"I was, I am, sort of. Welcome home." She rolled over and faced him. "I've been doing some thinking about you and me and this *we* thing."

"Thinking." He was hesitant. She was allowed to think, he supposed, but the thoughts weren't supposed to lessen his manhood or cause tension for him in any way. "Good thinking or bad thinking?"

"Just thinking. You know, considering some things about our situation and stuff." She was mentally becoming more alert and his face began to show fear. "I have some issues with the living arrangement and—J, you're really a great guy and you come from this awesomely great family and you have a great job and have all these really great things going for you."

"This doesn't sound great." He sat up; a slight paunch was beginning to show at the top of his boxer shorts that made her smile. "So I've got all these great things and you're the great icing on the cake, right?"

He leaned over and gave her a kiss, morning breath and all.

His left arm disappeared momentarily behind him and returned to produce a well-recognized robin's egg-colored box that she knew had a single point of origin: Tiffany's. Instead of grabbing for it as usual, she smiled and tried with her eyes to tell him it was over; that maybe she had met someone. Sure, it was only dinner and there was probably nothing to be concerned about, but that she was considering it—whatever *it* was. In fact, she had considered *it* all night as she polished each and every plate until her manicured nails chipped and hands wrinkled.

"No, no more gifts," she said sadly and pushed the box she desperately wanted to open from her reach. She loved his gifts. He always came back from a trip with a jeweled this or shining that or an expensive outfit from some trendy new designer. His thoughtful wallet drove her insane at times and calmed her at others. Even in her wildest fantasies, she never imagined living the lifestyle he had weaned her into.

"So that's it. I assume you're planning on telling me that you're leaving." He got up and started a frenzied pace around the bed. "Where are you going to go? Who is going to take care of you the way I do? No one."

"It's not that, J. Just sit down a minute."

"No, I've not only put up with your queen-bee attitude around here. I've gotten used to it. I even like it! I let you live here, use my car, use my credit cards—I buy you things, nice things, expensive things. No one else is going to spend six-hundred dollars on a dress for you that you'll only wear once."

"J, come on. Let's talk."

"Is it someone else? It can't be. It's not like you have a life outside of here. You go to school, you come home, and we go to Justin's—is it someone at school? Have you gone and fallen for another one of your teachers? What is it with you and your professors? Are you still looking for your father?" He stopped short, "I'm sorry, that was low."

"I haven't fallen for anyone."

"Then it's me?   What could I possibly do that is so aggravating to make you want to leave? I know I travel a lot—do you want to start coming with me? Is it the dishwasher thing? We don't need to use it—I'll do the dishes every night if it makes you happy."

"It's not the dishwasher."   The alarm on the nightstand started to buzz. She reached over and turned it off. "I've got to get ready for school. Can we talk about this later?"

"Just take these, wear them, and think about what you are doing. Think about me and us and this great thing we have going."

"J, this is all about me." She took the box and held it tightly in her hand without opening it. "I want to branch out, get a job, and be someone."

"I could get you a job—"

"I want to get my own job, J. It's not over between you and me; the deck just needs to be reshuffled. We'll talk later." She kissed his cheek and retreated to the bathroom as tears began to fall down her flushed cheeks, her brain reeling.

What was she thinking?

After class that morning, Cat greeted Wolf in his office with a new attitude, a fresh life plan and spectacular diamond earrings. Never once looking back, she knew it was time to put her life in second gear and become the person she once set out to be.

But where would the road take her?

The breeze was fresh on her back and the future was an open road of adventure.

Rose,

Yo. Sorry it's been so long without a letter, but I've been busy with school and washing dishes and breaking hearts and what not.

Let me tell you the latest—I've met someone. No, not J or one of those young ruffians from the bar, but a real man. His name is Wolf, Doctor Wolf—he's one of my professors at school and he is dreamy. I never thought that something could happen, him being a teacher and all, but it did. We ran into each other at Potash and went out for drinks and wham! I'm in love.

There are a few drawbacks, like the J thing. I am living there and being his whore and doing his dishes (don't even ask), and Wolf is separated from his wife of a million years, but he is getting a divorce, and being with him is phenomenal. We can talk about intelligent things and have this chemistry—I haven't had feelings like these since, well, you know when. I know that this whole thing is probably a stupid crush—oh, there goes Cat with another one of her teachers—but he is talking about getting my own place and helping me get a job!

I don't even know where to begin—me, speechless!

I'm too excited to go on!

More later,

Cat

ADG 226

4 years – 4,000 mile Bachelor of Arts warranty.
5 years - 5,000 mile Master of Fine Arts service contract.
7 years - 100,000 miles and you can call yourself a "doctor." Guaranteed.

What are the latest breakthroughs in safety? What is octane? Do you know when you lug the engine? Does this model offer exceptional roadside assistance for the over-educated? What happens if the luxury family carrier overheats or the radiator thingy steams up when you pop the hood like it does in movies? Four-wheel drive means what, exactly, in Shakespearean terms? Again, explain the importance of parallel parking in Middle English.

Every so often, the new car owner's questions are effortlessly answered. Most of the time, issues can be resolved moments after the dilemma has been brought up—especially if you have access to the manual—the nicer the car, the better the manual and the more languages it's printed in. If you aren't fortunate enough to be considered a "car person," it's good to have someone around who knows a thing or two when a moving violation is discovered, it needs to be lubed or jump-started when a battery dies or if a proper check of the air pressure in the tires is due.

Who even knew tires had pressure? Did this car read *Finnegan's Wake*? James Joyce is real pressure.

Cat never had a designated helper in the car arena, so when Wolf took the keys to her old Cavalier and returned a few hours later with a spotless, detailed, sky-blue sedan with a full tank of premium love, she was in heaven.

"You don't have to thank me. That's part of my job."

"I thought you were an English professor," Cat mumbled shyly. "*My* English professor."

"No, silly." He frowned when he pushed her curls behind her ear and viewed yet another high-priced gift from her previous lover, ruby earrings. "It's part of my duties. Making sure you get safely from one place to another is important to me just like you are important to me. Now, let's talk about this fantastic job you are going to get."

Cat grimaced, knowing her employment history was filled with titles like clerk and waitress and receptionist—things to pay cover charges and bar bills while in school. She had never prepared for the future like she was told; she never believed there would be a time she was not in school and now, not on someone else's dime. Or was she? Most of her belongings had moved from J's pad to another high-rise in an equally impressive building on the same block. There were more doormen who wore suits and knew her by name the second time she entered the opened door—one even carried her groceries to the loft she uneasily called home. She was old enough to know someone was paying the bills, but too young—or purposely naïve—to see a lease or ask the price of rent.

Moments later, they were entering an elevator in one of Chicago's tallest buildings. Wolf had talked wildly to Cat about a magnificent job at a top advertising firm and they were there to claim to it, and to see his "college pal" who ran the place. Like the new apartment building, there was an elevator operator who pushed the numbers and searched each face for familiarity to be met by name. As expected, "Professor Wolf" was welcomed with a smile and gloved hand to shake.

The doors opened and a buzzing office halted to greet "The Professor" as he was called by almost every employee in sight. Cat smiled at the receptionist, who quickly checked her make-up and stood to greet them.

"Professor," she nervously spoke, "Mr. R is waiting for you. He'll be glad to know you're here. It's good to see you again—"

"Don't bother ringing him. I know my way."

Wolf and Cat walked hand in hand past cubes and meeting rooms to what Cat always imagined to be "the corner office," where she saw a shoeless man practicing putting. Without knocking, Wolf dropped her hand and walked inside, shutting the door behind them.

"R, helluva putt, but it's still too far to the right."

The men shook hands and then exchanged a manly-type hug. Both stood back and looked at Cat with knowing smiles and devilish thoughts swirling in their minds that she could read. She didn't ask to read a lease, but she knew how to read a guy in man's clothing.

"So, is this the genius you told me about?" He held his hand out to her. "R's the name and nobody can use it without Mr. before it except you, understand?"

"Uh, yea." Her newly whitened teeth lit the room and she took his hand. "Catrin Moran. People call me Cat."

"This is the one, my best student." Wolf smugly put his arm around her. "One of the best minds you will find on the planet."

"That's what I'm looking for. I've got your office all set up and we work usually eight to five, depending on the project. Hell, I've got guys who stay here past midnight, but that's not going to be you." He put down the club and sat behind his desk while Wolf took a chair, motioning for her to do the same. "Tell me about yourself."

Cat looked apprehensively at Wolf. She was never good at interviews and worse when the subject hit close to home. What should she disclose first? Maybe she should start with a quirky tale of lesbian parenting, followed by her father's suicide or the days surrounding her rape as a teen? She had so many positive and uplifting stories to share with her new employer.

"Well, let me tell you," as always, Wolf gunned the engine and shifted into third gear. "She is almost finished with her doctoral thesis in literature, Ivy education, and whatnot. She is enthusiastic and a hard worker and the only thing I know of that she cannot do are dishes."

The men laughed. They laughed and shared that shrewd smile again making Cat feel like running out of the room, the building, the city. But she couldn't and wouldn't. This was now her life and she had to step up to the plate whenever she had the chance. She had left Team J for this ball club with the full intent of winning—losing was not an option.

"That's not true entirely," she piped in with a charismatic tone, "I can run a dishwasher. I just choose not to. I'm no old dog, but there are some tricks I don't care to learn. So, why don't you tell me what you're going to want me to do for you?"

"You don't mess around, I like that." R slipped into his loafers, stood up and led them out of the office and to a cube next to the window. "This is where you will be sitting and doing your work, copywriting and editing mostly, and over there is G, your secretary."

"Secretary?" Cat questioned as a girl her age ran over with a pad of paper and pen behind her ear. "What would I need a, excuse me, an assistant for?"

"My name is G, hi. I will be here before you and after you leave and get your coffee and lunch and dinner and dry cleaning and whatever else you need me to do." The girl was anxious for no apparent reason. "Do you need anything right now? Coffee? Tea? Do you prefer blue or black pens, or if you prefer pencils, do you have a brand and an electric sharpener or—"

"Isn't she great?" R was grinning at Wolf. Neither took their eyes off of Cat's body. "She'll take care of you."

"I'll be right back," Wolf whispered in her ear before returning to R's office.

"Listen, I don't know what I do here so I don't know what I need an assistant for." Cat smiled and tried to calm the over-caffeinated girl down with her eyes. It didn't work. "Did you ever think of decaf? Like actually switching to something less intense today or sometime soon? You're a little too wound up and it scares me."

"I'm sorry, Ms. Moran—I mean Doctor Moran or do you prefer Professor Moran? But Mr. R said you were new and important and to drop everything whenever you were around." She half smiled. "Since he's the head guy of like, thirty offices around the world, we all just thought it meant you were—or are—some huge client or vice president or something. You are someone big, right?"

"Ms. Moran? My mother isn't even Ms. Moran. Just call me Cat, and I'm not important in any way—no more important than you or him or anybody."

"Blue or black?"

"Blue or black what?" Cat was losing the little patience she had that day and the thigh highs that accompanied the garter belt that Wolf bought were in need of a lift.

"Pens. I need to know what you will be using." G was persistent. There was no way Cat would get out of this conversation without telling the girl in a knock-off DKNY suit her preferences on essential things like pen color and coffee flavor. "I don't mean to be a pain, but it's my job to get this information from you so that everything will be set up on your first day."

"Blue. Blue Bic pens, medium tip. OK? I never ever want

to see a black pen—they make me ill. I also like red for a change every once in a while, you know, to mix it up? Anything else?" Now she was agitated. There was no way Cat could stand looking at this girl every single day, let alone work with her. "I don't drink coffee unless there is whiskey in it, I like yellow legal pads and *People* magazine. And the tabloids are essential. I know I will bring in a radio for my desk and I'll need a calendar with big numbers. If you can, I'd prefer an Apple computer that can work with Windows programs." She didn't even know if it existed, but she felt like G wanted a challenge.

"And your coffee? How do you take it? What brand of whiskey would you like in your coffee?" She took a breath and looked around. "I'm sorry. Thank you. It'll be a pleasure working for you."

"G, you don't work for me—you work for R." Cat saw R and Wolf heading in her direction and knew G would run off before they reached her cube.

"How's everything working out?" Wolf whispered and put his arm around her waist. "I've got to get back to campus for the department meeting—I am the new head, you know."

Wolf had recently had been promoted to the head of the English Department and was planning on making some drastic changes in the curriculum. He wanted to slowly ease out ancient authors like Chaucer and introduce classes focusing on more current subjects like the Harlem Renaissance or Cat's favorite Vietnam era novels. He even planned an elective devoted entirely to recent best sellers and their importance or lack thereof. Medieval was out and pop culture was on the VIP list. It was going to be a hard sell to tenured musty book lovers who proudly taught early European epics and recited *Beowulf* from memory, but Wolf was confident that the new classes would bring the department—and school—a more well-rounded well-read student prepared for the future by thinking in the present day, but still learning from the past.

"Department head, eh? Good for you!" R shook his hand again. "Cat, there will be a car service to pick you up in front of your building at 7:45 each morning. That doesn't mean you have to be in it at that time—the car waits for you no matter what time you feel like coming in."

"A car? What time do most people get here?" A car service? What was that about? "When will G be getting in?"

"She is in at 7:15 every day. That way, she'll have everything in order and ready for you to join the team the moment you arrive. I expect you will enjoy your days here and might even get thrown challenging or interesting assignments from time to time. First and foremost, every morning, the whole staff completes a crossword puzzle in ink. The puzzle is distributed at exactly eight o'clock. That's how we start our days here."

"*Crossword puzzles?* Is that a joke?"

"Just a little brain food to get you thinking," Wolf again shared the sheepish grin with R who was blatantly admiring her short skirt and long legs. "We'll let you get back to your putting and Cat will start on Monday. I'll have her all prepped and ready to go by then—we'll even work on some crossword puzzles over the weekend—maybe the *Times*."

"It's a fierce competition and there's a bonus for the first to finish each day. You might tell G to get you a dictionary and thesaurus for yourself." He shook her hand with a strong grip. "Looking forward to working with you. Heck, I'm looking forward to just seeing you every day."

"A dictionary? I'm a Ph.D. and know six languages and—"

"What did I tell you? All of this and a Mensa membership." Wolf laughed as he cut her off. "She is remarkable."

Back at campus in the English faculty lounge, the mere suggestion of an atypical course schedule caused a head-on collision, blocking every outgoing lane. Red lights flashed and tempers flared at the suggestion of a unique or altered look at literature. Opposition expected, Wolf listened thoughtfully to concerns and fielded questions with answers slightly peppered with minor changes to the upcoming semester and each syllabus. He challenged instead of demanded each to shine a new light on the oldies and take a test drive with newer models to compare their significance and handling ability. He then stepped out of the conversation to retrieve a list of ideas and book suggestions he left in his office, but the banter continued between the professors and want-to-be professors.

"I don't know about all of you, but I'm not one bit interested in what that man has to say!" The Irish Renaissance professor barked. "We need to stand firm with this. None of us should budge an inch."

"That's easy for you to say. Your class wouldn't be changed a bit."

"Say goodbye to Chaucer, thank god." The Critical Theory Teacher added. "And not a minute too soon—year after year of teaching the same old thing gets old for us as much as it does for the students. Let's hear him out."

"*Wilcume*. I will happily retire Luther and Marlowe," Professor K announced. "Give me some Faulkner or Camus and you will see an improvement in student morale. That old material depresses even me."

"No way. I am proud to and will continue to teach Ancient Egyptian Literature," the old coot bellowed with pride. "The system has been tested and has proven successful for as long as I have been here, and any alteration will cause a collapse within our institution."

"What *exactly* do you teach?" Cat asked, without knowing her reason to be in attendance at this meeting. "I've received all my degrees from this school and have never taken a class taught by you. I've never even seen you before."

"Cat, what are you doing here anyway?" the Hawthorne know-it-all questioned.

Wolf returned. "Doctor Moran's presence, as you have

discovered, is here because she's going to be teaching an undergraduate elective on Seamus Heaney on Tuesday and Thursday nights. As you can see from the papers I just handed out, the changes will be gradual and we won't be eliminating Homer, just putting him in conjunction with contemporary thinkers."

"Contemporary like Scott Turrow? Stephen King?"

"As I said, I refuse and I speak for many in this room—I will go straight to the dean if this nonsense isn't put to bed." The coot was adamant. The fight was starting to look interesting.

"How dumb do you think I am, F? I have the dean's full approval and have been given the thumbs-up to do a little housecleaning." A secure and powerful Wolf took the group by surprise and Cat was taking note. This was not the happy-go-lucky Existentialist expert leading the meeting; this was a man with a clear objective and path to success mapped out; a sexy map. "Now look over the papers I just gave you and feel free to make suggestions or comments. As I said, this is just the beginning of a long process and there will be kinks to work out, but if we pull together, it might just work. Who's in?"

"I most certainly am not," the coot said and left the room.

"I think this is workable," the Bronte assistant professor said. "Anyone who agrees with F should make their concerns known now. F is clearly trying to start an interdepartmental war that I, for one, refuse to participate. Wolf has made an appeal to change what we are used to and know. This will affect each of our classes and even teaching styles. We need to work together. Should we take a vote or start out with questions?"

"Thank you, R, for your comments. It's good to start out on the right foot."

"Old F will come around when he realizes he is the only one in the boat." The Hemingway guru spoke up, "These changes are needed to keep up with other universities and I know I'm not the only one who thinks the tenure policy needs to be revised."

All nodded and a few chuckled. The suave Wolf seemed to have won over the group with his ideas and plans for the future, but Cat was concerned with her place in the department. Doctor Moran? Twice today she was called that and didn't mind. It wasn't until Wolf had announced her teaching status that she realized she *did* have a place at the informal meeting. Wolf had not asked her if she was interested in teaching, or if she had a slight knowledge of Irish poetry, but what was done was done and, like the crossword puzzle job, this was the woman she was destined to become. Grab your dictionary and start the engine.

For now anyway.

Like it or not.

Time to land the plane.

738 YES

Each fresh tank of gas in Aunt Jillie's hand-me-down car seemed to bring about the possibility of an adventure in her conventional and monotonous life—even if it was just for a joyride through Boystown or journey through the Gold Coast. The simple feel of her toe touching the weathered gas pedal kicked off a promising path to discover: new turns to take, short cuts to ignore, one-way signs to overlook; and routes to learn by heart. A laid-back ride in the Cavalier was a special occasion as she now had a "driver" in an elegant town car to take her to and from the only place she seemed allowed: work. She and Wolf never left the loft and this made Cat wonder if he was hiding her (which she was used to and accepted) or genuinely not interested in the world outside. He was always reading, preparing for a class or working the kinks out of an upcoming lecture by practicing on Cat, who paid little attention. The only thing she observed was his lack of personal effects in the shared apartment. This reminded her that he was a visitor, not an occupant. There were one or two or three pairs of khakis in the closet and hardly any other clothes of any kind; only a few T-shirts and bare essential toiletries—maybe a toothbrush and razor—were in the bathroom. More often than not, they would share a roll in the hay before he left and slept elsewhere. Wolf was adamant that her name was on the doorbell, not his. She knew that his wife was still the designated hitter in this game that was a daily reminder of her recurring role as benchwarmer.

Except on Mondays. *Melrose* Mondays at Justin's.

Monday was the only night Cat was free to be herself. All week she looked forward to Monday nights. She hurried home from work and changed from the business suit Wolf had bought into a separate outfit also hand-picked by himself. Cat was his doll and assumed she was not his first. Her appearance was evaluated daily and frequently based on his current fantasy or desire. He filled her closet with haute couture, dozens of knock-me-down and fuck-me heels and outrageously priced undergarments. Another Wolf whim was a demand to cut her long hair into layers—an outrageous fee Cat believed he could not afford. Curling was now a necessity, not a fun way to waste time while a cake baked.

But Monday erased everything.

Most feelings of indentured servitude were eliminated for a few hours of drinking, laughing and gossiping—that's what made living this depraved life worthwhile. Doctor Moran tickled the patrons with more than gossip; they adored stories of Cat's meaningless job and the co-worker morons she spent her days sipping herbal tea laced with whiskey with while reading a dictionary.

"Drinks are on me tonight!" Cat proclaimed as she bounced to the jukebox. It immediately began playing "Dancing Queen" and triggered a cheer.

"Did someone win the crossword puzzle contest?" J asked, his eyes lingering on what he considered to be his sole mistake. And she was. Everything in his life was going according to plans that had been mapped and folded years before: He was working in the family business, making large amounts of money, but living alone. He still believed Cat was the one and only. Perhaps she *was* the one for him and he spent nights praying for her return.

"I sure did—and this one was a total grab-bag of shit. I swear I'm going to start telling them I make the things up for cash. These people and their crossword puzzles—do you know that is the *only* thing I have to do for eight hours a day? I think once I was given some copy to edit, but no one gives me an important task or ask if I want to work on a project of any kind nor do I think they ever will *and* I have this secretary. *And* she calls me Doctor Moran."

"Is she single?" L was always on the lookout.

"Too high strung for you, but I'll introduce you to her. You guys do your dry cleaning at the same place. Mine." Cat gulped a triple shot of Bushmills and twirled to the disco beat. "She practically bows when I approach her—like I'm the fucking queen of England. Mick, another round. Make it something strong this time. Make mine a Doctor Moran."

"Slow down, Kitty Cat," Mick smiled. "The show hasn't even started."

He was right; *Melrose Place* was not yet on the screen; an altogether bizarre pile of soapsuds bubbled over the machine into the laundry room of hearsay. The TV was on, but a spectacle larger than a Michael Mancini divorce dilemma was about to begin. Wolf entered the bar, *her* bar; *her* protected palace in the neighborhood he had never visited. Cat didn't even hear the bells over the door as she and Rose danced to ABBA. During a double twirl, Rose pointed at the door. Cat was astonished and shocked.

"Wolf, hi, what are you doing here?" She was suddenly panicky and no longer bubbly.

"Hello, Catrin. I thought I would spend some time with your friends. I'd like to know the people who are holding you back and turning you into a drunk on a weekly basis."

"Professor Wolf." J held out his hand that Wolf not only ignored, but shot a frown at. "J, I had you for undergraduate Theory. You are an amazing teacher. Have a seat."

"I'm Mick, the bartender around here. What'll you have?"

"What are you wearing?" Wolf focused on a frightened Cat who reached for her glass of whiskey from the bar. "Didn't I tell you those shoes are for the faculty luncheon?"

"I'm not ruining them, just wearing them in a little." Just as she was about to swallow the cocktail, Wolf grabbed the glass and threw it against the wall. "Wow, you're a real asshole tonight. Have a fight with your wife again?"

"Catrin, put your coat on. I don't approve of this life of debauchery and the people you waste time with. You should focus on your work, *important* work, not the television." Wolf looked from face to face until he reached Rose. "And I know *you*. *You* are trouble. If I ever see or hear you near my Catrin again, there *will* be trouble."

Rose had a temper that effortlessly slid into gear. "*Your* Catrin? Who the fuck do you think you are, mister penny loafers and silk boxer shorts with extra starch? She has a mind and a right to do what she wants and right now, she wants to be here. Fuck you and the library card you walked in with."

"I know about your kind. Didn't bother with college because you know better, right?"

"College? What the fuck are you talking about?" Rose was pissed and liked a good fight—verbal or physical. "Just because I didn't go to your hinky-dink school, I can't be friends with Cat? Tell me why. Write a dissertation on it for me. Bring it on, Mr. Teacher Man. You've got no purpose here and no one needs to blow you for a grade."

"I really think I should go." Cat quietly put cash on the table after getting her jacket off the chair. "I'll talk to you guys later. It's cool, it's fine. No biggie. I'll catch the show at home."

Wow. What a surprise—a boy screamed orders at Cat and she followed. Many a man had attempted to saddle her in the barn and she knew that when the leather straps came out, she would fill her lungs with air making the saddle impossible to attach. The struggle would continue until one of the two exited the stable in control of the situation. She shouldn't be used to it or accept it, but it was the guy's method: her purpose has always been to make a guy look good by being dressed properly, answering politely and following the direction the herd was headed. She knew the story all too well and fell into his demands.

"How did you get here?" Wolf barked. "Don't tell me you took the El. Don't you even begin to tell me you rode the El."

"Then I won't tell you." She looked at J, asking for help with her eyes, but knew his empty can of confrontations would go nowhere. To the surprise of all, he managed to spit out a few words to follow her Irish inkling of being ill. "*Ag mothu tinn.*"

"Wait. Just let her watch the show with us. We never see her. Professor Wolf," J pleaded with this chance to be a knight in shining armor. Seize the moment. "We're just having a couple cocktails and talking about life. No one is getting hurt and one hour will not affect her performance at work."

"Come. Now." Wolf stormed out of the bar and Cat trailed. Trained pups at a dog show could learn obedience from Cat.

That night, she fell asleep on the couch watching television and Wolf slept elsewhere.

On her way out of the building the following morning, Cat noticed something yellow on the stairs out of the corner of her eye. She turned and found a small bird, probably a parakeet-definitely someone's pet—who had made a wrong turn at the balcony. It wasn't dead; she could tell that much, so she pulled off her scarf and wrapped the tiny creature the pricey silk Chanel. Without a thought, she tenderly carried the bird to her waiting company car. The driver had seen her pick something up and was attempting to get a better look at the object she was planning on bringing into his pristine black sedan.

"Whatcha got there, Doctor Cat?" He asked, turning to the

backseat for a look. He didn't care about the bird or its dirt; he looked forward to their conversations. She regularly had a joke or a story to share. He sincerely enjoyed her company and didn't mind picking her up or dropping her anywhere she went. In the year he had this gig, she and his wife had swapped recipes, volunteered to take his daughter to "kids at work" day, and, without fail, she never left the car without giving him a good chuckle. She was good people.

"It's a little bird and I think he's hurt."

"I'd have to agree with you. It *is* a bird. It's a parakeet. Not much good for anything but sitting in a cage and singing." He pulled the car into traffic for their short trip of six blocks. "The wife had one once—drove me nuts. *That* one shouldn't have been outside like that, on the ground. It's a house bird, not an outdoor bird. What do you think you'll do with it?"

"I'll do whatever it needs. I needed a friend and I got one." She smiled at the shaking creature. "What should we call him? I know, let's call him 'Driver.' So every time I look at him I will think of you. Our special pet will be our secret. Isn't he great?"

"Driver, I like that." He felt honored. "See you this afternoon and be careful of Driver. He might not be an office bird."

"Well, I'm not an office girl, but look where my ass ends up."

No one noticed the squirming feathers as she entered the building and not a word was mentioned in the elevator. It wasn't until the doors to her floor opened and the receptionist took note of the pricey Chanel scarf hanging from her shaking hands.

"Are you feeling all right, Doctor Moran? Be careful with that scarf."

"It's Cat and I am fine. I found this little guy and I think he needs help. Could you find G and have her come see me? I think I actually have work for her today."

"Doc, what's a five letter word for economic misery?" W asked impatiently. He was always trying to win the crossword puzzle jackpot.

"Illth." Cat answered while walking past him toward her cube. "With an I. Where did you go to college? Did you even go to college? Do you know anything? People like you should not be allowed to procreate."

"Doctor Moran," G was already there with a notepad and cup of coffee. "Rumor has it that you actually need help of some kind today. Let me just tell you that I have been waiting for this moment for months—maybe a year. Is that this season's Chanel? Do you have a dead bird in a scarf that costs more than a month of my salary?"

"I guess. Do you like this thing? I think it's a piece of shit. If you want to wash the bird goo off and like it, it's yours." Cat placed the handful of bird on her desk. "What are we going to do with it? Do you know anything about birds?"

"I can have that scarf? You're kidding, right?"

"I hate this thing. If I knew you liked it, I would have given it to you long ago." Cat was in awe of the humble piece of life that struggled on her desk. She had to do something, *anything*, to get this tiny creature back in shape. Who knows, maybe someone in the building was sick with worry about their missing pet? It had to belong to somebody and they must be horrified with its disappearance. "OK, G, you know that pet shop on like, I don't know, Halsted?"

"Yes, and I know of one that's closer if we are in a hurry." Her fingers were playing with the soft silk of the scarf she never dreamed she would own. "But Mr. R is looking for you."

A small group was gathering around her desk. Cat took a company credit card from her Versace wallet and handed it to G, who looked nauseous. "Fuck him. He knows where I sit. Now you need to go there and get me everything I will need to take care of this thing. His name is Driver, you know, after my driver?"

71

The small laugh from her jealous colleagues went unnoticed.

"What about Mr. R?"

"You're not going to keep that here. You *are* taking it home or to wherever you live, right? L told me those things carry diseases. How disgusting can you be? You just bent over and picked that thing off of the ground? Do you have any idea how dirty it must be? Who knows where it's been? It could have a number of incurable diseases that we are taking in right now and will pass to on our families. K, do you want to put your family at risk? Get it out of here. I'm going to do something about this mess right here and now. Everyone with me? I think he's cute. I can't see what the problem is. No one said it was going to stay in the office."

"Will all of you shut up?" Cat was concerned about Driver and his injuries. "G? What are you still doing here? Wait, you know that shoe place on Oak? The one that smells like leather and is by Johnny Rockets? Take my car and have Driver stop there before the pet shop and get yourself something fun. You deserve it. He knows the place."

"Leather shoes? For me? From you?" This was her first real assignment, plus she was getting a Chanel scarf and now a new pair of shoes. What a great day this was turning out to be!

"Moran!" R bellowed from behind the crowd. All held their breath as the shoeless man neared Cat's desk and little Driver. "I told you not to help anyone with the crossword puzzles anymore."

"I don't do them, but I *do* help sometimes."

"What's this? A bird? In my office? What are you doing with that thing?" He leaned over and petted Driver on his right wing. "Broken. We've got to get some attention on this."

"Already done." Cat smiled with R's acceptance of a stray bird in the office. She found it funny the way he went along with almost any idea she brought up. "G is getting some necessities this morning. Do you think he could come and go with me? I wouldn't let him out here, just to keep me company, you know? At least until his wing is all better or I find his owner? He'll be well soon."

"No problemo, little lady. Make sure she gets the little fellow a mirror, they love those things." He turned toward his office and walked. "Remember, no help with the crossword puzzles. It's not your fault these people are brainless."

"Cat, what's a six letter word for sorrowful?" P never listened to authority and desperately wanted to win the cash and again requested help with her sole task. "I'll help you with your bird, I used to have them as pets. I've had about a dozen or so over the years. Please help me."

"You have? You think you'll have some sort of bond with me because of the bird? How much do you know? You can help me with Driver?" He nodded and she smiled. "Dolent."

"How do you know this stuff? N said she went to Oxford or something. M thought she memorized the dictionary. It is so unfair that she can't be in the contest—I wish I could get out of doing this thing. It's like a chore every morning and I can't start my real work until this thing is done. We're not in school anymore and if Cat doesn't have to do it then none of us should. Cat should do *something*. Yea, bringing in lost animals is not smart. This is a place of business and she runs free. She doesn't follow any rules—why should any of us?"

"Don't you learn *anything* from the puzzles?" Cat asked, eyes never leaving the bird. "That's the whole point—to get your mind working in places it wasn't working before. It's not my fault I know a bunch of words. Get over it. Go back to your desks and leave me alone."

"I'll help you with the bird, please?" P was panting. He waved the puzzle to distract her from the bird. She looked up with a frown. "I know everything there is to know about these things and how to fix what's wrong with him. With my help, he will get better and live for years."

"Give me an hour on the Internet and I will too." She was

not quick to give in. At least not while there were others within ear space. As soon as they were alone she whispered, "Give me your puzzle, quick. Don't you go and tell anyone about this. You help me with Driver and I'll get you the winning money. We'll tell people I've been tutoring you or mentoring you or something."

"Anything you want, anything." She didn't want anything, especially from him, but loved a good caper. There was nothing better than pulling one over on a boss, especially if he was sometimes peculiar and never wore shoes around the office.

"OK, nine letter word to tear to pieces." He waited anxiously.

"Dilaniate. How many more have you got?"

"That was it. Thank you!" P ran off to R's office to claim his prize money.

Cat knew R would figure out the scheme with little effort. He had to know she had helped him because there was no way someone like P would comprehend one-tenth of the words that were used on the puzzles. Cat had been churning out the required company crossword puzzle every afternoon for R—this was her only assignment during her employment and she took pride in screwing with co-workers who treated her like crap. Who knew those words? She used vocabulary that hadn't been spoken in decades—maybe centuries. Did she feel guilty about messing with their heads? Not one bit. These people could decorate a used car showroom—they knew nothing but kissing ass and looking good doing it.

But now there was Driver. Now there was a purpose; a reason to wake up in the morning and embrace the day with her new best buddy, a little yellow bird with a broken wing and a heart of gold. She knew he was the best bird possible and that he was sent to her for a reason. Now she could focus on something besides Wolf and his wife and their ongoing disputes.

"Moran, get in here," R yelled.

Every eye in the office was on her, but no tension or apprehension was seen in her pace to the glass box he called an office. As always, he wore no shoes and was again practicing his putt into a coffee mug. There wasn't a single thing that would make Cat worry about her future at this joke of a job—she was the ideal employee: she was always on time and never left early. On most days she ate her lunch at her desk and always appeared to be occupied or busy with something. When she began creating the puzzles, R declared Cat employee of the year.

"Sit down, Cat." He missed his putt. "I've got an offer for you. As you know, my wife and I are beginning divorce proceedings."

"Yes, I heard that. I am very sorry." She didn't think or care about his personal life unless his signature was missing from a paycheck. "Is there anything I can do for you in this time of need?"

"Actually, you can do something wonderful." He put down the club and leaned against his desk, arms folded. "I've got a building—it's a brownstone I gutted and turned into a single family home. I won it in a poker game a while back and the wife doesn't know about it. Great location for someone your age—Southport and Roscoe area—you know where the Launder Bar is? Southport Lanes? Right in there. I need to sell it and sell it quickly and quietly."

"You want me to do real estate? That is the only thing I don't—"

"No, I want you to buy it."

It took more than a moment for Cat to take in his offer—this was not a suggestion; it was an order. The location was awesome—right by Justin's and all her friends. She would own land and not just land, but a rehabbed single family home from an old brownstone? How could she be against something so perfect? The catch? Price. Wolf. Life.

"I'm sure I can ask some friends—"

"No, Cat, I am going to sell it to you. No one is going to even see the place because you, my trusted employee, are buying it at an unbelievable price; a price that I should give you a mule to close the deal."

"Wow, my own forty acres. You seem to have thought this through. It's not like you just woke up today and thought I would make a great homeowner. That's a fantastic idea, but let me ponder for a while. At the moment, I am concentrating on my little bird and am content in my apartment with Wolf." She stood to leave, but he pointed to the chair for her to sit.

"Wolf is going back to Coleen. You are going to need a place of your own. I've grown to like you—you're almost the daughter my wife could never have. I need to get rid of property and assets—this one specifically—before the lawyers take over the mess. I've got to hide boats and houses and condos quickly." He was firm. "I am being honest with you about Wolf. They have split up a dozen times and every time they get back together."

"Then I guess I could stop teaching that annoying class." She joked, again attempting to leave the room and the crazy talk that accompanied the verbal diarrhea leaking from her boss. "Whatever happens with Wolf, I will be fine. You guys pay me really good and I am qualified to work anywhere with all my silly degrees and experience. This has been an excellent place to learn about the advertising business with the copywriting and editing and the crossword puzzles are a gas and I thank you. Right now though, I just don't think I can afford a house—I don't think I even need a house."

"Cat, I don't think you understand." He walked and stood face to face with her. "You already are the owner of the building. Months ago I transferred the title into your name and supposedly took out the mortgage from your salary—did you know you hardly ever cash your paychecks? That's not important right now, but this is not a question, it's a done deal.

Move your things from Wolf's condo and build a life in this place. It personally has nothing to do with you and Wolf—it has to do with my assets and my divorce and my money that I want to keep. My kids have homes and are educated and don't need anything from me. You are a bright light in this agency. I know Wolf, and I know he isn't going to be with you much longer. I'm sorry, but she agreed to have a baby, which is what he wants. I did this—the transferring of the title and all the legal bullshit long before you knew which way was up. Cat, I like you and this is my gift to you."

"Wolf is going to get rid of me to have a baby?" This was all she heard from his diatribe.

"He always does." He couldn't look her in the eye and stared at the mug bearing the company logo he used as the hole for putting practice. "I've known him for a long time and in the time I have known you, I have come to respect and even like you. You're different, Cat. There is something greater out there for you to discover. I can't believe I'm telling you this."

"Can I still keep my bird?" She was always on her toes for a laugh.

"Your bird?" He chuckled. The sick parakeet on her desk meant nothing compared to his wife's demands. "You can have your bird *and* a new house and a better desk only if you keep coming up with these crossword puzzles. You even have *me* stumped. But one thing, Cat."

She was hesitant; would the other shoe drop? "What?"

"You can't let Wolf know what I told you. I can see what he sees in you and it's everything he doesn't deserve. You are better than him—better than any man I can think of for that matter. You always talk about your car—"

"Because it's all I have."

"Well, let me put it this way. There's no long-term warranty on him." He moved to the seat at her left and took her hand. "I never thought I would choose one of his girls over our friendship, but you've changed me. Please keep this between us."

"Between us?" she joked. "I think you meant between you and me and the parakeet."

"Good girl," he sighed. "I never thought he would find someone out of his league, but you, you're something special. You can continue to work here as long as you like, keep all your company credit cards and your bird and your driver on one condition,"

"And that is?"

"He knows nothing of this. He can know about the brownstone that you *legally* bought from me—that's not a problem. If there's one thing he knows about, it's dirty divorces. Cat, it's one thing to lose a friend, it's another to lose a brother, and Wolf is like a brother to me. He'll let you down gently, but still be prepared. I actually think it might be the bird that sets him off—his wife loves birds."

"Nice coincidence. Karma even." She smiled and felt relief that her relationship was to come to an end sooner than she had predicted. "But not planned; just a twist of fate. I understand lawyers. My lesbian second mother is a lawyer, if you can believe that. I'll wait for him to get rid of me. This conversation never took place, right? Just give me my new address and I will slip out of the frame in each lens when he decides to send me off. That is, if you don't mind me helping him spend a little more money on me—he really dresses me well."

"I noticed. He always does that. Took off some pounds, too—gain them back."

"Did I tell you he totally embarrassed me in public? In front of my friends at my bar, but I'll just take that in stride." She was going to enjoy this one.

"My lawyer will be here this afternoon for you to sign papers for the building. You can fax them to your lesbian mother if you want a second opinion." He was relieved, and sighed. "This conversation was just another business transaction between co-workers and, if I may say, friends."

"Friends, I like that." She again stood and turned to leave.

"He embarrassed you in *front* of your friends? At a bar?" Curiosity killed the cat.

"Justin's on Southport and Roscoe—right near the house you sold me. The place even has a drink named for me."

"What's in it?"

"Bushmills. Just Bushmills in a tall glass." For some reason, she was proud of the liquor that bore her moniker. "Irish whiskey, three shots at once. Maybe I can buy you one sometime."

"I'd like that." He felt fatherly to her; he wanted her success with minimal suffering in the process, "I'd really like that, Cat. Now you get back to that bird. You say you found it outside your building?"

"Yea, it was the strangest thing." She followed his lead. "I was walking out the door and this little yellow speckle caught my eye. I hope I can help it or at least give it a good home for the time being. I think you gave us both a good home, but between you and me, I was planning on ditching the Wolf— can you believe I didn't have an escape plan on that one?"

"You are too good for that man."

"Please don't tell me I am smart like a lesbian. I am *not* my mom."

"No," he laughed. "There's no lesbian in you. You deserve someone who can make you shine, not someone who tries to shine you. Moran, you do not need a polishing. Aim higher."

She didn't know what to say. "I've got to get back to my bird. You know I named him Driver? What a great day today has been—I got a home and a pet and finally a job for that worthless G. Nothing against her, she just needs someone who needs her and I don't."

"Moran, I do have one concern." She stopped in her tracks. "Don't help these idiots with the crossword puzzles. I like them better when they squirm."

"One condition—I won't help them only if they are told I make them up—just to fuck with them."

"Deal." He smiled and she went back to Driver and a gathered crowd. H was poking at him with a pencil and K had taken him off the scarf and left him on the cold desk.

"What the hell do you think you are doing?" Immediately, she softly placed him back in the scarf and thrust H against the wall. "You see this bird? You touch this bird or anything of mine again and I will have your ass against the wall. Not the boss or security, but me. I will personally make you run home to your mommy and cry. Tell me you want a girl to take you and your ego to the cleaners."

"What can *you* do? Oh no, Doctor Kitten is mad at me, I'm scared!"

Cat grabbed his arm and twisted him around before ramming his face into the carpeted wall of her cube. Just for kicks, she again slammed his face into the carpet in hopes of causing rug burn.

"Understand? You don't mess with me and you don't mess with my bird." Somehow, she managed to take him down and it felt fantastic. "Do you understand? Do you? Because if you don't, I will fuck you in ways you have yet to discover. Understand me? If you don't, call R out here and I'll have your ass fired. Believe me, by the time he gets here there will be a bloody pile of your pride on the floor begging for mercy from this little kitten."

For once, the dyke moms had been smart and sent Cat to self-defense classes. R heard the commotion and ran over to the cube. He was more concerned with his new property owner than the male employee. He knew Cat was tough mentally, but not physically enough to think she could hold her own against this specific husky copywriter.

"Is there a problem here?" He acted uneasy, but saw that Cat had conquered which caused a smirk.

"I don't have a problem, R," she smiled. "Just a little tension over the crossword puzzle, you know. Nothing I can't handle."

He walked away without worry and Cat let the vulgar villain free after a final swipe of carpet.

"Don't fuck with me!" Cat was uninhibited and egotistical. All she cared about was little Driver and his security. "I will say it once more. If any of you touch this bird I will personally fuck you up. This is a warning. In case any of you didn't notice, I just took out a man more than three times my size and am ready to do it again. I don't fight like a chick. I am ready and happily willing to show you a side of me that doesn't own a dictionary. Dare me."

The area cleared. It was just her and Driver sitting at the cube and she softly stroked his head hoping he—a bird— would feel her concern and possible love. His little black eyes looked deep inside her. What did *he* see? Who did *he* think she was? Who did *she* think she was? Minutes earlier she was living in sin and now she was a bird lover and landowner with responsibilities. All her hopes and dreams were placed on this parakeet and its survival.

His survival, not hers.

YFN 899

The months of waiting in idle and hiding from Wolf's wife took the gleam from Cat's rustproof exterior. She had become an urban warrior, headlights able to scan vast distances in search of his better half that sought sperm; she looked beyond co-workers with crossword puzzle questions, and closed the door on her open-door policy with inquisitive and needy Irish poetry students. She transformed into a foot soldier in the jungle, peering for the ever-looming hazard that came in many disguises. The torture of hanging around for Wolf to abandon her like a heap of junk was nowhere in sight. Hidden hopes of his wife's pregnancy in the near future were cut short. The anticipation of moving past the bottleneck had grown old to Cat; like Wolf, himself. Rose-colored Gucci goggles were set aside and her eyes now saw a man who was worn-down, used up and haggard; he was no longer the sexy older man with rock star looks, but a Machiavellian guru with a never-ending hunger for students. His well-known admiration of students, preferably undergraduates, began to take time from both Cat and his wife, leaving them with nothing but their birds and motors running, stuck bumper-to-bumper.

She hardly minded time alone in her hidden high-rise, but

she did miss the extravagance of a new dress and Friday night at the theater. The overlooked Saturday dinner and movie added little restlessness to her tedious life, but she kept busy. Along with a new pet, Cat had discovered a new passion of painting birdhouses that she hung all over the balcony. Cat's "love life" with her live-in lover had become Tuesday dinner in the cafeteria and Thursday afternoon quickies, usually in his office before each taught their evening class.

This meant Monday nights were again hers.

No longer grounded or ordered to stay away from her weekly immoral diversions, she returned one rainy Monday night to hear ABBA, smell J's cigar and Rose's clove smokes, and see Mick's latest audition monologue while pouring a cold one. Cat anticipated taking a long drink of the bubbling life she never forgot existed; she had dreamed of this homecoming since the new television season began. For the sake of conversation, she brought along the papers from the closing and a picture of Driver. No one looked up when she entered— why would they? She smashed the bells over the door with her lambskin Birkin bag until the group stopped chatting and looked her way.

"Uh, hello?"

"Cat! Is that you? Are you alone? What are you doing here? That dick isn't going to come get you again, is he? What'll you have? We won't let him take you this time! Get her the usual! How have you been? Who are you wearing? Are you still living in 312? Have you lost weight? That is a great outfit! Where'd you get those shoes? How is work? Do you still do the crossword puzzles?"

"I've been lonely." Mick handed her a tall glass. "And need to be freed. Am I still welcome here? With you guys and all?"

"Abso-fucking-lutely." J pulled a chair next to his and motioned for her to sit. "What have you been doing with yourself? You *do* look like you've lost twenty pounds—are you sick?"

"No, I've been exercising. Wolf thinks I am getting chubby and wants to have a baby." She felt the heat from the whiskey fill her stomach. The first three shots went down fast and felt good.

"Chubby? Baby? You look sick is what you look!" Rose was sizing her up and pinching for the weight that was missing from her waist. "You need to eat something—how about some chili? You love Justin's chili, honey."

"Yea, let me get some." Mick smiled and walked to the kitchen.

"Did you say you were having a baby?" Q pondered.

"Of course she's not. How have you been?" J kissed her cheek. "I've missed you. What have you been up to? Are you done with Professor Wolf?"

"Yes and no, I guess. But I do have some news." Talking to the group was getting easier with each refilled glass. She pulled out the photo of her happy companion. "I do have a baby. I have a bird. His name is Driver and Wolf hates him which is good because then Wolf stays away and that's good because he is going back to his wife."

"That jerk!" Rose spit. "I never liked him."

"Well, he never liked you." They laughed at Cat's attempt to joke. "*And*, I own a home. It's big and empty and just about a block from here. All I need to do is move in."

"What are you talking about, Cat?" J sat up and grabbed the papers from her purse that proved she now owned and would never need to rent again. "You did this? Without Jillie or a lawyer or even talking to me? This is huge."

"Where is it?" Rose asked, "When can we see it?"

"I'm getting thrown out of my place. Can I stay there?" Mick questioned immediately.

"I've been there a couple times, but I have to wait for Wolf to dump me to move in and that should have happened a dozen years ago. There's this whole thing with my boss and his wife and their divorce and I almost got a boat and I'm supposed to let Wolf think he is the one doing the dumping because he wants his wife to get pregnant, but it's mine, right? It's all legal, J, right? The place is mine without a doubt, right?" She swallowed another glass and smelled the chili.

"Signed, sealed and delivered—it's all yours." J kissed her cheek again, taking in her hippie smell of incense. "You're not going to have a baby, are you? With *him*?"

"No, I'm not that dumb." She sank the spoon into the chili and did not stop until the bowl was empty. Six people jumped to get the plate away from the table before she looked up. "I just can't be the one to break it off. It's all a mess and that stupid woman can't get pregnant so he sees me a couple times a week and is going to break it off when she's knocked up. I'm not supposed to know about it because my boss is the one who told me and gave me the house because he is divorced and already has kids, but they're older. But it's taking too long for that woman to get pregnant—remember how easy it was to get pregnant—I remember trying *not* to get pregnant all the time because I think it got harder. This woman is ruining my life because she's too old or he's too old and here I am, sick of living there and seeing his old wrinkled ass is too much for me to handle anymore so I just go to the gym and ride the bike. I should just dump him. Why can't I be the one who makes the move? I should just go home right now, pack my stuff and move to this place, *my* place. I should just take my bird and go. What did Dolly Parton say in that movie? Remember? She said to go home and pack your bowling bag and start over? That's me, but I have a bird. Did you see his picture? He's yellow and had a broken arm, but I fixed it after I did all the crossword puzzles and took a leave of absence. And I can go somewhere for once. I have someplace to go that's not my mother or a friend to beg for help. I can paint it and play music loud and what's stopping me? Let's go, right now. I'm gonna get my stuff and move tonight and fuck him.

B'aoibhinn liom na hainmhithe!"

"Gaelic—she's talking about animals in Gaelic!" F had taken a few classes with her.

"She's drunk." Rose took the glass away from her. "Was that three?"

"Four—maybe five," Mick frowned. "I wasn't paying attention—to her drinking, that is. This is another great story."

"It's not a story," J pulled Cat over in a hug to calm her. "It's her life."

"How did we let this happen?" K was giddy from the princess' fall from grace. She had always wanted Cat's life, her clothes, her lesbian mothers, her education, J's affection—everything. If Cat took a wrong step, K was there to enjoy the moment.

"Let what? Let a ninety-pound girl drink a bottle of whiskey in ten minutes or let the thing with Professor Wolf happen? And what was that about her boss?" Rose's question was the last she heard as she fell asleep in J's arms...

...and awoke on J's couch a while later, her head on his lap.

"She should just leave. Move out. We can all help her."

"What happened?" She didn't try to sit up and Rose handed her a garbage can. "I've got to get out of here. What time is it? I need to get home before ten-thirty to feed Driver. I always give him a snack during Jay's monologue."

"Cat," J smiled at her side, stroking her hair. "It's not even nine. You fell asleep and we all came here."

"I always liked it here. But it was too nice for me. It was all too good. The mirrors in the halls and the elevators that you can jump in and the security channel on cable and the view of the lake and you, *you* were too good."

"I thought you didn't like the dishwasher." J was content on the couch, petting her hair the way she liked; wishing this moment would never end.

Cat sat up and ran her fingers through her layered hair. "I

hate my hair. Did anyone notice I look like Farrah Fawcett on a rainy day? He made me do this. He makes me do everything and I had no one to talk to because you all hated me. Please don't hate me."

"We don't hate you." Rose pulled a curly strand from Cat's face just as the bucket was being used. "None of us like being puked on, but no one hates you."

J went to get a washcloth and glass of water while Rose took his spot on the couch, still holding her hair out of shooting range. He returned and wiped the vomit from Cat's chin. "None of us knew anything like this was happening. We all thought it was what you wanted."

"You never called so we didn't think there was a problem." S was grinning. She was another of the Cat wanna-be's; she had idolized her since childhood and dressed like her and made many attempts to imitate her speech patterns and style of dress.

"I'd never call *you*, bitch." Again, Cat made them laugh. "I'm not kidding. I don't think I'd call any of you if I knew I'd end up looking like this. Who wants to see this? I sure as hell don't."

"You could have called me," Mick uttered.

"I'm always here," Rose agreed. "Our phone *was* disconnected for a while, though."

"I know it would have been hard, but my number hasn't changed. I'm always here waiting for your call," J assured after finding traces of vomit splattered on his couch. "Even if it means cleaning puke off my new leather couch. What is up with this? You never puke."

"I haven't eaten in a while. Or drank."

"Well, we all made a decision." Rose was in charge of the conversation. "We all think you should slowly move your things to the new place, but you have to let him break it off. He has to have *that* control."

"It's the only way right now," J explained. "Even if your boss *did* give you the heads up, you owe it to him not to break the secret. Trust is nowhere in the suit world and he trusts you, for some reason, over his best friend. These real estate papers were put together with precision for your complete and total ownership with no strings attached. If you promised—if *you* gave *your* word—then you play along and make sure he doesn't get anywhere near the situation with Wolf."

"But," Rose popped in, "we think you should all but move in. Make him think he is leaving you high and dry."

"But I *am* high and dry. Sitting around waiting for that old bastard to get his wife pregnant just so I can have a countdown to break-up is no way to spend my twenties—if I'm still in my twenties."

"Now, Cat, tell me the truth," J was sincere. "You said something before. Did you take a leave at work? Are you in some sort of trouble?"

"Yes. Yea, I took a leave and no, I am not in trouble." She frowned. "I'm not doing anything there and the place reminds me of an open casket. I sit in my cube waiting for Wolf to pop in for an afternoon surprise. R was really cool about it and I've never taken sick days or vacation days, so that's what I am using up. I did a month's worth of crossword puzzles and then just went home one day and I didn't go back."

"Getting back to your new home, what about the brownstone, Cat?" Mick questioned. "I *really* do need a place to crash for a while and then there will be someone there getting it ready for you. I can be like a security system while you don't live there. I know it's a lot to ask and you don't have to say anything right now—just think about it."

"You know you are welcome to the small bedroom, but not forever." She wanted to be alone with no one to please but herself. She couldn't wait for her days to be her own. This little building was doing more than provide a roof; without knowing it, R was handing her an adult situation with choices to make for and by no one but herself. "Then I will make you set up my fish tank and help install a real security system and water the lawn—if there is one. There will be no parties and I need a few rooms painted. So is that a deal?"

"Fuck yea!" Mick was safe again, this time under Cat's parachute. Over the years, Mick had become the gang's lead member of the sofa touring company. He was always about to be thrown out or evicted and inevitably ended up on someone's couch for a few months at a time—a few months longer than promised. More than once, Cat was there to help, financially or otherwise.

"Mick, I'll put you up for a while." J entered. "Cat deserves her own space."

"J, I gave him my word and my word doesn't back down."

"And your word is what you gave your boss and I don't see you picking out clothes for work tomorrow. How much faith did he put in your word? Your word is everything."

"You're right." Cat knew what she had to do: call her boss and go back to work like nothing had happened. She reached for J's phone and dialed. "Hi, R? Did I wake you? This is Cat."

"Do you know *who* she is calling *and* calling him by his first name?" P was in awe of Cat's job at the company he had interviewed with over a dozen times. Now he was amazed by the apparently close relationship she had with one of the world's richest men. "He invented pork!"

"No, that was my friend. He thinks you're some big shot with a glass office and spend all day golfing and whatnot. I know, he should see the big picture. The reason I'm calling is because I'm going to be back tomorrow, bright and early. No, I miss you guys, well, not really, but I do miss you. Should I call G? OK. I don't need a ride—I'll walk. I don't want to call him this late—his wife goes to sleep around nine. He does? That's so sweet. I will. I will. OK. Kisses to Richard. Bye."

"How did it go?" J, the businessman, inquired taking the phone from her hands. "Who is Richard?"

"His divorce attorney. He's the guy who helped me with the house." She smiled at the gang. "He says he was waiting for me to come back and missed the tension I created in the office."

"That's perfect." J kissed her cheek. "Business as usual?"

"You create tension at the office? Can you please get me another interview?" P begged.

"How can I get you an interview when I don't even have a title?" Cat rolled her eyes and looked at J. Everything's cool. I just have to call G and Driver and let them know, but I don't think I will. I think I'll let them sleep in tomorrow. The walk'll do me good. Can I go home now? Anyone interested in seeing the shack I live in?"

"Fuck yea. It's like the end of "Grease" when the whole gang is back together at the carnival." Rose hugged her. "We'll see your place and maybe take some of your things to the new pad."

After putting on their coats, they walked the block to the plush building Cat had learned to call home. J was impressed when the guards knew her name and asked to know their names for future visits. It was no surprise that Cat lived in a pristine three-bedroom loft. The loft was furnished, but the kitchen utensils were all plastic. Rose commented that there was nothing of Wolf's to prove he had ever been there. The place was tidy, Driver was singing, birdhouses were everywhere and Cat was proud.

"This is Driver!" Cat came out of the bedroom with the yellow bird on her finger. "He is the smartest and nicest and best bird I have ever known. He sleeps in his cage next to my bed."

"What's with the bird houses?" Rose asked looking at the dozens of multicolored houses.

"Oh, I paint them. Yea, I buy them from the Michael's by M's and paint them in case someone needs a new home, but the holes are too small for a real bird. I wanted it to be like a homeless shelter for lost parakeets, which is strange—you know I hate birds. I just sort of do it when I'm bored now."

"You must be *really* bored." Rose observed as she peered at the dozens of houses.

"This little guy loves you," J touched the top of Driver's head. He never saw affection from a bird, but Driver clung to Cat's shoulder and nosed her chin. "Look at how he trusts you."

"He's my little man, that is, if he is a boy. I don't know how to tell."

"Look at this view!" Rose threw open the balcony doors and the breeze surrounded them all. "This view is priceless. You can see the lake and the river and god-knows-what with a telescope aimed at the other balconies."

Cat put Driver on J's shoulder as she showed the gang her things that needed to be moved. The brick walls were empty, floors plain, two bedrooms never used and finally the boxes of books at the edge of her bed. She waved Rose over to the closet to show off her priceless duds. Without hesitation, Rose kicked off her shoes and started trying on pair after pair.

"Stop with the clothes," J interrupted. "Let's get out of here while there is still time and let Cat get her Leno fix. Besides, we never know if a Wolf is lurking in the bushes."

"Good luck tomorrow, baby." Rose kissed her cheek. "The end is near and we are all behind you. Especially me, if I can sesh these pumps."

"I'll be great. Driver and I are going to get through this—no matter how much shit I have to march through. If there is one thing I have learned is that life is all about walking through shit. You can either cry about it or wipe it off and keep going. I'm going to keep going."

2518810

If a limo drives by, you automatically wonder who is inside. Famous actors, successful athletes, the wealthy and their entourage are typically the crowd enjoying a smooth ride with a full bar, crystal glassware and other extravagant amenities. There are the seasonal everyday runs for proms, weddings and funerals, but the majority of the chauffer-driven elite are those whose lives are filled with importance, knowledge and deserve respect. Once in a while, a driver is rented for an airport drop-off, bachelorette party or to impress a date on a special night. No matter the size of the car or the politeness of the driver, a car service was all about status and how they view or want others to view their significance.

Cat was none of the above.

Wanting to feel the pavement under her feet, Cat decided the night before to let Driver have the morning off. The six-block walk through the crowded Loop streets felt longer than it should have, but she was wearing painful sling backs and carrying her birdcage, so each step was an uphill battle. She chugged along the busy streets, taking in the smell from the exhaust from honking taxis and an occasional bus. She watched the delivery guys on bikes darting in and out of traffic and smiled at the suits crossing against the light, trying not to get hit. The energetic odor of her city was suddenly replaced by a rancid scent coming from an over-perfumed woman who walked with a quarter between her cheeks, carrying a little dog in a designer bag wearing a rhinestone barrette. Aside from the fragrance, the woman was just like her; she was expected somewhere and refused to go without her trusty companion.

Her first steps off the elevator that morning felt normal, but within seconds she sensed meddlesome eyes glaring from every angle. She knew minds were filled with questions about her absence. Where had she been? Did she check into rehab or get fired or go just plain nuts and come back to beg for her job and dignity? K noted that she couldn't have gone on vacation because she was still pale, but Irish people are always pale. C thought Moran had something to do with Mr. R's divorce. Why would she want Mr. R when she had Professor Wolf? That was two marriages in shambles because of her wicked interactions. In the few weeks she had been absent, her co-worker's imaginations had flipped a semi and created a pile-up that held up traffic for miles. Every passing vehicle slowed to catch a peek at the wreckage in hopes of seeing a trace of blood or at least a leisurely drive past with the windows rolled down to hear the drivers fight of words about fault. At the very least, she was sure to be given a lecture from Mr. R. He had to say something about her unannounced disappearance and obvious insubordination. Cat was going to be fired and everyone would celebrate her loss as their victory. No one believed she temporarily traded in her Lincoln Town car for a beat-up station wagon with wood paneling—word on the street was that Cat did indeed go on vacation with Mr. R and then quietly checked into detox or a psych ward or just plain resigned. Faces glanced her way and then back to an imaginary project. Deafening silence and the smell of burnt coffee filled the air. What they didn't know was the truth; a few days earlier she had been given the keys to a new dawn. The dense employees wrestled to slow the passing lane and hoped for her to blow a tire on the expressway to the front office. Some actually thought she was taking advantage of the boss they hated and protected, Mr. R, and were envious of his generous nature toward no one but her. G followed anxiously to her cube, as always, with a pen and paper and another knock-off suit.

"Doctor Moran, you're back."

"Hey, Professor, where's Maryanne?" L hollered across the tension that didn't affect Cat.

"The name, for the last fucking time, is *Cat*." Over a year and she still didn't follow that one suggestion. "If I hear the words 'doctor' and 'Moran' from you again I will have to ask for a new assistant."

"I'm sorry. You're a mentor to me and I want to show respect." She was genuine and honest, and her display of loyalty disgusted Cat. "Did you go on vacation or do anything fun in the past two weeks?"

"Not a thing. I stayed home, ordered Eat-a-Pita and taught Driver some tricks. What did you do while I was gone?" Polite conversation was a bitch.

"Honestly? Nothing. No one needed anything so I just sat at your desk reading magazines. Can I get you some coffee? Tea? How about a Snapple?"

"No, I've got to check on R. I called him last night to make sure I still had a job."

"You called him at night? At home?"

"No, I called his cell." Driver was singing in his cage.

"He gave you his cell number? No one has that—not even his wife, err, ex-wife."

"Could you be a dear and keep an eye on Driver for a minute? I don't think everything is copasetic around here. This place has got a bad vibe going on today and it's got my name written all over it. Tell me, what has been the story about me?"

"Um, there's a couple going around." She did not want to

answer this question. "You were in rehab or vacation or broke up R's marriage—you know the gang."

"Yea, I missed them all."

Approaching his office, Cat noticed there was no putting or even a golf ball in sight. R was slumped at his desk, hands folded, deep in thought.

"Hey, R, you alive in here? Can I come in?"

"Sure, Cat. How are you? Have a seat."

Cat fell into a leather chair close to the desk. "What's on your mind? You look like you've got either the weight of the world on your shoulders or you just ate my bird. If you did, I will have to kill you as it's the only thing I have right now. But hey, it's pretty glum in here. Can I get you something?"

"It's really lifeless, isn't it?" He walked over and opened the shades that let the sun shine in from his view of the lake. He tossed a pile of papers toward her from his desk. "Well, here they are. Thirty-seven years of marriage—a decent marriage—all comes down to my initials on a few pieces of paper. I am suddenly alone."

"I thought you wanted the divorce." Cat watched her boss' emotions swish from sadness to joyful freedom. It there was one thing Cat knew, it was about being alone, but you just don't give into a conversation like this so early in the morning especially with someone like a boss. A boss would forever remember and use the words she spoke of her years of similar solitude against her. Trust no one.

"I did. I do. We really needed a change, but this was extreme." He picked up the papers, "I still love her."

"And you probably always will." Cat hadn't believed in love for years, but the concept had come into focus during her days with J. Wolf did zero to amend her nonexistence of love mind-set. "It's good to love someone and know someone loves you. At least that's what I have been told. Of course, I was told this by a man-hating lesbian who thought I needed to find a bald man in his fifties to be a happy heterosexual, but the bottom line is still the same."

"You'll find someone, Cat. I'm just a sentimental old fool; acting like a girl crying over losing a game of checkers. Do girls cry when they play checkers?"

"I never did, but acting like a girl isn't so bad—acting like a lesbian, now *that* is bad. And you can take it from me, letting out some fucked up feelings with a friend isn't the worst thing a person could do." She closed the blinds in his office to hide the scene from onlookers and then shut his office door for privacy. Cat knew the closing of the door would make tails wag. "Let's talk. You know me and you know you can trust me. Let it out. Do you want to get a drink?"

"It's the middle of the morning and you mick's have no problem having a drink any time and anywhere." He pulled a bottle from his desk drawer and found two clean coffee mugs. "Do you need water with that?"

"When I an drinking whiskey, I drink whiskey. When I drink water, I drink water."

"You know "The Quiet Man"? John Wayne? That is an all time favorite."

"Same here. I'm told my dad used to watch it every year."

"I bet I would have liked your father. You are an over-achiever with a sharp tongue and ability to stand up for yourself—you didn't learn that from your two moms. I loved watching you attack O about Driver that day." R looked out the window. "I bet your dad and I would have been friends. Right now, I could use a couple friends. Guy friends, no offense."

"No offense taken. I wish I could have met him myself." Cat wiped away a tear, "I think that's why I always fall for older men—I am obviously looking for a father figure. Bottoms up."

"To himself," he declared as the two clinked glasses before swallowing the full glass in a single gulp. "So, your dad took his own life? May I ask?"

"Sure, we're friends. Um, I was told he died in a car accident and then that he shot himself and finally that he hung himself in his office. It's kind of a tall tale so you never know the real story." Cat refilled the glasses. "It's always a shitty story so I never really pressed for details. I don't think finding out your wife is a dyke is a fun way to start the day, but—"

"You've always blamed your mom."

"Kind of." She thought and had a sip. "And I kind of never was told about the lesbian thing until I was in high school, which kind of messed me up. Yea, I think I do blame her for things she had nothing to do with, but don't we all blame our mothers for something?"

"I know I do." He thought for a moment as he peered out the window. "I really still love my wife. I don't want to go through this. What can I do?"

"Maybe the divorce will bring you closer." Cat was buzzing. "I have a friend who was dead set on getting a divorce and they went through with it and the next day they were back together. They said all they needed to do was clear the air and the whole divorce process made them see that. They never remarried, but their relationship is the strongest I know of."

"Really?"

"The only other working marriage I know of is my mother's and I've learned a lot from them." Cat finished her cup and poured more.

"What's that like? How long have they been together?"

"Well, since I was six or seven." She thought for a moment. "Can I tell you something?"

"Anything." He refilled his glass and sat down.

"I was in love once. It was in high school." Cat couldn't stop the words from leaving her mouth. This was a story only a few knew and she never spoke of. "There was a boy. His name was Tim. He and I were best friends—we did everything together. Our families were close and he was my first kiss and

I would love to say he got my virginity, but he didn't."

"You were raped, I remember." His eyes filled with tears.

"His older brother was the one who found me—he saved me. Later that same year, his brother was killed in a car accident and his family moved away." She couldn't stop now; she could have been a talk show guest unable and not wanting the confession to stop. "We wrote letters for a while, but you know how kids are. I lost touch and, I don't know. I have been looking for him since I was sixteen and if he walked into this office today, I don't know what I would do. Years have gone by, but I still love that crazy guy who wrote me poems and kissed me by the water fountain and always told jokes to make me laugh. Maybe that's like you and your wife. Maybe you are destined to be together and needed this bump in the road to remind you how good you have it."

"Maybe that's what I need." He put his glass on the desk and sat down. "I think I am going to call her. What do you think?"

"Neither of you were unfaithful and you have wonderful children and memories—even if she says tells you to drop dead, at least you tried."

"I tried." He picked up his phone and she turned to leave. "I can at least say that I tried. Thank you, Cat. You're a good friend."

"I'll kick your ass in golf if you ever ask me to play. I'm at a 78." She smiled proudly at the one thing she managed to learn from her days with J.

Before pushing a single digit, there was some sort of a commotion escalading outside. Cat and R looked at each other with confusion, and suddenly the door was kicked open. Wolf pounced inside and a surprised deer-in-headlights look covered their faces. He was sweating and out of breath.

"What happened to you?" Cat tried to talk this stray animal out of the neighbor's tree. "Sit down and have a drink with us. You look like you could use it."

"You two expect me to believe that the shades are closed and the door locked just so you can *talk*? What kind of *talking* were you doing?" Wolf grabbed the stapler from R's desk and threw it at the window wall. A small crack appeared and lines began to spread through the glass.

"What is *wrong* with you, man?" R was concerned and put the phone in its cradle. "Cat and I were talking about my divorce and then her father. That's all, nothing more, but you're going to fix that window."

"I know about the affair."

"Good for you. I was wondering when you would discover that I was secretly sleeping with R. Now the cat is out of the bag." Cat took a miscellaneous file from his desk and walked toward her desk. Wolf chased her, still screaming about the same nonsense. She pointed at G to take the bird out of the debris that was coming from all directions. Cat calmly sat down at her desk, ignoring his lecture that was getting louder by the minute. R followed, but was composed and collected. Wolf, on the other hand, turned her chair to face him; he stood over her with his veins popping; heart palpitating, forehead beaded with sweat. His fists were clenched and he began pounding the cube wall.

"Do you know how hard I work? I can't believe I didn't see this coming. Every dollar I earn goes into something for you, and you stumble onto R, the richest man in the city who just happens to be new to the singles scene. What did he do, buy you a boat?"

"No, an island in the Keys." She turned her chair to face her desk.

"You honestly think I am sleeping with Cat? You need help." R laughed and his anger began to show.

"He's a married man, Catrin." Wolf yelled. "What is your problem? Are you drunk?"

"Hello? *You're* married." Cat was bored with his one-sided banter and stood to leave. Wolf grabbed her arm and pulled her back, tearing the sleeve of her brown blouse. "Hey, big spender, I don't need my clothes fucked up the way you fucked up my life."

With that, Wolf exploded. His arms were wailing and he picked up and threw everything he could find around her and nearby cubes. Coffee mugs flew toward the elevator, her dictionary and thesaurus tossed into E's general area, keyboard smashed against the window and then finally, he grabbed her computer monitor and threw it cubes away. Her heart sank as she heard the Mac jangle to the floor. Then her desk drawers were pulled out and contents spilled around her feet.

"Cat, my god, what have I done? You choose R over me? Did I do something wrong or hurt you? I need the truth." Wolf turned to R, who was in shock. "And who are *you* all of a sudden? Fucking my mistress? I guess you know now that she's pretty bad in bed."

"Bad in bed?" Cat laughed. "I'm in my prime, old man."

Enraged and embarrassed beyond belief, R punched Wolf in the jaw sending him to the floor. The gathered crowd cheered and Cat was confused. Did Wolf deserve the punch? She knew many people who wanted a go at him in a dark alley, but this didn't seem like the best time to take a number. She told G to get some ice for R's hand and Wolf rolled on the floor moaning, blood coming from his nose. Cat knelt at his side, helping him sit up and checking to make sure his nose was not broken.

"First you burst into my office, then you go about making a fool of yourself with the most offensive comments about Cat and me. Company property was destroyed—including a top of the line Mac computer—not to mention everything else that was in your path. And now you tell me it is because you had some wild fantasy about Cat and me?" R was livid as Wolf got back on his feet. "Nothing you can ever say will make me forget this moment and the rage I saw in your eyes. Go ahead and try to mess with me, because you know you can't. I am giving you ten minutes before I call the police."

"I wish you could see how dumb you look. You should be ashamed." Cat said as she and G started picking up the contents of her drawers and putting them in place. "This is going to be a doozy of an explanation."

"*My* excuse? I just got out of a meeting with Professor X. He has decided to circulate a petition asking for my resignation. Then, I go over to *our* place and find your trashy blonde friend packing your books. Now, why would she do *that*? Her answer was shaky at best. She says she is taking some classes at UIC and was going to borrow your doctorate level books. Why would she have a key to the apartment? Then I find a box of your birdhouses packed and again, she didn't know why they were there, but in walks J to help Rose carry them out. Confused, I come here and find the two of you humping in his office."

'Humping?" She laughed. "Get your glasses fixed because we were on opposite sides of the room with a desk between us. How kinky do you think I am? Now I have *another* reputation to live up to, office whore."

"What do you expect me to think when the door is closed and blinds pulled? In my world, the *real* world, those are signs of only two things: performance review or romance. In one hour, my life has gone from unpleasant to horrific to dire. My whole existence is hanging by a thread and no one seems to care—look at you two having a drink and laughing the day away. I may be losing my job, my girlfriend is cheating on me with my best friend and *our* apartment is being emptied by your gypsy friends. I'm sorry, but I have just had the nastiest possible morning and expected you two would give me shelter from this one-man storm, but no. I come here and find *this*!"

"What the hell do you think *this* is? You've moved out of the place already and told me it's because your wife wants a baby. I sit here wondering if you are really going back to that minivan of a woman and promise her that everything between you two will be the perfect picture of happiness. I'm stuck in the middle here. Take another look at someone in a dire situation. See a fertility specialist and get a new hobby." Wolf had told her about the baby, she thought, so he could physically disappear from her life with fewer consequences and minimal heartbreak. "Wolf, you're a great guy and I would love to help you turkey baste your wife, but it's not my cup of tea. Can someone find my computer?"

The entire office was standing and watching with their mouths hanging open. Was Cat the bad guy? Did Professor Wolf actually want to try again with his wife—this would count as his eleventh rebound relationship—would he still sugar daddy Cat? And his wife couldn't get pregnant—she *was* in her late forties. And who would have thought they would ever see Mr. R punch someone? Office violence hit white-collar heights. What next? They were definitely ordering lunch in today—this was far from over.

Wolf went into R's office and the door was shut, curtains closed. Mumbles were heard inside, but it was the quiet sound of sobbing coming every few moments. Behind the broken door, they were no longer towers of industry, bosses or leaders, but two men forgiving actions, sharing fears and emphasizing each other's similar situations. The morning ordeal was now ancient history; swept under the floor mat in the front seat of a collective mind. In the future, all involved would look back on that day as a lesson learned in compassion for some while others acquired a new fear of R's unpredictable wrath.

"Cat," R called from his office door. "Can you come in here?"

For the first time in her employment at the company, she was nervous entering his office and pushed the broken door closed behind her.

"Yea, hey. How's everyone doing? Great show out there." She put on a calm exterior. Wolf was in a chair and R sat behind his desk. Both had mugs of what she knew was whiskey.

"Catrin, I am sorry," Wolf said in a small voice. "I know you're not having an affair. I know you are waiting for me to go back to my wife and I feel I owe you something."

"Continue," R persuaded.

"I don't know how to ask this from you." Wolf was in an unknown state as he handed her a brochure that she began to read. "As you know, my wife and I are trying to conceive. My wife, Coleen, however, cannot get pregnant. We're older and need someone to donate eggs for in-vitro and I was wondering—"

"Wondering what?"

"Wondering if you would donate some eggs for us."

Wolf was serious. R laughed. Cat was curious.

"No you didn't. You did *not* just ask *me*, your mistress, if I will help you go back to your wife and have what essentially will be half of my baby." She reached for a glass of booze that was handed promptly.

"Yea, he did." R threw a golf ball at his cracked window. "How the fuck do you get the balls to do that? That takes mighty balls—people put ads in the paper for that sort of thing."

"Where *do* you get the balls for that? I've seen your balls and they're not that mighty." Cat could not believe her ears.

"We looked through the paper and have seen specialists, but no one can tell you if the girl is educated or creative. We want to have a smart and funny baby. We want a baby with all of your characteristics and I decided to just ask you."

"And your wife knows my characteristics? She knows about me, specifically?"

"Yes, I was honest with her."

"What's the going rate for a dozen?" R asked, pouring more whiskey in each glass. It was ten o'clock in the morning and the three were nearly drunk.

"The closest we came was a girl for $15,000 from the University of Chicago." He sat back and sighed. He looked at

Cat with the same eyes he had given her that night at the grocery store. "Call me crazy, but I said I would ask."

"Are you kidding? In here, it says it takes three months of hormone injections that may cause weight gain and irritability. I will have weekly exams and finally a medical procedure that retrieves the actual eggs from the uterus and all you can come up with is fifteen grand?"

R was laughing and called G on his intercom. "Get in here, G, we need something."

Within seconds, G was fighting to open the door.

"Yes, Mr. R?" She was mortified. She had never been called into the boss' office.

"Go down to Sammy's and get a couple bottles of Jameson's and one Bushmills." He threw her a wad of cash before she ran off.

"We are willing to go to fifty." He was embarrassed. "But that is the number we came up with for Cat. She can have the condo for the duration and one of us will drive her to every exam and be available at all times."

"But there are some restrictions, right?" Cat was interested in the money. She had always wanted to play the market with J, or even start a little nest egg. What was she thinking? How could she even begin to imagine something so twisted? How could she put a price on something so personal; so intimate? It's not like she was ever going to use them, why not help someone else? "I'd be on some diet or some rules you made up, right?"

"No excessive drinking and no drugs."

"And I could stay at the condo?"

"You would be under contract to stay there for the duration. It's so we would be covering all your living expenses and know the roof over your head was acceptable."

This was the unexpected turn no one could imagine.

For Cat, it was just another cul-de-sac without a way out.

BVM511

No car with *Kelley Blue Book* value can promise complete safety under all circumstances; the industry workers usually win you over with brilliant marketing and page after colorful page of brochures to pick from. There are dozens of tests performed on standard features in case of inclement weather, air bag position when inflated during a dreaded broadside, accidentally parking your car through a light pole and other types of weather-related events. The office light was turning from yellow to red in a split second and Cat knew she would be side-swiped into a corner by anonymous colleagues, denting the entire left side of the vehicle.

But she couldn't let that happen. Not now. Not at this time.

"Let the games begin in exactly three months, G." She smiled and gave G a bag of scarves she never liked and an assortment of blouses from the last show Rose had worked. Rose worked at Marshall Fields in the make-up department and was often asked to work photo shoots and runway events. She liked her job, but she loved the souvenirs. The old slight of hand had been perfected over the years which had left Rose with tons of clothes that weren't even being sold in stores and hundreds of dollars in make-up—all of which she shared with Cat. Between the Wolf's buying sprees and Rose's slippery fingers, Cat had come to have one of the finest wardrobes in the city. "I hope these things fit you. My friend just got them last week and they're a little big on me."

Sitting unnoticed in an unmarked file folder on her desk were the papers from the Wolf and his wife that needed a final signature, hers. She had done all her homework on the in-vitro fertilization program, discussed its risks and benefits with Rose and Mick over a bottle of twenty-year-old-scotch and agreed the three could handle it. According to her agreement, Treasure Island would deliver food each week, a maid was hired to come in three days a week to do dishes and laundry—G still took care of the dry cleaning. Mick would be moving into the condo and was in charge of giving the shots, taking her temperature and monitoring the booze and smoking. Also taking up residence would be Rose whose role was to keep Cat clear of men and the thought of dating—eliminate the possibility of sex. With Wolf out of the pornographic picture and no one on the horizon, it seemed an easy fifty-thousand bucks with financial perks for the two in-house helpers. There were only a handful of people who knew about Cat's itinerary for the coming fall and they planned on keeping it that way even if it killed them. Cat had promised both Mick and Rose five thousand each to go through it with her and keep silent— neither could refuse. Mick had nowhere to live at the moment and the offer was too good to pass up. Rose was always up to her neck in bills and K had just moved home to save money for a new place—shacking up with Cat was a prayer answered and the money, hot fudge on a sundae.

"You know, I kind of miss him," Cat said in between bites of ice cream. "For all his faults, he was a decent guy and I still think he's hot."

"Hot or not, he is out of your life," Rose reminded her.

"I thought he was pretty handsome, for an older guy. He

looked kind of like Jackson Browne," Mick added, pouring more chocolate syrup in his bowl. "Maybe Peter Coyote."

"That is totally what I thought when I saw him at the store! Even you would have gone out with him that night!" Cat exclaimed. The buzzer rang and she got up to talk to the security desk. "Yea?"

"A Mister J is here to see you. May I send him up?"

"Does he have ice cream?" They laughed and listened to the guard.

"Ms. Moran would like to know if you have any ice cream with you."

"You can tell Ms. Moran that I have five melting flavors here."

"Did you hear that, Ms. Moran?" They were always polite.

"Yes, thank you. He can come up." Cat smiled and looked at her bowl. "J's a really good guy. I was stupid to leave him. Look how it turned out. Did I really think that Wolf was going to leave his wife and marry me? What a joke. I don't know what I was thinking."

"J is not the answer." Rose was firm and knew the hormones were taking over Cat's stream of conscientiousness. "Get him out of your head because he is just another guy with a wandering eye who was put on this planet to be your friend, just a friend."

J walked in the unlocked door and immediately kissed Cat on the cheek. Rose followed him to the kitchen to put away the ice cream and check the flavors he picked out.

"So this is what the three of you do? You sit around watching *Law and Order* and eat ice cream?" He took off his coat and joined Cat on the couch, putting his arm around her. "You're looking better by the day. I guess the ice cream diet is what the doctor ordered. May I use the facilities?"

"Go ahead." Cat blinked at Rose and whispered, "I want him back."

"No you don't. You just think you do, but definitely, you

do not want him back." Rose didn't realize keeping Cat celibate would be this demanding. "Try being his friend for a few months. Just a friend."

They all looked as the sound of something crashing came from the bathroom. Mick went to the door and knocked.

"J, buddy, you OK in there?" He asked. "Need some help?"

The door opened and J walked past Mick to the living room with a handful of hypodermic needles and a box of the hormone vials.

"Can I assume it's not for heroin?" J furiously looked at Cat. "Did that jerk-off professor have something to do with you becoming a junkie?"

"Don't assume anything," Cat shot back. "It's a long story and it's not drugs. Well, it *is* drugs, but they are legal and just trust me, it's nothing bad. Now give them back to Mick and get yourself some ice cream."

"Will you tell me what is going on? I don't like finding paraphernalia in a friend's bathroom cabinet—no matter what the reason."

"Then don't go looking in people's private places. What were you doing in my medicine cabinet anyway? I don't ever do that at other people's houses," she lied. She and Rose loved going through cabinets and discovering secrets or borrowing a couple prescription pills if they were the fun kind. "That is so rude."

"I was looking for toothpaste and instead found your stash. This is all *your* doing, Rose, isn't it? You were always into drugs and now you've got Cat hooked on something." J was pacing in front of the television. "I'll get you help, Cat. We'll get you into Hazelton as soon as I can find a phone."

"You use her toothbrush?" Rose was disgusted.

"Get out of the way! Briscoe was just gonna cuff that guy," Cat yelled as her mind was focused on the police drama, not J and his babbling mouth. "J, shut up and I'll tell you what that shit is if you move away from the TV. I love this show."

"Sure, OK, you need to share." He joined her on the couch. "We'll talk and then decide together what the next move will be. The four of us will—"

"Shut the fuck up!" Her personality flipped from giddy to irate. "I want to see this part."

The three held their breath until the commercial came on. All waited for Cat to make the first sound, each afraid of her next mood swing.

"Now, J, those needles are mine. I am donating some eggs to a couple and have to get an injection of something hormone-related every night. It's not anything fun. The needle goes in my butt and in case you didn't notice, I cannot control my emotions. It is going to be about three months of shots and doctor visits, but I agreed to help these people and am getting a ton of money to do something that is really simple. Now, if you would just hold your questions for the next commercial break, I would greatly appreciate it."

"Who are the people?" J asked.

"Wolf and his wife," Rose answered. "And they are giving her fifty large to go through the process. We all see it as a grand gesture and a windfall in one swoop."

"No one else knows, if you understand me." Mick needed the secret to be kept as much as any of them. If she didn't produce enough or many viable eggs, the contract would be cancelled and both he and Rose were depending on their share of the loot. The two had made a pact to wait on Cat and put up with her emotional yo-yo jumps, knowing she was not in control. They would do this for her as friends, of course, but the money sweetened the tea.

"Fine, my lips are sealed." J unhappily looked at Cat. "Why would you do this for *him*? He is the last person who deserves a favor."

"I'm not doing it for him—I'm doing it for her." Cat walked to the kitchen with her empty bowl. "Coleen is really great and always wanted children and Wolf put it off. Now she is older and can't get her girl parts to work so they are going to use mine. This was not a quick and easy decision and I have been irritating everyone I come into contact with for over a month and have to see a specialist every week and the shots are a real pain, but I know this woman and I like her. I hope this works."

"You're serious, aren't you?" J looked her in the eyes and held her hands. "Then I hope it works out. But doesn't that mean if she has this kid, it will be half you?"

"Yes. It will be mine and Wolf's, but that is what they have to deal with. Once I finish the egg retrieval, I am through with him completely. I will collect my payment for services rendered and move into my place and pave a new road. You can either jump into my car and go or step off my life until the ride is over."

"Your car," Rose yelled.

"Yours," Mick added.

"If this is what you want, then I'm shotgun." J did not want to agree, but did. He hated Wolf and thought this was the dumbest thing anyone could do, but that was Cat. If there was a crazy idea floating around, Cat would be first in line to give it a try.

Somewhere down the road after weeks of doctor visits, Cat had become friends with Wolf's wife. At first she thought the woman was wicked and wanted to see who her husband would cheat with; playing nice and enjoying the mental and physical discomfort the process brought Cat. But as time passed, Coleen and Cat became confidants—they even shared jokes about Wolf and his prowess and bedroom inadequacies. Coleen had a great sense of humor and seemed to know more about literature than her husband. To no surprise, Wolf was a student teacher when she took his class and ended up married. She spoke of her family money and admitted that to that day, she believed that was Wolf's motive not only for marrying her, but refusing a divorce. The fifty-thousand was coming from her personal savings that she hinted were in the millions. Living off his wife's money explained how Wolf could afford his neighborhood and all the expensive clothes and shoes and gifts he lavished on Cat.

Coleen tried to make the weekly doctor visits and unpleasant vaginal ultrasounds bearable for Cat. They would listen to her favorite music from Tom Petty or the Eagles while on the rides in her beautiful BMW. She tried to tell jokes, but the subject always found itself back to the doorstep of her dreams of motherhood. Cat admired the faith and love that already existed for this child. It would be blessed with a loving mother, a wealthy family and given every opportunity under the sun. She cried when telling Cat how the baby's room was being decorated with Dr. Seuss images and shared her ideas for the first birthday party. And then she would turn to Cat and remind her that none of it would be possible without her generosity. Coleen made her promise to call on them if she ever needed anything down the road; nothing was out of the question for the woman who was making her dream a reality.

"You really *are* a trooper, Cat." Coleen commented. "This cannot be easy on you between the shots and lifestyle changes and I can imagine your mood swings. I would give anything to be in your shoes right now. I wish I were young again, just starting out with new jobs and boyfriends and late night parties. As soon as this is over, I want—no, I demand—you go to your favorite bar with all your friends, drink like a pirate, dance on the bar, pick up a stranger and have as much fun as you possibly can. No, after this you should go on vacation! Yes, you and a couple friends hit Vegas and the spas and nightclubs. On me! I'll make all the arrangements and you'll be pampered like royalty. That's what you need."

"Vegas is fun, but I've never felt comfortable at a spa. The people were always kind of cheeky to me, like they were better than me." Cat had never revealed that she ever felt out of place—until now—to her new friend and confidant.

"Nothing and no one is better than you." The silver spotless car pulled up in front of Cat's building. "Have a good week and please call if you need anything. *Anything,* and I mean it!"

Cat got out and went inside. Did her mother ever have those feelings for Cat while she was pregnant? Did she spend every day and night thanking god for the new life growing in her belly? Did she even want to have a baby? All the stories told were about her father sleeping around and her mother being "stuck" with a newborn. She felt her birth was not planned or wanted, but the right thing to do under the circumstances. No one decorated her bedroom and she didn't remember her many of her birthday parties—she had been nothing but an inconvenience from day one, unwanted as a zygote.

Before reaching the security desk, Cat was in tears. One of the guards grabbed her and gave her a hug before she could fall over with grief. The one behind the desk called up to the apartment to see if someone was waiting for her. She sobbed into the security guard's uniform jacket and could not stop crying, and no one was answering the page. It was just at this moment that J was walking in to make a surprise visit.

"Ohmigod, Cat!" He grabbed her and held her close. "What is it? What happened?"

"She never wanted me," she struggled between sobs and words. "No one did or does."

"I've got it," J said to the guards after giving them a tip. He walked her to the elevator bank and pressed the button. "You think no one wants you? Where did this come from? Come on, look at me. You are so loved, it's astonishing."

"My mother didn't want me then and she doesn't care about me now. When was the last time she even called me?" She was calming down, taking deep breaths. "Wolf's wife is just so excited about this baby and she really wants to have it more than anything in the world. It made me think about M and how she says she was *stuck* with a baby when my dad left. *Stuck* is not a happy word. Even now, she doesn't care about what is going on in my life—I could be dead and she wouldn't know."

"M is self-absorbed, she always has been." They got in the elevator and J was searching for anything to say, knowing M was a miserable parent with no concern for her daughter's well-being. "But that doesn't mean she loves you any less. It just means she is proud you are independent."

"You are so full of shit." She laughed and hugged him. "Where'd you come up with that one? Even *I* almost believed you. Thank you for walking by at the right time."

Although no one had answered the security call, Rose had watched the scene play out on the security channel. They loved the security channel—it showed all the entrances and exits to the building that were monitored by the guards. Another channel showed the elevators and laundry room which was fun to watch on Friday or Saturday nights when drunks would wander the circular hallways or make-out in elevators.

"Cat, what happened to you down there?" Rose was wiping away tears.

"The fucking emotional basket-case just realized M will never win Mother of the Year award." Cat said.

J took Rose by the arm and into the kitchen while Cat sat on the couch and saw something interesting on the table: three little white lines of powder.

"What's that?" she asked when Rose returned.

"Coke. I got it from Q's brother who is suddenly clean. I think they threatened him out of the trust fund or something and he was giving all his shit away." Rose flipped between the two channels. "There's that black guy doing his laundry in his underwear again."

"How do you do it?" Cat knew, but wanted to throw Rose a curve and try some for herself. She had heard about it, but never was given the opportunity. Rose didn't answer and J was in the bathroom so she knelt over the line with a straw and sniffed. It kind of burned going in, but seconds later, she was on top of the world.

Her mind was suddenly clear and she felt in control and unstoppable, she thought, as she entered the bedroom to change. There were fewer and fewer of her things as the days passed; she was taking personal belongings to her home a little at a time. She found a grubby pair of shorts and a T-shirt before picking up the phone to call Q to see where she could get more of this stuff. Wait, she couldn't, she was supposed to be drug-free—but she knew it was out of your system in just two days and her test wasn't for another week.

Caution lights flashed in the distance, but the only thing Cat saw was a temporary fix. Day and night she rode over potholes that damaged her car in ways only a mechanic could understand. The outside refused to show signs of aging or rust bunnies, but the shocks and brakes were going to need to be repaired or replaced at the nearest rest stop.

Why was she sentimental about the old car? It had gotten her this far and took a beating every Chicago winter, but it was stable. Who knew how bad the weather would be this year?

The day was going to come when she turned the key and nothing happened. It would be that day she could see in the future and a part of her would die right along side it.

SPF 812

Next to the plethora of safety features, Cat's auto show hybrid offered out-of-this-world customer service and roadside assistance; the car went above and beyond expectations to please anyone who took it for a ride. With no particular place to go and time to waste, Cat jumped into her little vehicle; to her, driving was soothing—even in the Loop—and allowed a few private minutes to sing along with the radio, clear her mind and think about no one but herself. A simple joyride without a driver, or anyone without a license, was missing out on a good time as she proudly skidded through the snow and ice and slush of another Chicago winter.

The smell of burnt rubber and tire tracks accompanied possibly the biggest moment in her life because Cat was never on time.

There were plenty of "whoa moments" in her memory, but this was different. Cat was on time, for once. She wasn't the only gal in that zip code in need of a time management class, but she would benefit greatly from a lesson in big hand and small hand manners. Fast with the usual excuses (couldn't get a cab, directions were lost, a contact fell on the floor, etc.), Cat was always the last to arrive.

"On time my ass." She laughed at the ticket counter,

smiling at the time on her new Tag, a gift from J with a note that said something about checking the time before stopping to smell the roses. An odd note, she recalled, but an awesome gift, nonetheless. "I am totally twenty minutes early."

"Excuse me?" *The Second City* ticket girl questioned. "We've more than an hour before show time. Looks as though someone put your watch ahead so you wouldn't be late. I had to do that to my husband."

"Ohmigod, you are totally right." She smiled and felt her face flush. Cat compared the clock on the wall to her gorgeous arm candy. "And to think, I thought this was just a nice birthday present."

"Bar's open, if that's any consolation."

"That's always a consolation."

Cat took her change and stared at her watch in amazement until she reached the bar outside the main stage. The room was empty, of course, except for the bartender who was talking to an older woman sitting at the corner of the bar. After dropping her coat on the chair, Cat took a seat a few stools away. She politely smiled at the two.

"What can I get you?"

"Bushmills straight-up."

The woman looked at her and seemed to be sizing her up. Cat had nothing to be ashamed of; she was smart, employed, well-dressed, funny, and, most of all, her looks exceeded any supermodel girl-next-door. The Wolf had succeeded in getting her into a workout regime, healthier eating habits and dressing in tailor-made clothes that accented her curves. He had also filled her closet with the finest duds money could buy from shops on Michigan Avenue that had been hanging too loose while her attitude grew a tad higher.

And the drugs didn't hurt. She and Rose shared a new secret and craving.

"Bushmills, eh? You like a nip of the Irish?" The fifty-ish woman took her glass and moved the stool next to Cat. "Mind if I join you?"

"Not at all." She gulped her shot and dropped her change on the bar. "I've got to use the powder room and it will be a while before my friends get here, so sit on down. Cat's the name, what's yours?"

"Betty Doyle. I'll refill that." She held out her hand for a shake and nodded at the empty shot glass. "Bathroom is over there."

Cat went in the general direction that her older, possibly lesbian new friend had pointed to. Surprisingly, Cat did not have the gaydar you would expect from a girl raised in a lesbian household.

Warm, Lysol-fresh air engulfed her as she unzipped her jeans and plopped her bare butt on the toilet seat. More than a pee, she needed a line. A good, healthy, strong, pen-cap-filled, snow-white, brain-freezing line was required. The brand new eight ball bag angelically slipped from her bra cup and before she knew it, she was flying.

"It's too easy," she thought aloud while readjusting her bra and tucking in her shirt. She checked her face for loose specs and reached for her bag to get a dab of lipstick—it wasn't with her. Maybe she'd left it with her coat.

Returning to her seat, Cat saw that a few more people had arrived and were lingering about the bar area and Betty sat with a smile. It was a kind, welcoming smile that made her think of her third grade teacher, Mrs. Corcoran, who believed Cat was an angel sent to her classroom to help spread the good news of the Bible.

"So, Betty, what brings you to *Second City*? Are you a big fan of comedy?"

"Well, I'm in the city visiting my son."

"He brought you here? How sweet. This is a great time." Cat swallowed the shot from Betty and continued as she offered Betty a cigarette, "How old is he? Is he single?"

"Why, yes, he is," she said with a sparkle. "He's my baby

boy and he lives right downtown and works here at *Second City*. If you stick around, I'll introduce you to him. Who knows, maybe the two of you will hit it off."

"Excuse me, ladies and gentlemen," a voice louder than life came from the ticket area where a man, larger than life, stood. "Someone seems to have forgotten their pocketbook at the ticket counter and I have been assigned the task of delivering it to the rightful owner and judging by the driver's license picture, she is righteous."

Cat looked through her coat, in and out of every pocket. "Shit, I think it's mine."

"Let's see, an Illinois driver's license, surprise, surprise," the man with the baby face continued. He was maybe six feet and well over three-hundred and seventy-five pounds on a good day. But he was adorable and had a smile that Cat wanted to look at forever. She was suddenly smitten and didn't care if it was her wallet or her rap sheet he was looking at and announcing its contents to the filling bar. "This young woman, a good-looking fair lass I must admit, is five foot seven inches, weighs about a fifth of me and owns a Ver-sase wallet with Chanel lip gloss and a tube of Carmex."

"That would be me," she yelled above the chattering crowd as she reached for her wallet. She could smell his Old Spice cologne as he handed it to her, just like she imagined her dad used to wear. "I'd forget my head if it wasn't locked into place."

"Well hello there, pretty lady." His smile was huge. He held out his hand, but she already wanted a hug, a soft, safe hug. "You must be Catrin Moran. Pretty name for an even prettier lady."

"This is my son, the one I was telling you about," Betty chimed in. "Daniel, this is Cat. She and I have been sitting here getting to know each other."

"You know my ma? All right! That's one major stepping stone out of the way." He gave his mother a squeeze and winked at Cat. "Listen, gals, I've got to get ready for the show, but would you—and you too, Ma—be interested in having a drink later? Do you live around here? I could walk you home or share a cab with you. Am I being too forward?"

"Yes. I mean, no, you're not being too forward and yes to everything before that. I live on State, on the river."

"No way! I'm on Michigan, north of the river!"

"Great." She told herself not to sound too excited. This was a nice, genuine, seemingly family oriented man whose mother was on the cool side. Maybe someone she could clean up her act for. "I'll see you after the show, Daniel."

"My friends call me Danny, Catrin."

"Mine call me Cat."

"Can I call you Kitten?"

"Only *you* can call me Kitten."

He meowed and walked away.

Rose and the gang ran up behind her. She handed them each a ticket and tried to join the conversation about seeing "that comedian" in person.

"Do you know who that *is*?" Rose was in awe.

"Yea, Danny, and this is his mom, Betty." Cat thought he was just another guy. "Betty, this is my friend Rose. Rose, this is Danny's mom, Betty."

"Nice to meet you." Betty leaned over the bar to talk to the hostess who was starting to seat people. "You want to sit at my table, right?"

"That would be great." Cat replied.

"He is the biggest thing in comedy right now." Rose spoke under her breath. "He has been on Leno and Letterman and Conan and is supposedly going to *Saturday Night Live* after this show closes. He is big, Cat, and I mean big."

"Yea," she whispered. "He looks like five-hundred pounds."

"Follow me." The hostess led them to the table at the edge of center-stage and took Betty and Cat's jackets. "I'll hang these for you. Will these seats work for you, Mrs. Doyle?"

"Yes, just fine. Could you get a waitress over here? My glass is almost empty."

The hostess walked off and they took seats around the little tables. Rose kept babbling quietly about how this guy was the next god of comedy and if Cat didn't like him, she was supposed to introduce him to her. He was going to make it big-time and his life would be fabulous.

The show was just what Cat needed. Two hours of nothing but laughter and comic bliss filling the room erased any thought of her IVF schedule. And, as Rose had said, Danny was huge. Every time he walked on stage, he was met with thunderous applause and everything out of his mouth was hilarious. Cat had never dated someone who could make her laugh. He could and did.

At the end of each show, the performers take suggestions from the audience and act them out. Most of them were directed at Danny and he was a pro at improvisational theater. Cat thought she caught him looking at her a few times and it felt good being the center of attention to the center of attention.

"Tell us something no one else knows!" someone yelled out.

"No one else knows? I've got to be careful. My mom is here tonight. Stand up, Mom. Take a bow." Betty stood up and waved at the cheering fans. "OK, I know. Tonight I met the woman I am going to spend the rest of my life with."

The audience was intrigued.

"Does she know it?" another called out.

"I'm looking right at her." Danny had his eyes fixed on Cat. "So I think now she does."

The cast left the stage and the house lights filled the room. The gang was staring at a surprised Cat who was speechless. Betty turned to her.

"Well, welcome to the family." She hugged Cat. "Let's get back to the bar and find my son before the drunk groupies eat him alive."

The lobby was filled with people who wanted to meet the cast and just as Betty had said, Danny was the main attraction. He waved at his mother and walked through the crowd to join them. The first thing he did was kiss Betty.

"How'd you like it?" Cat saw his need for her feedback and support.

"I loved it and I loved you and everyone else could use more training." Betty stood with Danny's arm around her as proud as could be. "But what's this about you meeting a woman to spend the rest of your life with? Do you plan on getting married?"

"Hi, Cat." He was embarrassed. "I didn't mean to put you on the spot or make you uncomfortable. And I never said married."

"Uncomfortable? Me? Not at all. I just need to know when the rest of your life is going to start so I can get my ducks in order." She laughed. He leaned over and kissed her cheek.

"We're heading to the condo. You coming?" Rose knew the answer, but asked anyway. She whispered, "No sex. None. Not now. Not tonight."

"I think I'm going to hang out here for a while. Someone owes me a drink." She smiled at Danny who never took his eyes off her. "Does that offer still stand?"

"Absolutely. Do you ladies want to wait here for me to get my things? It'll take two minutes." Danny disappeared at the backstage door and the two were again alone at the bar.

"Another Bushmills, Mrs. Doyle?" the bartender asked, even though the bar was closed.

"Yes, I don't mind if I do and let's have one for my new daughter-in-law."

"Did that take you by surprise?" Cat asked. "Or does he find his future wife from the stage pretty often? Is that his thing?"

"He's never said anything like that before and it wasn't intended to get a laugh. I take it he means it." Betty, an impressive drinker, downed her glass. "And this old lady is going to catch a cab and go to my hotel so you lovebirds can get to know each other."

Danny returned just as Betty was putting on her coat.

"You're not leaving, Ma, are you?" Danny was losing his backup.

"Yes, I am. I am going to the hotel where I will probably have a couple more drinks and then go to bed." She kissed his cheek. "I'll see you in the morning. Besides, you've got more important things to do right now. Cat, it was nice meeting you."

"You too. I hope to see you again soon." She meant it as she gave a goodbye hug. Suddenly, she was alone with a man she did not know, who incidentally wanted to spend the rest of his life with her. "Well, what should we do?"

"The place across the street is still open. I could use a couple drinks—girls make me nervous." He waited for her laugh.

"Then don't think of me as a girl." She smiled and grabbed her coat. "Think of me as someone you've known all your life."

"It already feels like that."

"It does, doesn't it?"

Tequila Road House was wall-to-wall with sweaty, drunk people, and finding a table wasn't an option. Instead of pushing through the crowd, Danny motioned the bouncer who led them to a roped off table in the back. Cat imagined this was where he took all his groupies—why did she have to be so negative so soon?

"So, Kitten, how'd you like the show?"

"It was really good." Drinks were brought out and she didn't remember seeing a waitress or telling someone what she wanted. "I haven't had a good laugh in a long time so you are like some magic medicine for my blues."

"Speaking of blues, your eyes are a beautiful green." He held his pint glass up. "A toast to us."

"Us?" She clinked his glass.

"The *we* we are starting tonight." They both drank. And drank. And laughed.

"You know, I'm surprised they let me in here." She was more than buzzed. "I was in a fight in here and got punched in the nose by a guy!"

"A guy hit you? He must have been really mad."

"No, just stupid. The best part is that I didn't fall when he hit me! But they told me to never come back." Cat looked around the thinning crowd. "What do you say you walk me home? Where do you live again?"

"On Michigan and you are on State, right?" She nodded. "A little fresh air might do me some good."

They started walking south on Wells, both knowing a taxi was in the near future.

"Can I give you a call sometime?" He was nervous.

"I was hoping you would." She wrote her number on his hand. "Now, I'm not one of those girls that you wait ten days to call because you are playing it cool. If you want to go out with me, you need to call. No call means you're not interested."

"How soon? Like tonight?" He held the cab door open for her.

"Not tonight, but soon." She gave him a quick kiss that he held for about a minute. She smiled and got inside. He waved as she drove off into the night.

J693313

Waiting for a tow truck seems like a lifetime. Minutes—even hours—can fly past as you stand next to your vehicle steaming on the shoulder, praying the problem isn't going to be expensive. Sometimes the dilemma is nothing but a flat tire and you're highway-bound in no time. Other times, you embarrassingly run out of gas or need a jump-start. If you know the tow truck driver's cell number by heart and send him holiday cards, it might be time to admit the obvious—the snag isn't as simple as the battery. If you know the driver's birthday, it's time to start browsing the brightly-lit lots and look for a new car.

A better car.

Knowing that Danny had put Cat into a wonderful mood that week made Rose keep track of the amount of time that had passed since Cat met Danny. Rose and Mick boosted her confidence, inflated her tires and told her Danny was a celebrity and did things differently, at his own pace; the hours he kept were the opposite of theirs and a call might come when they were asleep or at work. Cat did not like waiting for the wiper fluid refill and wrote him off. If he had been interested, he would have called within a few days as suggested—maybe she shouldn't have suggested anything. It had now been a week since the show and not a word.

From the start, Rose said he was different.

Not good or bad, yea or nay, up or down, just different.

That night the group had discussed the subject at length, coming to the agreement that he definitely was not her *type*; what was her *type*? How did they know her type if she didn't, or even if she had one? The regulars shook their collective head and passed the young Mr. Doyle as nice, but "no way."

Cat knew this wasn't a simple textbook case of opposites attract; it was an actual collision of worlds. He was a performer, a comedian, a significantly overweight comic-book reading, "Caddyshack" quoting galoof who didn't like to call every day.

That didn't fly.

This simple call-a-day plan was a fact that both annoyed and distressed the emotionally needy Cat whose existence fed solely on daily affirmation from that special someone's message on her machine or even a number on the caller ID. Against the wishes of all, she had led the loud-mouthed horse to her sweet well of water, but now it was Cat who longed for a taste of his intoxicating drink of mutual admiration. She sensed his wonderment when she caught him studying her like an O'Keefe floral at the Roadhouse; delighting in the simple extravagance of a quietly sexual orchid. But that was only her mask—what about they way her heart skipped the first time he nervously slipped his hand hers that night outside the bar as they were preparing to go their separate ways?

"He could have washed his hand and lost the number—that happens to me all the time," Mick suggested. "Stuff like that happens. You should go to the theater and surprise him. He probably doesn't know your last name to call information."

"Hello? He had my driver's license and knew the tickets were in my name and number." Cat sighed. "I'm just not celebrity material. Maybe I'm not up to his standards. Maybe I am the one who should take the hint and get into the slow lane. Today is the limit; if he calls today with an excuse then I will consider seeing him again."

"You know he's going to call." Rose yelled from her room as she tried to hide the smell of pot by puffing her clove cigarette. She smoked in her room with the radio pretending none of the smoke would reach the supposed sober and drug-free egg donor. "He's a busy guy doing his shows all over the country. Why don't you just call him?"

"Because I'm *not* that girl. And because I can't have sex for another five years."

"Turn on XRT!" Rose screamed. "He's on! He's talking about the show!"

All three gathered around the living room stereo and heard Danny's voice.

"You're right." Cat kissed Rose and grabbed the phone with her hands shaking. "Why don't *I* call him? I'm not damaged goods, right? Put the car into gear, right?"

Rose fell onto the couch and Mick bounced in place.

"Uh, hello? I have a question for Danny Doyle," she told the producer. He put her on hold and they listened to the show.

"Well, well, Danny, my assistant is telling me that you have a call. Do you want to talk to a fan?" D, the DJ asked. "It's a young lady."

"Sure, I'd love to."

"OK, caller, what's your name?" D asked.

"Cat, but Danny calls me Kitten." Cat smiled when she talked. "Remember me?"

"Cat! Sweet Jesus! I've been trying to find you for—"

"A week. A whole week."

"What's with the week? Do you two know each other?" D tried to get the back-story.

"We know each other," Danny laughed. "I am going to spend the rest of my life with this girl and I am a very lucky man."

"I'd rethink that rest of your life thing. It's been a week and I don't like running in circles, for anyone." Cat would not back down. Rose joined Mick in the jumping in front of Cat. "Of all the things we talked about, what was the most memorable thing I said?"

"That you got into a bar fight with a guy and won." Laughs. "No, it was that you aren't one of those call-me-whenever girls. I was supposed to call you and ask you out and I never did, so I bet you think I hate you, which I don't."

"How could anyone hate you, Danny?" The DJ kept cutting in. "Ladies and gentlemen, if you are just joining us, we are with Chicago funnyman, Danny Doyle, who is appearing at our very own Second City and various other comedy houses throughout the country, including an upcoming *XRT* sold-out show at Zanies. At the moment, it seems he has his eye on our female caller who he forgot to call after they met. Am I getting this right?"

"No," Danny said. "I don't have my eye on her—it's nothing like that and this isn't the best place for me to be saying this. If we could let Cat go, or if I could talk to her in private—"

Cat was petrified. Rose and Mick were holding hands and stopped jumping.

"I can take it, Danny. Go on. It was the kiss, right?"

"She *did* ask for it," the jockey prodded for something juicy.

"Cat, I don't just go around falling over for women. I get a ton of offers every night from gals who see the show or my act, but I have never gone off with any of them."

"Good for you." Cat had no idea what to expect.

"And I never will." He paused. "Because I no longer have control of my heart. You stole it that night and I haven't been the same since."

"Sweet sentiment, but save it for the stage." She hung up the phone and threw it on the floor before screaming. "What did I just do? Ohmigod! Fucking Jesus—why didn't one of you two stop me before I did something stupid like that?!"

"You just hung up on Danny on live radio." Mick turned the stereo up.

"Wow, Danny. That hurt." But it was making for great radio.

"She's just upset. Can we call her back?" Danny sounded uneasy. "You must have gotten her number when she called, right?"

"He's going to be sick." Rose laughed. "I need a drink for this."

"She's right, Cat. You just threw him out of the field." Mick put his arm around her. "Why don't you call him back?"

"Because I'm not *that* girl."

"But you weren't *that* girl before and you did it anyway." Rose poured vodka into three glasses and each took one. "You have been in the best mood this week and I think it's because of him and then you dump him *on the radio*?"

"Cat," the DJ begged, "if you are still listening, please call back. Here kitty, kitty."

"That won't get her," Danny was right. "That's going to piss her off."

"Can we play a special song for her? Do you know what kind of tunes she likes?"

"OK, Danny, if you remember this, I will call back." Cat talked to the speaker.

"Uh, we were in the Roadhouse and said she hated the music, but I guess there was different music in the bathroom because she came back singing, uh, something about a Maserati" He was straining his mind to remember a moment from a week earlier that was hazy from booze.

"Come on Danny, remember this for us!" Rose cheered.

"My Maserati drives one eighty-five—Joe Walsh—she was singing Joe Walsh "Life's Been Good" when she came back." A sigh of relief was heard. He continued and you could hear his smile through his words. "She said she loved The Eagles."

"Do we have some Joe Walsh or Eagles handy?"

"Yea, she asked me what kind of car I drove because she has a driver—"

"Whoa, hold on. The lost cat has a driver and car? And you haven't called this girl? Give me her number and I'll take her out. But first, your wish is my command," the first notes of "Life's Been Good" began to play.

Rose, Mick and Cat screamed and jumped up and down the room.

"Call him! Call him!"

"You said you would! Get the phone!"

Cat grabbed the phone. "What's the number?"

"Redial, you fuckhead!" Rose screamed.

"OK, everybody calm down," Cat had to sound cool. She took a deep breath and spoke, "Hi, XRT, this is Cat. No, I really *am* Cat. How many calls? He wants to what?"

"What are they saying?" Mick questioned.

"I guess the phone lines are full of people claiming to be me and Danny wants to ask me—and all the other ones—a question to see who's the right one."

"Do it. You remember that night, don't you?" Rose refilled the glasses. "Drink this and think about that night."

"OK, mister radio man, bring it on." They waited on hold for the song to end. Cat was pacing and Rose continued to add a couple shots in her glass as it emptied.

"All right, Joe Walsh may have made a love connection tonight." D's scratchy voice came from the stereo. "And according to our producers, there are dozens of delicious ladies on the phone claiming to be Cat. How should we weed out the strays?"

"Stop it with the cat jokes, for one. Cat would know my mother's name."

"Betty Doyle!" Cat yelled into the phone.

"And what my mother drinks."

"Irish whiskey, Bushmills!" she yelled again and the producer told her to hold on. She walked back and forth until she heard the click as her call was put on-air.

"And what brand of wallet she carries." Danny waited.

"It's pronounced Versace, but you said Ver-sase." She smiled into the phone. "And you called it a pocketbook and that my picture was righteous."

"That's right, it's Versace!" Rose's screams came over the air. "I stole that for you last season! Versace!"

"We have a winner!" Danny laughed.

"And a thief," D laughed.

"One more thing—can I see you tonight?" Danny asked.

"Fuck, yes! Tell him to come over!" Rose continued, screaming into the phone. "Danny-fucking-Doyle, get your ass over here!"

"Sorry about that. We've been doing some drinking and she never stole anything." Cat laughed. "Do you remember where I live?"

"Before we go any further, should we keep the other numbers in case this one doesn't work out?" the jockey asked.

"No. Not for me. Cat, how about if we take this conversation off the air?" Danny was snapping back to himself. "It was great to be here and I look forward to coming in again if you'll have me. Go XRT!"

The sound of headphones hitting the table and Danny leaving the studio were heard behind the DJ's send-off and return to music, more Eagles. Cat was put on hold and a few seconds later he picked up the phone.

"Cat? I am soo sorry."

"What did you do, wash the number off your hand?"

"You wrote it with a Sharpie—how could I?" He laughed. "I was scared. You are completely out of my league. I'm just a comedian, but you're a professor so you're smart and really pretty and you can make me laugh. No one has ever made *me* laugh."

"*I* can make *you* laugh?"

Cat was back in her game.

Rose disappeared to Cat's closet and began putting an outfit together and Mick was in his wallet pulling out a twenty dollar bill. Cat looked at them and knew something was out of alignment.

"What's up with you two?" She fell onto the bed and watched the money change hands. "OK, I have never seen Mick pay anybody for anything—no offense—but what's the bet and how do I fit in it?"

Rose was wild-eyed. "He planned it!"

"Who? Planned what?"

"Danny, dummy!" She was dancing in circles with a bottle of vodka and a handful of scarves. "He told us about it days ago. We had to go along with it."

"What? I'm lost. If you knew he was gonna call me, why did you let me get so down about myself? I thought I was suddenly ugly or unattractive to everyone but J?"

"So that you would know how special you really are." Mick smiled.

"Tell her the truth." Rose frowned and handed him the bottle. "He said he needed at least a week to clean up his act—not his comedy show thing—to clean up his life and his apartment and buy new shoes and check out some literature. He wanted to impress you."

The security buzzer rang and they jumped up again.

"I'll get it!" Mick ran for the phone.

"Rose, do you have any?" She blinked.

"Sure thing. I needed to get some powder on your cheeks somehow." They closed the bathroom door and went to work. "He really adores you, I swear. A thousand different ways than J does or Wolf or anyone ever did or does or will. He spent this whole week trying to think of ways to impress you into dating him."

"But he thinks I'm practically marrying him." She inhaled.

"Right? I mean, he's serious about that long-term thing, right?"

"Completely. Totally." She put some gloss on Cat's lips. "And he thinks you're into celibacy, which he thinks is cool. You know, because you're waiting for the right time?"

"Wait a minute." Her mind cleared. "You two knew all about this and didn't tell me?"

"We bet that it wouldn't work—especially not this well." She looked at herself. "How am I? Do I have anything? Boogies?"

"No, you're fine. Me?"

"Clean as a bug."

"He's on his way up!" Mick banged on the door and it opened. "Me too!"

There was a knock at the door.

"I'll get the door," Cat assured as she shut the door behind her. "Just don't be long!"

She felt fine walking to the door until she realized that she was wearing flannel boxer shorts and a Northwestern T-shirt— not very put together or even cute in the collegiate sense. Another knock told her to go "as is" and take her chances.

The door opened and Danny was waiting. He was wearing khaki's, a sweater and some sort of L.L. Bean jacket. In his hands was a bushel of daisies and yellow roses.

"Well, hi."

"Hello, Catrin." He was polite. "May I come in?"

"Sure—of course." She held the door open for him. Rose and Mick conveniently appeared behind her in the hall. "I gather you remember my friends. I know you met Rose last week, but I don't think you met Mick. Danny, this is Mick. Mick, Danny Doyle."

"These, my lovely, are for you." He took the yellow roses and handed them to Rose with a kiss to her cheek, and from his jacket pocket he pulled out a bottle of Bushmills Black. "And you, kind sir. For you I bring this."

"Details. Details." Cat put her arms around him and

kissed him. Again, she smelled the Aqua-Velva or whatever Walgreen's bargain aftershave he wore and felt safe. He gave her the daisies. "So you've crossed the moat."

"I've made it this far." He gave her a gentle kiss in return. "Now all I've got to go on is looks and personality. Oh, and this!"

He pointed at his jacket pocket and Cat put her hand inside with his and pulled out a tiny mirror; a tiny mirror made for a bird cage.

"This is for Driver."

"You remembered Driver?" Cat was astonished.

"No, that one Mick told me. But speaking of *your* Driver, the guy in the car, he's downstairs waiting for us."

"Waiting for us to what? He never works this late." Cat was worried about the lines they were crossing. "He's just for going to work and home and maybe shopping."

"He was in on it, too." Rose laughed and finished her glass and led Danny into the living room area. "Come on in, Danny. Why don't we hang out here for a while? The Kitten has to change."

"Change for what? What are we doing?"

"Danny, do you party?" Mick was asking as they ignored Cat.

"I've been known to, unless that's a bad thing." Danny looked at Cat. "We're going fishing."

"What?"

Rose walked in with the mirror and its pile of white. "I put out some clothes for you. Just put them on."

Cat went into her room and found her size 20 overalls and a flannel button-up on her bed. They must not have been kidding about the fishing, but what was with Danny partying? Did she want to get involved with someone who did what she didn't want to be doing? *Let's just wait and see*—who was she to condemn? She changed clothes and grabbed Driver's cage. When she entered the living room, Danny was inhaling a line.

What the hell?

"Get me one." She knelt next to Danny and put down the cage. She put her hand inside and pulled him out. "This is Driver and he loves your mirror. Want to hold him?"

"The bird is the calmest thing you will ever encounter," Mick answered. "I was terrified of him until I slept here and he flew in and gave me a kiss goodnight."

"Well, I guess so." Danny hesitated, but put his finger out for Driver to step on. "He seems pretty nice. He doesn't bite?"

"No." Cat took her line. "He does a little nip as a joke if I tell him to."

"Well, take him back and let's get going." He watched her put him back in the cage and the cage safe in her bedroom. "You guys keep things under control. We will return."

A buzzing clear head was on her shoulders as Cat and Danny hit the elevator bank.

"I didn't think you were going to call." She stood on her toes and kissed him. He kissed back. "I really thought you didn't like me."

"I adore you. I can't stop thinking about you." They stepped into the elevator going down. When the doors closed Cat jumped up and down. "No, you're not one of those people, are you? Are you an elevator jumper?"

"Caught me." She stopped. "These are great for jumping, especially with the mirrors on the ceiling. Did you ever try it?"

"No way, I would break the cables with my weight." He smiled as she continued to jump.

"So, we're going fishing? Where'd you come up with that?"

"Rose." He held the door open for her and greeted Driver. "She said you were a wonderful fisher-gal at a trout farm on a school trip."

"Hi, Driver." She was uncomfortable. Many times she had

made it clear that he would not, under any circumstances, be the designated driver outside of the office runs. "Sorry about the late night. I had no idea—"

"Not a word, Ms. Moran. This drive is off the books."

They sat in silence as the car took them to the pier at Montrose Harbor. Danny jumped out and the trunk opened. Cat saw him grabbing a couple of poles and a Styrofoam cup of what she imagined were worms, then slammed it shut. Lake Michigan isn't really a place for shore fishing, but she assumed Danny had something else in mind.

They walked in the darkness to the tiny cement pier that went out into the lake. He jumped around the small pier and danced with the poles. Laughing, she took a pole and grabbed for the worms.

"You can bait a hook," Danny said. "*This* I need to see."

"No problem." She opened the cup of worms, grabbed a slimy creature and pushed the squirming thing through the tiny blade. The waves were coming in with a wind that made her rethink her footing. "We might fall in if we stay here."

"This is the perfect place. Will you bait my hook?" He held his pole to her. "I can't bear to do it. There's too much violence in fishing these days."

"Sure, but how are we going to see bobbers in the dark?" Again she hooked a worm.

"With these." Danny pulled a clear bobber from his pocket and turned the bottom that made a little yellow light in the center start to glow. "We can fish in the dark."

"You thought of everything." She cast and fought the wind. "Man, I wish I had something to drink or do something with."

"Your wish is my command." He cast his line and a bottle of Absolute Citron was in one pocket and a baggie was in his shirt pocket. "I'm not a druggie."

"Me, either. I want you to know I don't do this all the time. I really *am* wholesome." She reached for the baggie and pulled a pen from her overalls. "This isn't like a regular thing—neither is nighttime fishing."

"Me neither," He took a drink from the bottle. She shielded herself from the wind and used her pen cap to take a hit, then another. "How'd you learn that?"

"Rose." He followed her lead. She took the bottle and drank. "Plus I always have a pen. Are we really going to fish?"

"Sure, this is one of my tests." He laughed and put the bottle on the walkway. She sat up and took off her shoes. "No shoes?"

"No, I want to feel the water." She dipped her feet into Lake Michigan and then jumped down. "It's warm. And didn't I pass enough of your tests for one night?"

"Be careful. Don't get wet."

She didn't listen as she handed him her pole and walked on the sand into the breaking water. Each wave pushed her body back and caused her baggy pants to get wet. He jumped down and caught her in the next wave that soaked them both to the waist. Wave after wave came in and Cat pulled Danny out further into the water. After a few more waves crashed, they were soaked from head to toe. Both jumped back on their pier laughing. They left their fishing poles and worms and ran back to the waiting car. Again the trunk opened and they grabbed beach towels before getting into the car.

"Man, I owe Rose fifty for that!" Danny laughed as he inhaled twice.

"For what? For me going in the water?" She laughed and followed suit. "She knows I can't stop myself around water. I was like a mermaid in another life."

Driver laughed as he headed in the general direction of the apartment. He seemed to know Danny's plans for the evening and since it was almost after ten o'clock and *The Tonight Show with Jay Leno* was almost a religious event that Cat would not miss. To say the least, Cat should probably be getting home soon. However, the apartment was in full swing and the whole gang was relaxing and waiting for the return of Danny and Cat.

"Is this a shindig?" Cat asked as she walked into the filled living room.

"Gee, Cat, why are you all wet?" Rose smiled at Danny who pulled cash out of his wallet and tossed cash in her direction. "I already ran you a bath if you want to warm up."

"Don't mind if I do." Danny laughed and followed Cat to her room. She didn't notice him as she stepped out of her soaking overalls. "Should I be in here?"

"Uh, I'm going to take a bath so I don't know." She wanted him to be everywhere she was, but knew he couldn't for obvious reasons. She stood on her bed and kissed him as she pulled off his jacket and sweater. "You know how I feel about, you know."

"I do." He continued to kiss her and began to unbutton her shirt. "But I just don't want to be away from you right now— I don't think I *can* be away from you. I just want to smell you and kiss you and touch you and feel you."

"Whoa." She stepped back on the bed and yelled. "Rose!"

"What?" Rose ran in.

Cat was out of breath. "Is my bath cold? I may need a cold bath."

"Danny, boy." Rose looked at the two who were inches from intercourse. "I've got a shower in my name with your room on it. But first, may I offer something from the alcohol or drug family?"

Cat was kissing Danny's neck and ears when he stopped her. "Yea, we need to put this car in neutral. Cat, I understand your beliefs about sex and respect your wishes. Rose, show me the money."

"This may calm the hormones for the time being." Rose held out the plate with white lines. Both took turns and instantly took a step back. "Danny, a shower and Cat, your bath awaits, but hurry, Jay is on in fifteen."

"Jay? You mean like Jay Leno? You like Jay Leno?" Danny was wasting time. "I know him! I've been on his show a couple times. I'm gonna be on in a few weeks—would you like to come with?"

"Cat's only purpose in life is to watch Jay Leno's monologue." Rose laughed, "I don't see what the hubbub is all about, he's so boring."

"Meet Jay Leno?" Cat shot a glare at Rose and then realized she was in love with the fishing, drinking comedian. "Rose, can't he at least take a bath with me? Maybe he could wash my hair."

"I wouldn't even have to be in the tub if I washed her hair." Danny pleaded.

"Absolutely not." She pulled Danny by the arm to her room. "Not a chance."

Cat shut and locked the bathroom door. It was a quick bath—she needed to get Driver and prepare his Leno snack. Wearing flannel pajamas, she joined the party with the yellow bird on her shoulder. Danny was nowhere in sight.

"We like your friend." J smiled and put out his cigar. "Fishing and swimming in the lake in this time of year?"

"You always liked my fishing style." She smiled at J while putting some seeds on a little plate. Danny came out of Rose's room with a towel on his head. "You know the rules, smokes out while the bird is in the room."

Danny cornered Cat in the kitchen and began to use his towel to dry her long hair. "How was your shower?"

"Cold and necessary." He laughed. "I want to be with you, but I know I'll have to wait."

"Not only wait, but see if she chooses you," J laughed.

"Ignore him." Mick handed Danny a glass of the Absolut saved from the fishing. "J is our bubble-buster in the group when Cat is involved."

"I am the truth teller," J interjected. "When Cat is ready to get back in the saddle, who knows who she will choose?"

"I have a clue." Rose watched them staring at each other over the plate of seeds. "And with the way my luck is going tonight I'd bet money on it."

Leno turned into Conan and Conan turned into the security channel and the security channel turned into dawn. They had stayed up all night watching TV, telling stories and fooling around with party favors. Most of the crowd thinned out when they realized it was a school night. Cat decided to order in some breakfast, but no one was hungry. At long last, she was tired and fell asleep on her bed, waking to find Danny sitting at her side, petting her head and hair.

"I love that," she smiled. "You could do that forever."

"If you'll let me, I'd be happy to."

That night out turned into a weekend of togetherness. Danny and Cat were now an item and she was sitting in on his shows, he was partying with her friends and Sunday dinner with his parents in his condo was prepared by the two who couldn't keep their hands off of each other. She already knew and liked Betty, but it was Danny's dad who gave him the comic bug. The two were always trying to upstage one another with silly jokes and childish humor. Betty and Cat just watched, sometimes grabbing the spotlight from the zealous father-son duo with a one-liner. Cat felt oddly at home. For the first time she was where she was supposed to be. She had felt wanted before by J and Wolf mostly for their selfish reasons and even M and Jillie shared a little comfort, but being with the Doyle's made her feel like part of the team—win or lose, they stuck together and looked out for every member.

The only lingering question was when Cat would be done with the cycle.

ALD514

The first time you enter a car dealership, there should be no hesitation. No one knows your name, where you live, your salary or even what type of car interests you. A few trips later—after you have chosen your color and make—when greeted at the door with a smile and first-name salute, that is the time to put on a poker face and get down to business. This is when you challenge the necessity of little perks, realize undercoating is bullshit or that the warranty isn't worth its weight in free gas.

Cat knew none of the questions to ask or the art of haggling and was terrified, but for no reason. Believing she was never nervous, Cat was horrified of buyer's remorse as she second-guessed her decision to allow Danny to invite his friend to Justin's for a night of drinking and laughing and hopefully gaining approval of Cat. Danny didn't seem the type to have had a bursting black book or even a handful of ex-girlfriends to compare her to, but anxiety remained.

To most people, Cat was top-of-the-line; the showroom model in the window under the hot lights that caused people to slow down and take a longer look. He, however, had memorized the *Consumer Reports Car Guide* and knew *Kelley's Blue Book* value on his gal and liked what he saw when behind the wheel enough to bring a friend to take a look.

Knowing her gang, it was his turn to introduce a friend. Even though he won hers over with his comedy and easygoing personality, a touch of concern remained. He just knew that someone—probably Q, who didn't even like Cat—would discover his reckless driving and convince the group he was nothing more than a stolen car stripped for parts, no longer good for anything, but taking up space in a salvage yard.

Justin's was over-capacity as everyone in the neighborhood was out and about barhopping. Basketball season was in full swing and another thrilling go-around with Michael Jordan making the game look easy, promised Chicago fans the season would be ending in another victory. At the Godfather table with J and W, a few Launderbar shots of Cuervo confidence were had before heading to Justin's to meet up with Danny, the gang and Danny's stage partner and best friend. The three pushed their way past the bouncer, Justin himself, only to hear the roar from the usual suspects whom Danny now considered friends.

Little did he know.

"Kitten!"

"Kitten!" the entire bar repeated.

"Fuck you all," Cat said under her breath as J took off her Versace faux fur collared jacket that had a homemade splatter of colored glitter, and kissed her cheek. Danny took her hand before giving J a dirty look. "Hey there." She returned his kiss. "You know I'm not the Norm Peterson of this bar, right?"

"More power to you. I just get so excited to see you I want to scream it from the mountain tops." He smiles. "Hey, where were you coming from? You and J? And your coat looks expensive. Did he give you that?"

"Danny, my darling," she put her arms on his shoulders for yet another round of reassurance, "I was across the street with W having a quick drink because I am terrified that I am going to fuck up meeting your friend and J was there because you needed me to score. As for the jacket, it's last season and I told you Rose swiped it from the show she was working. Remember, it matches that mini I have? She is the leading lady of fashion felonies and I have the merchandise to prove it. All good friendships have illegal secrets and jail time to serve. Satisfied?"

"You know, someday I'll have the money to buy you all those fancy clothes so you won't have to be an accomplice."

"I know you will." She kissed his cheek, not knowing he was glaring at J.

"How much did you get?" he whispered in her ear. "And don't tell Tim. Don't talk about it at all."

"My lips are sealed." She nuzzled his neck.

"No they're not." Danny pried open her mouth with another kiss and his smell of the plastic-bottled aftershave turned her on. For some reason, she wasn't only falling for this guy, but falling at a lightening fast speed. She frantically felt like taking him to the celebrated undisturbed spot in the alley where many late-night drunken attractions had been consummated, but knew she couldn't. For starters, her three months were not up. Secondly, she wouldn't until she was given a sign that this was not another one of her stupid flings with Joe of the Day who wanted arm candy, a break from his wife; a housewife or a mother to his busload of children. They stopped and smiled at each other. "Cat, I've never felt this way about anyone before, I—"

She put her fingers over his lips. "I'm feeling something too, but shouldn't you be introducing me to someone? Don't forget your little friend."

"Oh, Jesus, Mary and Joseph—I almost forgot! Kitten, this is the most important person for you to meet since you already passed the mom test. This is my stage partner and best friend, Tim." Danny tapped the little guy behind him on the back who was ordering something from Mick. "Tim, this is the most important girl I have ever met, Cat."

A small man who was Cat's height and weight turned around and handed Danny a beer and Cat a whiskey in a tall glass. His hair was blond and he looked like he was about fifteen with big blue eyes—he could have been the elf who dreamed of being a dentist. She immediately fell in love and found someone new to take to the alley.

But wait.

"The guy behind the bar said this is *your* drink, Professor. Pretty impressive to meet a chick who has her own drink. *And* a place where everyone yells your name when you walk in, but I take it Kitten is not your preference."

"You could have asked my mom what she drinks. That's how they met, remember? And that's how we met." Danny put his arm around Cat as he took a long drink from his bottle while Tim drank from a pint glass.

"So, Cat, that's an interesting name." He was making nervous conversation. "I used to know a Cat when I was growing up. Her name was, I think, Kathleen or Catarina or Catrin Moran and her mom was a lesbian and everyone knew it but her." Tim looked up from his glass and into her piercing grass-green eyes that were wide with amazement. Their eyes locked and hours passed before she could force herself to speak.

"Timmy? Little Timmy? Timmy Reece? Reece's Pieces? Ohmigod, you and I are still the same size we were when we were thirteen! I haven't seen you since—." She stopped and turned away as the memories of first love, puppy love, inundated her brain, tears flooding her eyes. Danny put down his beer and turned to her immediately as she blinked away the warm trickle before he could catch a glimpse.

"That can't be my Kitten. Her dad died when she was little and her mom lives in the suburbs with her aunt. You're way off on this one, Tim."

Cat turned around and faced them both.

"Looks like I've got some 'splaining to do." Cat knocked

back the triple shot in a single swallow, but it was Tim's eyes—not the booze—that jam-packed her with heat and she knew he was feeling the same. This had been the road she should have turned on years before, but for some reason, had stopped for gas and never got back on the highway. She would regret this for the rest of her life.

But maybe tonight was the first night of the rest of her life.

"Allow me to refill that for you." Tim was unable to take his eyes off of her and was thankful for the proximity to alcohol. He gave an apologetic smile before reaching for her glass; his hand touching hers, and then quickly turned back to the bar.

"You know Tim? What's all that stuff with your mom?"

"Well, it looks like no one has recognized him, but every person in our group—even Mick behind the bar serving him— went to school together when we were kids. He'd probably be happier if they didn't; they teased him for being a small pint. After his brother died, I kind of lost touch with him, but looks like he turned out OK—especially if he found a friend as good and true as you."

"And your mom?"

"Danny, I can't begin to explain *that*. I don't know where to even *start* to begin to explain that. You come from this big wonderful family and have brothers and sisters and a mom and a dad and I have none of that. Your parents aren't even divorced for chrissake! You grew up normal!" Tim turned and handed her another glass, able to read the story being told by the expression in her eyes.

"Should I leave?"

"No, explaining how we know each other is easy. It's the whole life thing that can't be defined that I'm having trouble with." Cat forced herself to smile but could not believe what and whom she was seeing in front of her. "Tim, by the way, behind the bar is Mick, one of my oldest and best friends that you may remember. And over there are J, Q, R, S—the whole gang, and I take it they didn't recognize you. If you're worried about seeing them, or think less of me for being around them, I would understand."

"Cat, Cat, Cat," Tim pleaded as she grabbed his beer and knocked it back. "You and my brother and Mick were my only good memories of those years. You used to stand up for me. What you and I went through— "

"But what about your mom?" Danny *had* to ask; he *had* to press on.

"Yes, Danny, I did not know for many years that my mother was a lesbian and I am sorry that when you met her, I didn't do it at a more appropriate place like the Pride Parade or a lesbian bar. So I guess you now know that my aunt really isn't a relative. Well, not legally in this state." She finished the drink and leaned into the bar to get Mick's attention. All the while, J had been taking notes from only a few feet away.

"What's up, sugar? You're leaking and not waterproof," Mick asked, wiping gently under her eyes as she leaned into the bar.

"This is little Timmy from school, remember him?" Quietly in Mick's ear, as she grabbed for her jacket, "Put him and Danny on my tab for the rest of the night. Versace, last season. Keep them busy, I am going to the bathroom and then kitchen exit and then home. Tim—god I can't believe it's him! After all these years and now—what the fuck? But he told Danny about M and Jillie and now everything is fucked up and I am horrible and a bad person for not wearing a T-shirt that explains my mother's love for muff-diving. Can you believe it's Timmy?"

"Timmy!" Mick looked at him and took the spotlight off Cat. "You haven't changed a bit! It's great to see you!"

"You too, Mick." Tim took a stool next to Danny, who was confused.

"Why do you have your coat? Are you leaving?"

"No, just the bathroom. I'm sure my face isn't that great

right now and I know I could use a pick me up. I was not prepared for the M conversation, but I'm glad we got some things covered before the family Christmas letter. Oh, by the way, my dad committed suicide, but they told me it was a car accident." She was on a roll and could not be stopped. Mick began to pour another glass of Bushmills and handed it to Tim so he would not miss a moment of the drama that took precedence over MJ's jump shots. "And then I lost my virginity to two high school boys who liquored me up and kicked the shit out of me before I was found unconscious in the boy's locker room by Tim's older brother, who actually *did* die in a car accident, but all of that is irrelevant because I have lived the life only Marilyn Munster or Patty Hearst could comprehend."

She slammed the almost full glass and put it back in Tim's hands.

"Happy? There it is, Dans. My nutcase life in a fucking nutshell. Compare your cookie cutter life to mine—we don't fit. I am a circle and you a square. But feel free to use my life in your routine; to think of it, I've got more comedy material than you do."

"Cat, wait!" Danny yelled as she walked off.

"Give her a minute, Danny," Mick said, trying to calm him. "She's real touchy about all that stuff and bringing it up all at once may have shaken her up."

Cat took her jacket and headed to the ladies' room, powered her face and exited through the door that led you to the beer garden. Instead of trying the kitchen exit, she went out in the alley and walked that the two blocks to the brownstone to find J sitting on her steps.

"I am *not* in the mood." She walked up to her door. He followed.

"To talk? How hard was it for him to accept a lesbian upbringing? Or was it you seeing Little Tim and remembering the love you had for someone before me?"

"I don't really know just yet. I don't know how of all the people in the Midwest who are actors—fucking comedians, especially—Danny finds Tim." She unlocked the door and the two walked inside. "I don't know how I ever lost Tim, and I dreamed of this day for years, and never in my mind could have imagined it would turn out worse than it did."

"I saw the way the two of you looked at each other—it's still there. I'd put a bet down on your dumping fat boy for Tim within the week." She ignored his comment and tossed her coat on the couch. "What is it, buyer's remorse? Wishing you hadn't jumped in headfirst with the oaf before meeting his eligible and more-attractive friends? How soon after you met that comedian did you sleep with him? On the first date or was it that night after his show?"

"Fuck you. I told you I wasn't in the mood for this." Cat poured whiskey into a glass that was sitting on her living room table. "I'm sure your take on all of this is me forgetting them both and running back into your arms."

"Getting you back is a dream I will never let die. No one can replace you and I will go to my grave a single man—it's you or no one, Cat. And I'm not the only one who feels that way judging by the look on Tim's face when you left."

The doorbell rang and both knew the night was about to get more interesting. Neither moved as it rang again and fists pounded on the wooden door. Cat opened the door to what she knew would turn into either a house party or a world war. Danny and Tim stood on the porch, while the rest of the crew waited on the stairs.

"Let us in, bitch. It's fucking freezing out here!" Rose yelled and pushed past all to enter, then stopped dead when she saw J. "What have you got to drink?"

"I'll run over and grab some bottles from Mick, hard OK?" X excitedly jumped into action. "Your tab, Cat, right?"

"Be my fucking guest."

"Cat," Danny was heartbroken and stayed at the door,

"why'd you leave? Didja think I would be upset that things were fucked up when you were a kid? Did you think that I would judge you because your ma is a dyke or because some guys roughed you up way back when?"

"I don't know what I was—or am—thinking." She was buying time. "I was sorta planning on coming back."

"Nice door you have here, Cat." Tim couldn't look her in the eye as he prodded to be invited indoors. "I bet you have a knack for interior design, and I imagine you have heat."

"I'm sorry, come in."

As soon as the two entered, Danny saw J. He was sitting comfortably in a lounge chair with a glass of something and waited for the anger to enter Danny's emotional gumbo. To his surprise, Danny turned to Cat, staring at the floor, and fell to his knees.

"I am so sorry that you had to live through a single moment of pain," he pleaded and hugged her legs. "But I'm here now and I'm going to take care of you and I promise that nothing like that will ever happen again. You're safe now."

"What are you planning on doing, Danny boy, turning her mom straight?" J callously called out. "What's done is done and if she was too embarrassed to tell you in the first place, what else do you think she may have hidden away? Have you heard the one about her first true love? The one about the boy she has spent the past ten years pining for and wishing she could get back? The one man who is a bigger threat to you than I will ever be? The one she will leave any man for the minute she finds him? It's got a great punch line, Danny—you'd love it."

"Who wants to watch the game?" Rose roared, realizing Tim's identity and J's path to Cat's breakdown. She grabbed the remote control, turned the television on and blasted the sound. Her eyes searched the board game shelf until she found a deck of cards. She held them over her head. "Bulls were ahead when we left and who wants to play poker? Put your money on the table. I'm feeling lucky."

R turned on the stereo and Cat's too-often-played Eagles CD began while Glenn Frey coincidentally defined the evening ending in heartache.

"I'll play," Tim said softly.

"What is he talking about, Cat?" Danny rose to his feet with the face of a crushed man and looked from her to J and back to her. "Who is this guy he is talking about? Do I know him? Is he here?"

J let out a fake laugh.

"If she has been searching for him, then he isn't here," Rose fibbed, while dealing cards for Tim, Q, P and herself. "Or if he was here, you wouldn't be. I think that's the point J was trying to make."

J laughed again.

"Cat, tell me what he is talking about. Who is this guy? You would dump me if you ever found him?" All color left Danny's face. "I believed you when you said we had something special here, but how special can it be if you would run to this other guy the minute you saw him? And what kind of a man would let someone as special and wonderful and beautiful and smart as you get away?"

"He's got you there, J," Rose snickered.

"You'd just walk away from what we have?"

"You've only had her a month or so, Danny boy." J was fuming. "That's not a lot of time for a relationship to be as strong as you may think."

"Danny," Tim stood up from the card game. "Let's get some air and talk. I think this whole thing is being blown way out of proportion—J is and always has been an asshole in need of a good beating. He's trying to hurt Catrin, not you. Believe me, I know him."

Everyone noticed that Tim had called her Catrin and no one spoke.

"Danny," Cat pleaded as he walked out the door, slamming

it with such force that the house shook. She looked at J, who grinned with delight. "What is wrong with you? If Danny thinks I would leave him, what makes you think I wouldn't leave you?"

"Leave some shit here so I can stay awake—it's going to be a dilly of a night," Rose said before looking at Tim. "And you, fucking calling her *Catrin*? You're the only person in the world who ever called her that. I hope Danny is as stupid as he looks or there will be a multiple homicide on the Gold Coast tonight. Fuck, your best friend is in love with your first girlfriend. Tell us, Tim, do you still have feelings for our little Kitten? Do you stay up nights wondering where she is and if she is happy?"

"I always thought you were gay," Q added.

"I just tell people I'm gay," Tim said quietly.

Cat tossed a baggie on the table, grabbed her coat and ran out of the house to search for Danny. In one direction was X carrying a box of booze to her place. In the other, was Danny. He was halfway down the block when she spotted his jacket and began to run, calling out his name, to no response. When she finally caught up with him, he didn't stop, slow down or even look at her.

"Danny, you have to stop and listen to me."

He didn't.

"Tim was right, J was trying to get you pissed and it looks like he succeeded. I haven't been waiting or looking for someone from the past." She sounded like she believed her words, "He would do anything he could to break us up."

Danny stopped.

"Why?"

"Because he always gets what he wants and he can't get me."

"Why didn't you tell me about your ma being a lesbian? I'm OK with homosexuals. Tim is gay!"

"For one thing, it embarrasses me. Secondly, I don't care

to talk about M's sex life and think what people do in their bedroom is their own business. Did I ever question you about what position your parents use most often? Or if your dad ever had an affair? And J's sort of right. We've only known each other for a little while and are just starting to get close. I was afraid something like this—something this fucked up—would be a deal breaker." She was cold and out of answers. If he wanted to walk and pout, let him. "I have a lot of baggage and that scares away new people—why do you think I'm still friends with the same ones who lived through it all with me? They are my security blanket and I don't need to explain to them my issues with men or problems with sex or my misunderstanding of family values to every person I meet. I haven't hurt anyone and I've turned out pretty good and I don't need to apologize for anything I've done. You know my number."

"I leave for Vegas in two days, Cat." he called. "I want you there with me."

Cat turned and walked away.

Danny didn't follow.

Back at the brownstone, Tim was sitting on the porch smoking.

"I didn't know you smoked."

"I don't, but I needed something and Rose gave me this." He handed it to Cat, who took a puff and coughed.

"Timmy, you little moron, you're smoking pot!"

"So that's why I don't care about Danny or your mom or J or the strip poker game or the drug buffet. All I want to do right now is look at you—are you real? Is it really you?"

"Yes, it's me. What do you want, Zuzu's petals?" She helped him up. "Let's go inside. It's fucking freezing out here and I'm not wearing shoes."

"Wait. Is it true what J said? Have you been looking for me and dreaming about me and, as they say, carrying a torch?" He looked at her and reached for her hand. "Don't answer.

Even if you haven't, I have."

"Let's go inside."

The living room looked like backstage at a Rolling Stones concert. There were beer cans in every open space, two pizza boxes were on the floor, bottles of hard booze scattered about, ten people she didn't know sat watching the game, and Rose was in her bra.

"*That*, I expected." Cat smiled, referring to Rose as she walked to the table. "May I ask who the silicone gals and frat house zombies are?"

"P let them in. He said he knows them. I wasn't wearing a shirt so I couldn't throw them out." She put her blouse back on and stood up to yell while pointing at Cat. "Does anyone know who this is?"

"No," a blonde said. "Is she like famous or something?"

"No, it means you are leaving." Cat went through and tossed out a bunch of people who had just walked in off the street.

"I know you! You work at R's ad agency! You were the reason he and his wife got divorced and then back together," some guy answered in her face.

"Yea, that's me." Pissed, but calm. "What kind of host am I? Where's your jacket? Let me hang it up for you."

"That's what I'm talking about." He threw her a leather coat which she took and tossed out the front door. "Hey, bitch, what the fuck are you doing?"

"It's either me asking you to leave or the cops insisting."

A few more people left and Cat fell into a chair at the poker game. The entire time, Tim had been on the couch staring at Cat who had become more beautiful than he ever imagined. She was smart, bold, funny, and could still kick some ass. Why did he never make that call? All this time he had kept in touch with another school buddy who filled him in regularly. He knew exactly where she had been and never picked up the phone. What was he so afraid of?

"You in?" Rose was dealing.

"Yes, it's too hot in here. Is there anyone left who I don't know or like?" She and Rose looked around the room. A disheveled P and an unknown gal came out of the bathroom. "Who is she?"

"She is, uh, K." P was out of breath and recognized the look on Cat's face. "And we were just leaving. Anyone up for Nookies?"

"I think she's hourly," Rose joked. She looked at Tim. "It's him, honey. It's really him. How do you feel? Want to talk? Rethink celibacy for one night?"

"You haven't slept with Danny?" The room inquired.

"Did anyone *not* ask that question?" Cat laughed.

"Not me—I know the secret." Rose winked at Cat.

"No and no, I can't let my house be free to strangers any more tonight." Cat got up, grabbed a garbage bag and started to toss out the empties and then sat back down next to Rose. "And what about Danny? Things were going really well for about a month or so—I can't fuck up his career. I've fucked up a lot of things in my life, but never a career."

"The career isn't with me." Tim stood by them. "I'm going to New York. I've been asked to audition for *Saturday Night Live*. He's got offers in Vegas. We've got a script for some buddy movie that we were talking about doing in a couple months."

"I knew about that," Cat noted. "He says he won't go if I can't go, and only wives are allowed on the set and I'm never getting married."

"I can't believe that for the past month, he has been talking about this wonder girl and it was you the whole time. *You're* the one he took fishing and fell into the lake with? *You're* the one who makes crossword puzzles at work and it was your boss who sold you this place that you fill with birdhouses? You paint birdhouses? I thought you hated birds!"

"I just like one." she pointed at Driver's cage. "Him."

"*You're* the person he bought new clothes for and hired a maid for and cancelled all his Monday night football plans for? *You're* the one his mother likes? She hates me, but she adores you. She even talks about you when she's around, which has been pretty often since she wants you two to hook up and she knows he needs a little help." Tim just stared at her perfect face and then touched her chin. "All the advice he has gotten from everyone we know has been for you, Catrin. *My* Catrin. And did you say celibate?"

"As of this moment, I am no one's Catrin." she yelled over the television. "You hear that J? No one's Cat."

"You'll always be mine," J shot back. "Always and forever."

"Go write a Michael Bolton song, creep!" Rose shouted.

"And mine." Tim locked eyes with Cat.

"I can't take this." She looked at Rose. "Toss everybody out when the puking starts and give me that baggie. It's not even mine."

"Just a little?" Rose poured a small pile of white on the table. "Danny won't mind."

"That's for Danny?"

"No, it's for Dennis Rodman after the game tonight."

She took the bag, grabbed Driver's cage and pointed toward the back bedroom. "Clean up after yourselves, please! Timmy, we need to talk. Alone."

She led him past the kitchen into the breakfast nook-turned library. She flopped on the futon and motioned for him to join her.

"How are you?" she could barely speak.

"Thrilled to see you," he whispered. "Where did you end up at college?"

"Let's see, I went to St. Norbert's—"

"I transferred there my sophomore year after starting at the school we talked about."

"St. Mary's, right." She remembered fighting to go there,

but M wanted her closer to the city and home. "We just missed each other."

"Then I signed up for acting classes at Northwestern and saw a Sheamus Heaney course last semester, but the professor had moved on and wasn't teaching there." He looked down. "I dropped it."

"I did too." Their faces were getting alarmingly close and she felt his soft breath on her mouth. "So you were stalking me? That is so fucking hot."

"Still talking like a pirate's wife? Who would think that a girl with a doctor's degree would have a mouth as filthy as yours." He smiled. "I missed every bad word in your everyday vocabulary."

Cat pounced onto Tim's lap and they began kissing. She could not stop and he didn't try to hold back. She was unbuttoning his shirt and feeling his heart beating faster than it had in years. He stopped and looked at her; took her face in his hands and pulled her back into the moment. Out of breath, Cat backed up and looked at the situation.

"Timmy, ohmigod, I can't."

"I know, we'll work it all out tomorrow, but right now I need you."

"No, it's the hormones." She tried to explain. "I'm soo ovulating right now that I'll get pregnant if I even think of your dick."

"So we get pregnant and we have a family." He was in that guy-begging mode. "Or a condom—I'm sure Rose has condoms. I'll wear two!"

"All you have to do is take your pants off and I'll get pregnant." She stood up and paced. "I'm fertilizing eggs for a couple and have been on hormone shots for three months and am like a drunk virgin on the date rape drug. It's like two days before I get them taken out and I can't—"

Rose threw open the door and poured a cup of water on Tim's pants.

"What are you thinking? You know you can't even use a public toilet right now!" Rose tossed Tim a towel. "Sorry, but she won't be able to catch your bus tonight."

"What?" Tim was deflating. "You're donating your eggs to someone? That's a noble thing to do, but I thought a few of those had my name on them."

"You screw her now and you'll have nine-tuplets or something outrageous," Rose laughed. "It's kind of funny if you think about it. Oh, Danny called. He wants you to call him tonight. He needs someone to go over and talk to."

"Me?" Cat thought she had another chance.

"No, Romeo. I take it things in here are a little cooler?"

"Goodbye, Rose." Rose closed the door behind her. She turned to Tim. "Don't go. Don't go to him tonight. Stay with me. Just sleep with me and let me feel you. Let him wait— this might be our last chance."

And so they sat, hand in hand until the dawn talking about all of the plans they once had, their childhood dreams and the hopes of a reunion sometime in adulthood. Cat felt every muscle in her body sizzle when he stroked her hair and had to remind herself that it was Danny she was destined to drive the road of life with, not Tim. If Tim had been serious, he would have called her years earlier and they would probably be married by now with a yard filled with kids. But he didn't. He chickened out. By sun-up, both grudgingly agreed a friendship was all that could happen because of their mutual admiration of Danny and unless he should suddenly get sick and die— only then would she be back on the market.

"Just promise me that you won't turn to J for comfort," he half-joked.

"J? Are you kidding me?" She smiled and ran her fingers through her hair. "That train left the station hours ago. He had his chance and blew it."

"I always warned you he was a cheater."

"Yea, but I thought you meant on math tests, not women."

She opened her arms for a hug, "I love you, I really do. Let's keep in touch Mr. *Saturday Night Live*. Besides, you know how I feel about New York."

She hated it. Any city larger than Chicago caused fear and a feeling of being lost. Aunt Jillie and she were accidentally separated in London once and M had taken a wrong turn on the way to Disneyworld on a trip to Los Angeles which still gave her nightmares. New York would be out of the question.

"I would give up the show to be with you, but that's neither here nor there." He hugged her back and she caught him smelling her hair. "You still make your own shampoo?"

"I sure do. I make shampoo and paint birdhouses."

The fresh pavement signaled that the road ahead was open and begging for tires.

Was she ready?

ZPS315

Miles passed on the odometer and there was no visible sign that Danny was double-parked or waiting on an off-ramp or a weigh station. The night with Tim had been magical, but his plans for the highway ahead blindsided Cat who didn't need to bleed the brake fluid for the direction he was headed. New York to her was a Denver boot—even with the promise of love and happiness from Tim as insurance. He was taking the city head-on with or without her. Kept safely in his glove box, Tim had his future mapped and if the directions included Cat, he would be a lucky man. Years were spent getting to this point in his career, and the days yet to come did not require her companionship. Sitting in idle, the aged Cavalier managed to push forward at a predictable pace in the cash-only lane, letting the cars in the left lane fly past and fade into the horizon.

Her eggs were retrieved and the agreement was final. The money was deposited into her savings account and Cat finished moving into the brownstone in record time. Mick and Rose weren't tossed out in the cold; they each took a bedroom with the promise to move as soon as their personal highways cleared of traffic.

But Cat had to switch lanes first.

It was hard to tell if Danny was angry or confused at the road block the night at Justin's created for all involved. He didn't call before he left for Vegas, but his reckless driving and courtship continued; fresh flowers were in Driver's car every morning, Potbelly sandwiches for her and G arrived at noon each day, and almost every night when she returned home from work, there would be a gift with a card celebrating an anniversary, like their first kiss, first date and even the first argument. He didn't say it in any words, but his actions showed he was not giving up without a fight.

"Hello, may I speak with Danny Doyle?" It was a fuzzy long distance call to the stage manager to find Danny who was practicing for his upcoming week of shows. "This is Cat Moran."

She waited and listened to the multiple voices calling out his name. After a minute or two without an answer, feet were heard running to the phone.

"Cat? Is it you?" Danny was out of breath. "You called! You found me and you called—does that mean you want me? Do you want a relationship with me? Is that why you called me all the way out here?"

"Yes," she smiled. "If you'll have me."

"Only for the goddamn rest of my life." He laughed. "Did you get your tickets? I wasn't sure if you were going to come or not, but the hotel insisted they send them to you so you could. You *are* coming, right?"

"Yes. And I have some other good news." She took a breath before she continued. "My ban on celibacy may have ended. I mean, it's still a risk, but I think I am willing to take a chance if you will."

"This is the best phone call of my life!" he screamed. "I'll meet you at the airport tonight or I'll have someone pick you up if you land during the show. OK? This is fantastic! I can't wait to see you!"

"Me neither." He sounded genuinely excited which made

her feel more at ease at the thought of chasing him across the country. "I'll see you in a little while."

If Cat acknowledged a fear of anything, it was flying. Before she got to the gate, she took a couple of Xanax with three shots of whiskey from the friendly bartender at an airport lounge. She would have given anything to just drive to Vegas or Greyhound the trip, but it would have taken too long and Danny would be back in Chicago before she got there. Right now, she needed a car ride; something that she would be in control of and take responsibility for if there was an accident. Who knew who was flying this thing?

And why was she in first class?

Passenger planes were always cramped and filled with an unruly assortment of people you hope to only see once. She stared out the window and watched the clouds go by, one after another; peaceful and billowy. She guessed a plane was a step up from her car fantasies; everyone had a place to go and people to see and they chose this means of transportation.

The flight attendant was friendly and noticed that Cat was a basket case. She brought her a pillow and blanket and suggested she take a nap. When that didn't work, she brought Cat a glass of champagne that was gulped before she walked away. Headphones were not wanted and there was nothing left for her to do but wait it out with Cat. She asked about her plans in Las Vegas and how long she would be staying. When Cat said she was going to see her boyfriend, Danny Doyle, the girl got excited and said she had tickets for the following night—could Cat possibly arrange a meeting between the two? The stewardess was a big fan who told the other first class flight attendants that Danny Doyle's girlfriend was the anxious flyer and they all clamored around her asking questions.

"He talks about you in his act! He says such nice things!"

"Really, like how I need a few cocktails to ride a plane?"

"Is that all you need?" One disappeared and returned with a handful of assorted brands of airplane bottles of booze and a couple small cans of pop. "Pick one—or have them all! What the heck? It *is* Vegas!"

"Can I use the bathroom? I think I am going to throw up." Cat stood and they walked her to the first class bathroom. She didn't need to puke; she needed a line to clear her head. If she was going to spend the next hour answering fan questions, then she needed to be alert. After checking for spots, she returned to the chatting gals. "Nope. I'm fine."

"He says he met you in Chicago with his mother. Is that true?"

"Yea, we were drinking together before the show and—"

"And you lost your wallet! It's such a cute story, but I never knew it was true!"

"I never knew it was part of his act," Cat added. "What else does he say—that we went fishing on our first date?"

"No, but that's out of the ordinary—just like him." The girl produced another handful of bottles and a can of orange juice. "He doesn't seem like a fisherman."

"He's not." Cat drank until she didn't realize the plane had landed. All the girls had chatted her through the end of the ride and she promised to take Danny to meet them the next night at some round bar in the MGM by the gift shop.

Her hopes of Danny meeting her were crushed when she realized it was nighttime and he was probably onstage. Cat then saw a man in a suit holding a sign that read "KITTEN."

"I think that's for me." She smiled at the guy who took her luggage. "Not even a doubt? How could you know it's really me? Danny always makes me take tests like this."

"Because I have your picture." He opened his jacket and inside was a photo of Danny and Cat and Driver at the condo taken some miscellaneous night. "He did ask me to get you liquored up before his show ends. He'll be getting off the stage about the time I walk you to the stage entrance. So start your drinking."

"No need. I am on the ground so I'm fine."

He tucked her in the backseat and quietly handed her a baggie. "He also thought you might be in need of a lift."

"What kind of place is this Las Vegas?" She took the bag and the limo door closed.

Cat had somewhat of an idea of what to expect. She had heard about Vegas and the stories told always involved *something* considered illegal in Illinois, *someone* considered illegal in Chicago and a loss of money all around. She was so excited about the comforting car ride that she completely missed the bright lights and neon signs. Here she was, in Sin City, dressed in her favorite Prada mini-dress—the new lavender eye-popper with beaded layers that Rose found special for the trip—and being driven to see the man she only recently decided to be her one and only—how could it get any better?

She saw the room.

Danny had finished early and was upstairs in their suite. She didn't know he had been pacing and changed shirts a dozen times, not knowing which to wear. Cat was led through a golden lobby past banks of elevators to a private elevator door that had a personal guard. The limo driver handed him her things and she was taken inside the restricted elevator with the doors shutting behind her. They opened into a living room. In a mirror, Cat saw Danny walking back and forth and she stepped into the room.

"Dans?" She was quiet, thinking it was someone else's big-time hotel room.

"Cat!" He ran toward her, jumping over a sofa and knocking over a table until she was in his arms. "My darling, wonderful, sweet-smelling Cat!"

"Danny, you are a celebrity!" He was nuzzling her hair and smelling its long curls. "All the girls on the plane gave me airplane booze and I have to take you to meet them tomorrow. And then the limo driver was cool and there are posters of you at the airport—do you do me in your act? The flight attendant's said—"

"It's wonderful to see you." He kissed her unlike any kiss they had shared before. Tingles went down her spine and she knew Danny had one thing on his mind. "You ready to meet Las Vegas?"

"I was hoping to meet someone else." She looked into his eyes and kissed him.

"I'm too jacked up for that right now." He smiled. "Well, maybe a little lovin' won't kill me. Follow me."

"Whose place is this?" He led her to the bedroom where a maid was unpacking her bags and placing her toiletries in the bathroom. "Who is she? Why is my stuff being put away in this huge place?"

"This is our suite. It's a penthouse. This is a good one— they make 'em bigger, but I got this one. It's got two stories, five bedrooms, six bathrooms, a kitchen, a chef, a butler and maid, a private balcony, hot tub, living room, dining room— everything you need when you are away from home." He pulled her toward the bed. "How un-celibate are you?"

"Almost completely," she teased. They began to kiss and fell onto the bed. Danny had never touched her bare skin and when he pulled up her dress and felt her thigh, he panted. "One thing I know for sure is that you're the one I want."

"I'm so nervous about it." He sat up, but continued to play with her hair. "It's been so much fun thinking about making love to you that I'm afraid I won't—"

"You won't do and be everything I want you to be?" she smiled. "You already are. No matter how bad either of us is at it, we're all we've got and we'll make the best of it. Deal?"

"Deal." He smiled and they shook. "Now, a drink, a line and my town. Later, when I get my courage up, I might try to get to second base."

It was a plan. He led her by the hand out of the opulent hotel and onto the strip. It was filled with beautiful crowds dressed to the nines—she fit right in. Tan, thin, expensive and drunk people packed the streets and the neon lights above them finally caught Cat's eye. Danny was busy pointing at the different hotels and talking about their respective shows or specialty buffet open around the clock. It was after two and they were still walking tall, hand in hand. Danny was stopped for autographs every so often and was asked if Cat was the girl from the show.

"Danny, seriously, what do you say about me in your act?" She was curious as she kept hearing bits of stories from a variety of people.

"Nothing bad. I just tell the ladies I am taken." He swung her around and kissed her. "Sometimes I tell how we met—"

"That's what the stewardess' all said." She smiled. "We can go to the MGM and meet them tomorrow, right? They talked me through the plane ride."

"Of course we can! We can do anything your little heart desires."

"Well, right now my heart desires some sleep." She kissed him. "Is that on the menu for tonight?"

"Sleep? Maybe we can fit that in."

Cat did not want to have sex and was lucky enough to have found a guy who didn't need full intercourse to, well, you know. Kissing and touching finished him off.

The next morning, Cat woke up to a room filled with trays of fruits, pastries, eggs, sausages, and everything ever consumed as a breakfast meal. Wearing only Danny's T-shirt, she walked around taking bites of melons and strawberries, and a waffle nibble before settling on a lobster tail and champagne. The maid entered and surprised her.

"I'm sorry, ma'am. I didn't mean to disturb you." She started to back out of the room with her head down, eyes staring at the floor.

"No, hey, come on in." She apprehensively walked back in. "We didn't really meet. I'm Cat and this is way too much food for me. Why don't you grab a fork and join in?"

"You want me to eat with you?" She was uneasy. "Mr. Doyle couldn't sleep and is at the blackjack tables. Can I get you something?"

"Yes, you can sit down here and eat some of this food. Who were they expecting to eat all of this?" Cat poured butter all over the lobster and the maid slowly sat down. "I know Danny is an eater, but this is too much for even him."

"Mr. Doyle wanted to make sure you had anything you might be hungry for." She took a seat, unwrapped a silverware set and began cautiously cutting a pancake, nervously glancing at Cat every few seconds. The butler entered the room and the maid stood up. "Ms. Moran—"

"It's Catrin," She swallowed another bite. "Please call me Cat."

"Cat wanted someone to eat with." The maid was terrified of his seniority.

"Why don't you grab a plate and get your grub on?" she asked the man. "Can we call Danny to get up here and eat with us? There's enough food for a small army."

"I'll ring Mr. Doyle on the floor for you, Cat." The polite man left. The woman sat back down.

"This food is soo good, I never imagined." The maid was cleaning her plate.

"What's your name?"

"My name?" Why would she ask that? Should she interact with the guest? "It's Maryanne, ma'am."

"Do you work all over the hotel? It seems really big. How many rooms are there?" Cat could not eat fast enough. The thought of a line crossed her mind and knew it was lying out in the bathroom. "I mean, I don't want to get you into trouble by keeping you here."

"This room is my only assignment." She smiled. "And Danny is very generous and wonderful to work for. He has really been excited for your arrival."

"That's funny your name is Maryanne," Cat said as she

walked into the bathroom and scoped out the stash. "Did Danny tell you I was a professor and people always ask me where Maryanne is and now I finally know a Maryanne? You know, from *Gilligan's Island*? Can I call you that?"

"You can call me whatever you like."

Just as she was sniffing a line, she heard the elevator doors close and Danny calling her name in the foyer.

"I'm right here. You don't have to yell." She kissed him. "Blackjack?"

"Yea. I took a couple hundred out of your pocketbook and played for a few hours. I hope you don't mind." He was taking casino chips out of his pockets and dropping them on the bed before taking a hit in the bathroom. "Hi there, Maryanne. Taking a break?"

"That was my souvenir money, geek." She poured Danny a glass of champagne. "I asked Maryanne to eat with me. I don't like eating alone."

"The table was on fire—I won it all back and a few hundred more so you can get even better presents for your friends. I could have stayed there all morning."

"Having a party, without me?"

Cat's thoughts raced to Q, back in Chicago, who took out personal ads in *The Reader* looking for dates. Weekly, she would publish her alleged weight and height and favorite movies in hopes of finding someone to have a meal with. She dreamed of the rare occasion and meeting the right guy who would sweep her off her size-7 feet. They would fall in love and she would become a happily married person, or at least a cheerful relationship person. Usually, she ended up paying for both meals and returning home with a doggie bag of shame. Q, with all her hateful qualities and buckets of family cash, was a nice girl who wanted simple things, but guys couldn't get past her extra twenty pounds and walked away without the second call they promised to make.

What was Danny doing having a party without her? Was

she now like Q and he became the guy too good to pay for his own meal or embarrassed to be seen with her at his side?

"Not at all." He kissed her forehead and grabbed a plate. "You were sleeping and I didn't want to wake you."

"Can I ask you something?" She was trying to be funny. "Since I am the Professor and this is Maryanne, could the butler be the Skipper?"

"Skipper?" He rolled with laughter and pointed at the butler. "Do you mind if we call you Skipper?"

"Not at all, sir." He stood firmly at the door. "Might you be Gilligan?"

"Gilligan! Now that's fucking awesome!" Danny laughed. "I have to go down to the stage and check on a couple things that fucked up last night. Why don't you get dressed and come with? You can meet everyone."

"What should I wear?"

"I'm wearing this smelly shirt and jeans," Danny proudly proclaimed as he went into the bathroom again. "No one has a clue what a goddess you are, so you could probably go down in that."

Cat quickly washed up and changed into a pair of jeans and an Isaac Mizrahi cashmere top and a little make-up. She knew she looked good and with Danny at her side, she felt like she was on top of the world. He went into the bathroom as she was putting on mascara. She turned and looked at him as he stared at her through the mirror.

"You know you don't need any of that stuff, right?"

"I always need a little something." She powdered her cheeks.

"You know I love you just the way you are." He brushed her hair. "You are too perfect for a schmuck like me. No one is gonna believe some gorgeous babe like you is dating someone like me."

"*Like* you? What are you like?"

"I'm all overweight and smelly and a slob." He looked

down. "Why would someone like you want to be with me? You deserve the best of everything."

"I have the best of everything." She turned to him. "You are everything I want. I can't believe you would be interested in someone like me. I'm the one with all the baggage and crazy hang-ups and issues."

"I'm just telling you." He led her by the hand to the elevator. "No one is going to believe you are with me. They'll all think you're a working girl and I'm playing a trick."

After their elevator ride, Danny led Cat to a back entrance to the theater and the stage he performed on nightly. The theater seated 2,500 and was sold out for the whole week. Ticket prices were $85 apiece and the casino had been talking about signing him on as their main attraction as long as he packed the seats. He was a great act, easy to work with, always full of energy, loved meeting his fans and, most importantly, filled every seat at every performance. In her mind, Cat did some math and figured Danny brought in over $200,000 for the casino nightly, not counting drinks—of course they wanted to hire him if the payoff was this handsome and the patrons kept drinking. How much did Danny get a show?

"Everyone, can you come out for a minute?" he shouted from center stage, and people began to appear from the lighting and sound booth, up by the spotlights, and from different places in the backstage area. "I want you all to meet Cat. She finally came out to see the place and decide if I am going to stay here and work with all of you for the next few years."

Cat shyly waved.

"So, if any of you see her around, be friendly," he shouted. "She is very important and it is her decision if I stay here. So, if you like working with me and like the show, go out of your way to be nice to Cat."

He took her by the hand and led her to stage right and the stage manager's desk. A squirrelly guy with a headset and a pony tail sat on a stool looking at her.

"So, this is her?" His words were sharp and hurt. He pointed at her. "You do anything to fuck with him or the show and I will personally kill you. Don't test me."

"Happy to meet you, too." Cat smiled to piss him off. "If *you* do anything to fuck with him or his show, I won't kill you. I'll hurt your family. Are we in agreement?"

"I like her. I'm S." They shook hands. "I am the stage manager and the only person you need to go to if you are looking for Danny or have any questions about the show."

"He just acts rough," Danny said to Cat. "He's actually very nice and has a beautiful wife and kids. Isn't she gorgeous, S? Didn't I tell you how pretty she was?"

"Yes, you did." He spoke into the headset microphone. "I'm busy right now, but we will see you later, Danny. Nice meeting you, Cat."

The two walked hand in hand to the floor that buzzed with energy. Cat looked for the slot machines, the only gambling she knew about. She reached into her pocket and pulled out some chips and remembered he had been at the tables all morning while she was in the room. They found their private elevator after signing a few autographs and went to the suite.

"Danny, why didn't you take me to gamble? Do I embarrass you?" Q was on her mind and unwanted singleton life was weighing on Cat's conscience. "Did you go alone because you wanted to meet someone else or maybe I was bad luck?"

"Absolutely not!" He kissed her forehead. "I wanted you to sleep off the airline booze in case you would be hung over today. Maryanne, what should the Professor wear for our visit to the floor?"

"I've had her yellow dress pressed and hung in the bathroom. All of her other necessities are with it." Maryanne stood when she spoke to him. "Will that suit you, Professor?"

"It's Cat and yes, the yellow thing will be great." She shut the bathroom door behind her and began reapplying make-up and primping. The yellow dress was another Prada that Rose had pocketed about a month earlier. Cat was lucky to be the same size as runway models and fit into almost everything Rose got her. After curling her hair, she opened the door to see Danny still eating. "Dans, will you call Rose or Mick and check on Driver? I'm really worried about him missing me and our Leno time."

"Sure." Maryanne brought him a cordless phone and he dialed. "Hello? Rose? How the hell are you? Me? Fabulous. The new dresses you got Cat are beautiful, but you have to start being careful—I had to wait this long to finally get her and I don't think I could handle a prison term. Yes, I am calling to check on Driver. Did he watch Leno with a snack? It was a rerun? How dare he do that to Driver? OK, good. Is he singing and flapping around or whatever he does? Good. Are you and Mick doing OK? You have got to get him to move out. He is a slug. No, I don't mind you there. I just think Mick is overstaying his welcome. Got it. You, too. Bye."

"Well?" Cat asked from the bathroom.

"She thinks Mick is taking advantage of your generosity." He stuffed an egg in his mouth. "I do too. Is there anywhere else can he go?"

"He never goes anywhere. He is always shacked up with one of us." She stood in the doorway and spun around. "How do I look?"

"Too good for a drip like me." His eyes bulged. "Maryanne, remember to call Marty at the front desk to get Kitten some new duds from the Forum Shops. You know her size."

"New clothes? For what? I'm only going to be here a couple days." She was confused but excited to own clothing that would never put her in front of a judge. "How was Driver? Did he see the monologue last night?"

"Driver is fine. He slept in Rose's room and woke her up at 6:30 this morning singing for his breakfast." Danny wiped the egg dripping from his lips and joined her in the bathroom with a kiss before a hit. "Maryanne, make sure everything she gets is the best and the newest and the most expensive."

"Danny, I have clothes and you don't have the money for things like that." What was he up to? Was Las Vegas like a drug that altered the small part of your mind that was still sane when you landed and fizzled out when your feet hit the ground? She hadn't spent any money yet and didn't think she would be getting anything but postcards and key chains for the freeloaders watching her castle unless something extraordinary caught her eye.

"I have plenty of money, Cat. I signed a contract and this suite is my new home—*our* new home." He was excited and waiting for her enthusiasm to kick in. "They are going to remodel that stage we were on and name it after me, and I will live right here in this penthouse and anything I want is mine. This is going to be our home!"

"*Our* home?" He had jumped a few feet ahead of the line drawn in her mind. "Did you forget that I *have* a home and a job and family and friends and responsibilities and people who depend on me in Chicago?"

"You will meet new people and you don't need a job with the money I'll be making and I get breaks to tour and do that movie with Tim and—what?" He stopped when he realized she was not thrilled with his news. "What is it? If you don't want to move, you can keep your house and just bring the things you want here and come and go as you please. The hotel has given me free reign of the private jet so you can go home every week if you want. You know you hate Chicago winters and were planning on leaving your job. This is a new start."

"I'm not a follower." Cat said quietly. "I'm not the person who packs up and runs off after people. I'm a leader. What about Driver and Rose and Mick? What about M and Jillie and my job and *Melrose Place* and Justin's? Do you really think I can just pack up and move across the country without a plan or map?"

"*I'm* your map. *I'm* your compass." They stood face to face. He was genuine and willing to do whatever it took to keep Cat in his life. "This is the chance I have been working for and you are the girl I would wait a lifetime for. If you really think about this and decide you don't want it, I will stay in Chicago with you. I would choose you over anything."

"Can I think about it for a while?" she softly asked.

"As long as you want." He heard possibility from her question. "I am here for the rest of the week and then we go back to Chicago. After that, I have the movie and maybe when I am done, you will have an answer for me."

Again Q came to mind. She would jump through flaming hoops to get a man to pay attention to her. Rose moved from Chicago to Dallas to be with K, but ended up back in the Midwest when it didn't work. They took chances, brave chances, to find happiness and love. Cat had never been in love before and still did not believe it was a realistic phenomenon. She had built a life in Chicago; she knew her city and felt at home in any neighborhood. If she decided to stay with what she knew, Danny would lose everything he had spent years working for. If she moved to Vegas she would need to buy a new street map, plot out the good and bad places, meet new people and basically hand her whole self over to a guy.

Or was he a man?

One thing was certain, she needed to take a test drive.

16435A

After weeks of debating, Cat decided to sell the Cavalier. Tears flowed as she carefully took dancing turtle stickers from the windows to save in her journal and removed the license plates. The lazy blue machine had been a durable companion since college and had seen her through some of what she believed were the hardest times in her life. Cat made the dealer who bought it promise to sell it to a good home where the people were nice and had available garage space in the winter and the sense to change the oil or rotate the tires every couple thousand miles. She had kept it in good shape and made a few bucks on the deal, but the sadness that accompanied her handing over the keys caused uncertainty in her decision altogether.

She was questioning all her decisions these days. Her miniscule job had been perfect and explaining her reason to leave to R—who had gotten back together with his wife—caused her to vomit in his trash can. Along with a job in the Las Vegas office, he promised there would always be an opening for her there if things didn't work out. They finished off a bottle of whiskey and officially retired her non-position at the agency. She promised to fax crossword puzzles daily—she *had* to do something to keep busy since she hated swimming pools and gambling. R assured her that Danny's job would make them plenty of money and she would be showered with luxuries if the casino owners were happy and selling tickets. By the time the movie was finished filming, he was going straight into three months of sold-out shows which would make any big shot pleased with his investment.

M and Jillie were excited about the move and immediately checked their calendar for a free weekend to visit. Not a single question popped up about living arrangements or Danny's career taking them across the country, the subject was all about a vacation. Cat had hoped one of the two would be curious about her reasons for following him or if a new job was in her future. Of course, M was positive Caesars would comp them as they were guests of Danny Doyle, the main attraction. Neither asked if this was a step in the right direction for her future or if she planned on marrying the man now referred to as Cat's better half. As always with M, it was all about her and how the subject at hand would affect *her*. Her only child was leaving the Midwest and all she could talk about was free hotel rooms and the days that were open to travel.

The gang at Justin's had mixed emotions. J, of course, was against the entire idea. Mick thought it would allow him more time in the brownstone, which Cat was leaving in Rose's capable hands. K would be moving in with her and keeping everything in working order with the understanding that they were out the minute she returned. *If* she returned. The overall reaction was surprise and disbelief. After M's conversation, she was overjoyed to be asked if she would start a career or do volunteer work or teach at UNLV—something she hadn't even considered. Would she be leaving most of her things here? How long was Danny's contract for? When is he going to be on TV again? What is his movie about? Is it really with Little Timmy from school? Did you read the script? Is it funny? Are you sure you know what you are doing?

The uncertainty ended when she took a little test.

Luckily, she had two months to slam the door on the life she had built before the private jet would be taking her and Driver to their new home in a spectacular city where time didn't matter and every day was a celebration. Danny filled their days apart with flowers and cards and gifts—she got something from him every single day. She was moving to a town filled with tourists and the people who served the tourists. Cat had no idea where she would fit in with her already odd lifestyle of insomnia, ABBA, drinking, Aaron Spelling and crossword puzzles. If she got there and was miserable, she would have the jet to bring her right home the minute she decided that life on the strip was not a page in her book. She wished there was a psychic in her neighborhood to offer spiritual guidance or present a suggestion from her crystal ball about the final verdict she had to make, based solely on love. This time, however, all she had was Rose, the girl who would happily follow K to the ends of the earth without a dime or plan. To Rose, Cat didn't need to think twice: she *was* going and she should be prepared for the time of her life. Falling in love with Danny was the best thing to happen to Cat and Rose was certain he would forever be at her side.

Cat didn't believe in love or forever, so she flipped a coin.

Tails.

She was going.

She had thought their suite at the hotel was over-the-top until she got on the private jet. It didn't have seats or rows or crying babies or even another passenger. The interior was white leather with gold accents and had seats for maybe six or seven high rollers. There was a dining table for four and televisions built into the walls. A woman dressed in a Chanel suit greeted her and asked if she needed help with the birdcage. Cat said she didn't and took a seat at the window, Driver on the floor in front of her. Another woman came from behind her carrying a silver platter with a glass of champagne.

"You don't have anything stronger, do you?"

"Whatever you like, ma'am," she replied.

"Then I'd like a lot of whiskey." Cat explained, "I don't like flying and I will do or take anything to make this ordeal end quickly. No offense to you. I'm sure you like to take off and land and watch the skies zoom by, but I don't."

"Don't worry, Ms. Doyle—"

"Wait a minute, Ms. Doyle?" Did she get married and forget?

"Yes, you are a guest of Mr. Doyle. I just assumed, I'm sorry." The woman looked as if she had just said the words that would end her career.

"I'm Cat. That's it. Just call me Cat."

"If you watch the screen," the champagne woman said, "there is a special video on all of the attractions and things to do while you are in Las Vegas. Will you be staying long?"

"I'm kind of moving there." She took the crystal glass of whiskey from her and swallowed in one gulp. The stewardess was in awe. "Danny—err, Mr. Doyle has a huge job and refused to take it unless I moved there with him."

"He would have turned down his job for you?" she questioned while refilling Cat's glass. "He is the biggest name on the strip right now."

"Yea, that's what he said and I believe him."

"He's a really great guy. He's flown with us a few times and always leaves us in stitches." They were trying to talk her through the flight like the flight attendants had done on the last trip. "Then you must be the girl he met with his mother."

"Does everyone know that story?" She laughed. "I really should see his show to know how much of my life has turned into his comedy bits."

"Well, the last time he was on the plane, he said that the minute he saw you, he knew you were the one." She took a seat across the aisle. "Do you mind if I sit down?"

"Sit away."

A couple more glasses of whiskey later and the plane had landed. Instead of looking for her luggage, she went right to the arrivals gate, where Danny was standing with flowers. He ran over and swung her around in a hug.

"What are you doing here? I thought you had a show tonight." She checked to see if Driver was damaged from the spin.

"I do, but it doesn't start until nine." They walked hand in hand toward the waiting limo. "All your stuff got here. Shipping it was a good idea. You're filled with good ideas. What do you want to do tonight? Want to see my competition? How about a magic show? Maybe do a little gambling? The world is your oyster and Vegas has it all."

"I'd kind of like to go to bed early. I think I drank too much on the plane and I've hardly eaten a thing and I think I am going to be sick."

"Drank too much? You? I've never seen that." He was concerned. "But if you want to go back to the hotel, get in your jammies and snuggle all night, that would be fine with me."

"I don't think I'll be doing much snuggling."

Before they reached the hotel, Cat had thrown up twice in the limo's ice bucket. She was sweaty and clammy and Danny was worried she had alcohol poisoning or eaten something that was making her ill. From his cell phone, he called the hotel to have chicken noodle soup and a grilled cheese sandwich along with Alka-Seltzer and Gatorade sent to their suite.

Greeted by most of the staff, Danny gave a little wave to all as he carried Driver's cage through the lobby to their private elevator. She ran for the bathroom and continued to throw up. After each hurl, she would lie on the cold tile floor and pray silently for death. Danny brought in a pillow and blanket.

"I'm calling the hotel doctor." He stood next to her. "You never get sick from drinking. Did you eat *anything*—anything at all? What did they serve on the plane?"

"Nothing, I'm fine." She sat up. "I just went overboard to

cope with my adventures in the sky. The girls on the plane knew you and I got the idea one of them was planning to steal you away from me."

"That will *never* happen." He looked at his watch. "The show starts in twenty minutes, but I don't want to leave you alone when you're this sick."

"Go to the show, Danny." She took her blanket and pillow and nestled in the tub. "By the time you get back I'll be feeling better."

"Are you going to take a nap in the bathtub?" He smiled. "You are one unique, eccentric and peculiar person, Kitten, and that's why I love you and want to marry you."

"Marry me? Was that a proposal? I have vomit all over me and you decide this is a good time to propose?" She laughed. "This has got to be another joke for your show."

"I'm serious, Cat. Let's do it tonight, after the show." He pulled a ring box out of his pocket and held it in front of her. "Will you marry me?"

"You mean it, don't you?" Inside the box, she found a huge pink diamond—tear drop cut—on an antique setting. She was speechless. She was nauseous.

"I picked out the stone, but the setting was my great grandmother's and then my grandmother's and finally my mom's, and now it is yours." He slipped it on her finger. "I love you, Cat, no matter how much you smell or puke. I love that you paint birdhouses and jump in elevators and bait a hook and eat hot wings without messing up your face. I love that you make up crossword puzzles and read all those old books that are printed in French and how your feet are always cold. I love you sleeping in a tub, worrying I may find someone else and especially because you are funny."

"Dans, fuck, you really just dropped a bomb on me." She didn't know what to say. "If I wear this, does that mean we are engaged or is it a promise ring?"

"Call it whatever you want, but I am serious about getting

married." He looked down. "You don't have to accept it. I didn't realize the temerity of the question."

"Temerity? Have you been using my dictionary again?" He smiled. "Yes, it is a huge decision that I will probably be up for, but I need a little time. I just got here and need to settle in, you know, find my place. Maybe stop puking."

"Oh, totally! I agree." He had gotten a positive response. "We'll just get comfortable for the time being and then we'll talk about it again. Is there anything I can get you? Anything at all?"

"A gun. I want to kill myself—I will never drink again."

"Now you're just being silly." Maryanne stood at the door. "Hey there, will you keep an eye on her while I'm gone?

"Yes, sir." She was timid, but Danny's mammoth size scared off more than a few people. "And Mr. P is waiting at the elevator to take you down. Perhaps if she is feeling better, she could come down and sit backstage."

"Nope, this little lady does not leave the suite until I come back." He kissed Cat's hand and admired the ring. "I think I did pretty well today."

Danny ran to the elevator and was gone.

Slowly, Cat walked around the suite. She went to the second floor for the first time to find a full kitchen with a cook who leaned against the oven. She greeted him, but heard nothing in return. More bedrooms and bathrooms and a game room with pinball machines and a projection screen television. Did they need all this room? Of course, M was planning on visiting and keeping her out of sight would be easier if she had a room the furthest from the master bedroom. Cat was now used to and enjoyed the lack of interest her mother had for her. If and when M visited, Cat would go out of her way to steer clear of her in the city she now hung a shingle.

Feeling better, she started to get dressed and thought about seeing Danny's show.

"Maryanne, would you come with me to watch the show?

No one knows me and I doubt that anyone will let me backstage."

"My job is to keep you in the suite, but if you *want* to go, *you'll* go." She smiled, but never looked Cat in the eyes. "I will take you and we will watch it together. That way Danny can see I didn't leave you alone. Are you sure you feel better?"

"Maybe I need a couple drinks. What's that they say about the hair of a dog that bit you? Let me wash up quick. And you need to get out of that uniform. Why don't you pull out the new pantsuit my friend gave me—it'll look perfect on you."

Quickly, she washed her face and brushed her teeth. More importantly, she took a couple hits, closed the baggie and put it in her bra along with a pen cap. Maryanne was good at picking out clothes and left out a pair of Seven jeans, peasant shirt, and a long knit scarf that when used as a belt, the ends would hang near her knees. She tossed on her flowered Doc Marten's and the two were off.

Getting backstage was easy—everyone had met her or seen her photo—and opened the doors without hesitation. Chairs were placed in the wing and Danny was only a few feet away doing what he did best. The crowd was cheering and laughing with every word that came from his mouth. He glanced off-stage and saw Cat watching him with a smile.

"Folks, can I have a couple seconds to greet my personal guests?" He ran backstage and hugged Cat. "You're here! You came!"

"I always said I knew my life would end up in your act. Feel free to borrow anything from my funky history."

"I love you." He kissed her and went back on stage.

"Mr. Doyle really cares for you. He wants only the best," Maryanne noted." But can I warn you about something?"

"Herpes?"

"No," she laughed. "The performers in Vegas are often plagued by fans who go a little too far. I have heard that

Danny likes to sign autographs and pose for photos, but he has groupies. They come every night and wear the skimpiest clothes and always wait to talk to Danny."

"Girls? Trying to hook up with Danny? *My* Danny?"

"Some are persistent." She pointed at a gorgeous blond in a sequined tank top drinking a martini; her eyes followed his pacing and she was just plain enamored. "That one is trouble and I *know* you *know* who I am talking about."

Wanting to see her first official meet-and-greet, Cat and Maryanne waited for the crowd to thin until all that was left was the blonde. Maryanne tugged to take her back upstairs as not to start a fight, but she stayed to check out her competition and get the real score. He kissed her hand and she whispered something in his ear.

"Danny," she had to jump in; she had to keep him to herself. "The show was great. Who is this, one of the gals from the sound booth?"

"Who are *you*? You don't talk that way to people like me," The buxom blonde growled.

"I'm Cat. You know, the *girlfriend*, partner, wife— everything."

"Cat, this is not what it looks like." He did not leave the blonde's side. "She was just inviting me to a party tonight. Ask her."

Maryanne tugged her again and this time, they actually did leave the stage area. Maryanne ran up to the room and Cat sat at the bar closest to the theater.

"Can I get you something, Cat?" Asked the bartender.

"How did you know my name?" This wasn't Justin's where she had a reputation; here in the desert no one should know who she was.

"We were briefed on you. All Danny's guests are to be treated in a specific manner." He poured a glass and put it on the poker machine built into the bar. "Your official drink, Ms. Moran—Bushmills."

"Thanks." She swallowed and looked at the bartender. "What time does Danny usually come through here to get upstairs?"

"He already did. Now you can find him in the VIP room, but you *might* not want to go in there. Things are orgy-like tonight. I think I saw Joe Walsh go in, if you want to meet him."

"I'll take my chances," she said. "But if I see something I don't like, I will come straight to this seat with a cup filled with quarters to play some games. What's your name?"

"It's B, and you can find me here every third shift if you ever need something to drink or someone to talk to."

Cat smiled and walked to the curtained off VIP room. She was not stopped at the door—they all knew who she was. It was a dimly lit room with bottles of champagne, full bar and late-night snacks. Lounging on a velvet sofa was Danny having a good laugh next to the blonde. They were holding hands.

She walked over to the couch and spoke." "Danny? Am I interrupting?"

"Oh shit, Cat, let me explain."

Moments later, she had cashed in a hundred dollars in quarters for the bar's poker game. B greeted her and started mixing a blended drink. When he put the icy glass on the table, he shook his head.

"I knew that was coming."

"Is he sleeping with her? Are they serious?"

"According to V, the bartender in the lounge, she is usually trying to get his attention and has not succeeded. They end up talking most nights. He was here for so long before you came; he was probably lonely. "He pushed the drink closer to her and explained. "This is a special treat of my own. A couple of these and you will forget about Danny, who, by the way, is heading right for us."

"Shit, what do I say?" She took a sip and turned to Danny.

"I'm talking to B right now. Do you know he only works 3rd shift?"

"Cat, that woman and I are nothing more than friends."

"So, she is a buddy, like Tim? You don't hold hands with Tim or do you? And silly little me, I thought I was the one you would be spending the night with. Welcome to Vegas—meet my groupie. You know, maybe *she* will marry you."

That's right; there was a ring on her hand that she took off and handed to him. She waved goodbye to B, grabbed her cup of quarters and ignored Danny's shouts of her name. She went to their elevator and up to the suite. Before she could take off a shoe, she began to vomit the booze in the bathroom. The elevator doors closed and Danny was yelling her name until he found her on the bathroom floor crying.

"Get away from me. I'm in town for an hour and you already have a lady friend who can be allowed to put her hands all over you."

"She's just got a crush on me, that's all. She's a student at The Second City here."

"So you're leading her on or you maybe are leading *me* on. I'm not so great after all." She stood up and began to fill a bag with toiletries and called the front desk.

"Yes, I need a room for the night." Danny motioned for her to put the phone down. "Yes, I know I am calling from Mr. Doyle's suite, but I need a regular room for a regular person for the night. Yes, I am sure. Danny is going to have a woman over and, call me crazy, I expect they were planning on fucking in the master bedroom. OK, thank you. I'll be right down to get the key card. You could do that for me?"

"Do you honestly believe I would sleep with someone else?" he pleaded when she pulled a few things from the dresser and into a bag. I would never cheat on you."

"You already did. I shouldn't have come here to be with you while you are cheating on me. You confide in her when it should be me! You share jokes and laughs and stories that should be shared with me. And don't think people don't talk around here. The word around the hotel is that every night after your show, you and the blonde go to the VIP lounge. I'm not sleeping here so that you can have your privacy. Go ahead, get your gal and canoodle in what was going to be *our* bed, but don't come crying to me when you discover she wants nothing more than celebrity status."

"Cat, hear me out."

The elevator doors opened and she got inside.

"One last thing—I'm pregnant."

The doors shut and she stepped out on the 14th floor. Waiting for her was a bellboy who was sent to make sure that she knew if anything was needed it would always available and to call the front desk at any time.

She needed Danny.

Hours later, there was a pounding on the door. She looked through the peephole and saw Danny's face. He was nervous. Cat opened the door and he entered.

"We're having a baby?"

"Unfortunately we are." She was stubborn and went back to watching TV. I may consider coming back up to the suite if you promise to stop leading women on and answer one question."

"I never touched her."

"Holding hands is touching and that wasn't even my question. Buh-bye."

Heavy thoughts weighed her down as she changed from her pajamas to the outfit she had on earlier. She went to the first face that was nice to her, B. He greeted her and poured her a drink.

"I've got a cup full of quarters, so I may be here all night."

"Then you'll have me as your company." A waitress came over with an order. "E, have you met Cat Moran? Cat, this is E. E is going to school during the day and working the late shift so she can see her kids more often."

"That's me, all right." E, dressed in a skimpy toga, smiled and held out her hand and shook Cat's.

"What are you studying?"

"English. I want to be an English teacher. I'm going to trade in this flimsy cocktail dress and work a real job with regular people." She smiled.

"If you ever need help with that, I'm an English professor back in Chicago."

"Thanks, I might take you up on that. I'm having a devil of a time with Chaucer."

"Who doesn't?" The two laughed. "I mean it, I would love to help you."

"Thank you, really." She garnished her drinks. "I may take you up on that."

"Where'd that ring go that you were wearing earlier?" B asked Cat, while filling E's drink order. "It was gorgeous."

"It was an engagement ring. I gave it back to him."

She sat and played video poker until her quarters ran out.

"I suck at this. See you tomorrow, B." She waved.

Instinctively, she went to their elevator and then had to go to the regular people elevators. Sitting on the floor next to her door was Danny. She helped him up.

"Where have you been? I was worried you had left. I know that what I did was wrong and I'm never going to do that with anyone but you." He shrugged to speak. "I've never had such good-looking ladies pay attention to me, and I guess I got carried away."

"You *guess*? The only thing you *guessed* was that that I would never find out. I only heard about the one, but the floor is buzzing about your arm candy, Miss Blondie Blonde, and you, night after night—even the bartender knows your story— laughing into the wee hours. Heck, there's some more crap for your show. Once again, my bad luck will fill the crowd with laughter. I'm done with you, please leave."

"I make one mistake—"

"OK, that means I can make a mistake! Does that mean I can go off and screw someone else so we'll be even? Will we be even Danny?"

"No, I don't want anyone else touching you."

"Then at least have the decency to stop whatever it is that you were *not* doing when I get into town. You made a fool out of me." Cat was full of anger and jealousy and nothing would stop her rant. "Do you know how hard this was for me to move here? I gave up a great bullshit job, I left my beautiful home—I gave up my life just so waitresses in toga's can giggle and point at me, the loser, who made the mistake of following, not leading. I'm going back home and will start dating J within minutes. At least he owns up to his infidelities. This isn't going to go. And why did you go to the bar knowing full well that I was sick and needed to be with you to feel better? At this point, you're like gum that sticks to your shoe and you can't get it off without ruining the shoe."

"You can't leave. Promise me that you will come back upstairs. Right now. I'll get your things." He tossed everything into her bag and she ignored him and sat on the bed. "We have to work this out. I'm going to be a dad! That is awesome news."

"It's still early and I don't want people to know. It feels like something is wrong and judging by tonight's episode, there's a lot that is wrong."

Without further thought and unable to fight, Cat followed Danny to the elevators and finally their suite. She immediately fell onto the bed in the master bedroom and got under the covers. She knew something was wrong with the pregnancy. She never should have told him. She should have just gotten it taken care of in Chicago so something like this wouldn't be looming over every decision the two would make. He had claimed they were destined to be together before, but now without a doubt, they were going to have a relationship for life because of a tiny pill that fell down the drain.

The only cars in Vegas were taxi's that were always zooming people from one casino to the next. They knew their way around and didn't hesitate for a moment. Those yellow cars that had little yellow brains.

At that moment, Cat didn't have a life purpose or a yellow anything.

No life; no purpose.

Why bother asking for directions at all?

Rose,

Yo! Sorry it's been such a long time since my last letter—I actually prefer the telephone but since you don't have one, I must resort to this. May I ask why there is no working phone in my home? If you need some cash, let me know—no questions.

Yes, I am still with Danny and I am pregnant, but it feels all wrong. Not just the baby thing, but the Vegas thing and the marriage thing and the living in a hotel thing and the me thing.

I hate me!

Danny wants to get married—wait until you see this ring. And Danny really wants this baby and I don't know if I can go through with it. I never wanted one and now I don't have a choice. I wish I had never told Danny so I could have just erased the whole concept without him knowing. You have to admit, it was a pretty funny way to tell him—very dramatic. We were fighting and just as the elevator doors closed I shouted it out and they shut. I can just imagine the look on his face—do you think he was worried about us breaking up or happy that we were going to have a little family?

As if.

And the groupies—I hate them. You know how you and I hang out after concerts to meet the guys in the band? We never pushed this hard and these girls throw themselves at Danny's feet. They all want him to autograph their boobs and some ask him if he can tell if they are real or fake—anything for a fan. And they are so much prettier than me and they are thin and tan and have beautiful hair and all I am right now is bloated with split ends. If I were him, I would probably cheat, but let's hope Danny isn't like me. Or you.

How's work? Got me anything good lately? I'm running low on Chanel face wash.

How's the man? Are you guys working and living and laughing and still in love? If you're in love, tell me what it's like. I don't think it ever happened to me—the closest I've come to love is Danny (in person and not in old letters from Tim), but out here, everything is different. Everything is the opposite of home. Skanky girls are the ones people want. You sleep all day and are awake all night. Money means nothing. All that is important is selling tickets and keeping the bosses happy.

But I'm not happy.

Sorry I'm so down.

It just doesn't feel right.

I need to talk to you.

Please get the phone turned back on.

Can you get a couple days of work off? I could send the plane to get you.

Let me know.

Cat

17912C

People who work in the automobile industry have their own language—just like Vegas folk. This lingo spoken at repair shops is used as a weapon to intimidate the gal who thought she just needed an oil change. The poor girl knew what she wanted done before she arrived, but was talked into a new filter, brake pads, wheel alignment and a custom-detailing job. The advertised price for an oil change was $19.99, but the clever mechanic mystified the naive woman with potentially harmful non-issues and created a list of things that needed fixing; he said he was worried about her safety on the road. Believing his concern, she agreed to the parts he deemed necessary and after the work was done, she left the station. With her mind at ease, she had happily gambled away hundreds of dollars on useless and unneeded extras to "keep her safe" on the streets. But fuck, he was on commission and she should have known better than to go into his world without backup or a translator. She would never catch him in the tampon aisle or bothering with the penny slots.

Her loss. His gain.

Danny had left town to do something with the movie. Alone at last, she had the opportunity to check out the shows

190

and showgirls. She finally had a few free nights and saw an Eagles concert, checked out Danny's main competition, Danny Gans, grooved to a mind-blowing group of female impersonators that reminded her of her birthday party way back when, hopped on a few roller coasters and took in a few of the many magic acts.

One magician stood out in the crowd.

For the past four nights, Cat had been sitting in on his show, searching for a flaw or an idea of how each trick was being done. His final trick was being held upside down in a straightjacket and then submerged into a water-filled tank that was locked. No matter how many times she saw his act, she held her breath to see how long she could make it without air. He rarely spoke, had no rabbits in a hat or doves flying from his sleeves. He wore a pinstriped suit and took off his jacket before the straitjacket trick and did the rest of the show with his white shirtsleeves folded up to prove he wasn't pulling anything out of his sleeves. After being amazed and filled with questions, Cat went to his meet-and-greet to see if he would teach her a trick or two.

He came from backstage and into the souvenir shop, where fans were getting autographs and taking pictures—the same things Danny did after his show. But T looked around the store filled with magic wands and decks of cards and spotted Cat in the back, waiting her turn. Their eyes locked while he continued to sign autographs and walk in her direction.

"Catrin," T said with a smile. "I was wondering when I was going to have the pleasure of meeting you."

"You know me?" Vegas players were like the FBI and knew every tidbit of information and gossip that was available. "I guess you must have noticed that I have a slight crush on you."

"As I do you." He pulled a rose out from behind her head and handed it to her with a shy smile. "Slight of hand. Would you like to have a drink or maybe some coffee? I've got plenty of things to choose from in my dressing room. Follow me."

He was in his fifties and to no surprise Cat was falling for his charm. He led her by the hand and they entered through the house, took some stairs to get onstage and then a right at the water tank to his secret room. Behind a screen, he changed into dry clothes—another dark suit, same shoes, same tie and same adorable smile.

"I hear Danny is off making a movie. That must be exciting for him." He poured two glasses of champagne and sat down waiting for her to answer.

"Exciting for him, right." She rolled her eyes. "I'm just happy to have some free time to do all the things I haven't done yet. There are so many shows—"

"Tell me why you always come to mine." His eyes sparkled.

"Like I said, I have a huge crush on you and can't sleep nights knowing you are trapped in a tank of water without air." Was she flirting?

"*I* make *you* lose sleep? That's an honor." Was he flirting back? "Listen, Cat, everyone is talking about Danny's groupie problem—"

"We got that all straightened out. It was a misunderstanding and Danny is really devoted to me." She tried to believe what she was saying. "What's this I hear about your casino wanting a new comedian? I love the gift baskets, and the Bentley was fun, but why Danny?"

"Because he's the best in town. Do you have any idea the amount of money the casino makes every night from him? And wouldn't you like living here instead of that old Palace?"

"Has anyone made him an offer?"

"I think they are just courting him at the moment." He poured more champagne into her glass. "Aren't you afraid of his weight and substance abuse? It's not healthy for him or you."

Cat's cell phone started to vibrate in her purse.

"I have to take this. Excuse me." She stood up and walked by the door with her back to T. "Hello? Yea, it's me. What's wrong? *Arrested*? I thought you were in LA doing a re-shoot. Obviously you lied if you got arrested in Mexico. Mad? What is there to be mad about? I'll call the grand master and have him get you out. What were you doing in Mexico? OK. I'll talk to you later. Bye"

"Trouble?"

"Yea, I'm sorry. I have to go." She kissed his cheek. "Danny seems to have gotten arrested in Mexico and I need to figure out who can get him out."

"The general manager of the hotel will handle everything. Just call him and Danny will be back in no time." He smiled. "Will I see you at the show tomorrow?"

"Plan on it."

Danny had been missing for three days. This might have worried some people, but Cat was used to his disappearing act, believing he was working on things for the movie or possibly off reading a new script or on the road doing a show here or there. No matter what he said or did, Cat loved him and accepted his faults. No guy was ever completely faithful—the lesbians taught her years before and she still believed and accepted it. Danny was a hit in town and everyone wanted a piece. Along the way, he hosted *Saturday Night Live* where he and Tim recharged their dead battery of friendship. He was often a guest on *The Tonight Show* and made the talk show circuit. His popularity was as big as his growing stature and nothing was going to slow him down and no one was going to suggest a change in weight, booze and drugs. All of his vices, however, were done away from the very pregnant Cat who had been trying to get his blood pressure tested and to start a diet.

And now he was in a Mexican jail.

T was right and the head guy of the hotel had Danny released and driving home within hours. They assured Cat that it was a misunderstanding and drugs had been planted on him, not to mention he was trying to get a new car over the border, which was supposedly illegal. But Danny, the drugs and car were on their way back to the Palace and she would hear his side of the story shortly.

"Cat? Are you awake?" Danny got off the elevator.

"Yea, I just got back from a show." She hugged him. "Are you OK? What were you doing in Mexico? Why were you taking a car from Mexico?"

"Come with me, you're going to love this." He took her by the hand into the elevator, down through the lobby and out the main entrance. Parked in the limo lane was a yellow Volkswagen Beetle, an old one. "I got it for you. I know how much you like them and this is the style from the seventies and that's what I was doing in Mexico."

"You got me a car?" She was in love with the thought and the car. "You got arrested to get me a car?"

"Yea, they still make them in the old way down there and I wanted to surprise you."

"It's a surprise all right." She walked over to the bright car and hugged Danny after looking inside at the dashboard and seats. "It's stick. I don't know how to drive a stick shift."

"Then I'll teach you. So, do you like it?"

"I love it." He swung her around in the air.

"What's the story about the drugs?" Cat wondered.

"Nothing important. They got it all figured out and it was a mistake. It'll probably be in the papers, but there were no charges pressed. Wait! I forgot the best part!" He waved over the valet who was holding license plates. Danny took them and showed them to Cat. They were vanity plates that said "KITTEN."

"You named my car Kitten?" She was surprised at the thought he had put into this adventure. "This is too much!"

The car was parked in the employee lot and they went back to the suite. Danny was looking through her scrapbook and gazing at all her ticket stubs from the attractions she had been visiting while he was gone.

"You did all these things?" He held up the four tickets from T's show. "You liked this one enough to see it four times?"

"Yea, I love it." She finished washing her face and dried it with a towel. "I *even* got to go backstage tonight and talk to T for a while. I was trying to find out how he does those things, but he wouldn't say."

"You were in his dressing room?" Was Danny jealous? "Did he try anything with you? Did he try to kiss you or make any moves?"

"No. Not at all. We just talked about slight of hand." She rethought. "And about how his place is trying to buy out your contract here. That's why they gave you the Bentley. Did you know they wanted you?"

"I've thought about it, but they already have a main show, *him*. I would be second fiddle there and here I'm at the top." Danny kept reading all the stubs. "Did you do anything else with a man while I was gone?"

"I had dinner with Siegfried and Roy and played with their tigers. Do they count?"

"Seriously." He saw the Eagles ticket. "Did you hang out with the Eagles after the show? Did you go to their after party at the MGM?"

"Actually, I *did*. I talked to Glen Frey about his volunteer work and Joe Walsh is a funny guy. He has got some stories to tell and you cannot shut him up. Did you know he's been sober for a million years? It was easy hanging with him since I can't drink or smoke now."

"How are you doing with that?" He went over to her and put his ear to her belly. "Hey there, little guy, how're you doing? Has Mama been good since Daddy was gone? How far along are you?"

"Like five months. No one has noticed because I've been wearing big clothes." She was sure the Vegas FBI knew about it. "Did you know that everyone here knows *everything* about *everyone*? Do you know any secrets?"

"Sure, when we talk backstage you hear all the gossip." He was getting his clothes on for his late show. "The tech crew guys from all the shows hang out and talk to each other and then the juicy news is spread among the rest of us. Like that magician friend of yours, T? He's supposedly into guys."

"I didn't get that impression." She felt a pain in her abdomen. "That hurt."

"What is it?" He pulled on a T-shirt and ran to her side. "Are you OK?"

"Just moving around, I guess." She was lying. She hadn't felt a movement in days and knew something was very wrong, but she didn't have the guts to tell Danny who was already buying baby clothes and diapers and toys. She also neglected to mention she skipped her last three doctor visits. "Nothing to worry about. Get to your show, it's almost eleven and the fans will be chanting your name if you are a minute late."

"OK, one thing before I go." He looked at her. "Did you see Carrot Top while I was gone? *Anything* but Carrot Top."

"Not a chance."

He kissed her and ran off to the elevator. Cat went to the bed and sat down. After a few moments, she yelled for Maryanne. She came running.

"What is it?"

"I think I need to go to the hospital."

"Should we call Danny? We should get him before he goes on stage."

"No, I'm going to call a friend to meet us there. Can you just call downstairs and have a car waiting for us? You're coming with me."

Cat picked up the phone and called T's dressing room. Surprisingly, he answered.

"Hello?"

"T, hi, uh, this is Cat."

"Catrin, darling, what can I do for you?"

"Can you tell me which is the best hospital out here? I need to go and don't want to take any chances."

"The hospital? What happened?"

"It's too much to explain now. Just tell me one that has quality doctors and privacy."

"Does this have to do with your baby?"

"How the fuck did you know that?" She was pissed that the secret got out. "Yes, there is something wrong and I think I am in trouble."

"Valley Hospital has a neonatal intensive care unit. I'll meet you there."

He hung up.

Cat went down to find Maryanne waiting with a limo. Both got inside and sat down.

"Is it the baby?" Maryanne knew, but still asked.

"Could we go to Valley Hospital? They have a special neonatal unit."

"Of course, of course." She told the driver where to go and put her arms around Cat. "I *knew* there was something wrong. I knew days ago—maybe weeks. I just had a feeling it was something bad. I *should* have done something. I *should* have said something."

"How am I supposed to know what it should feel like? I've never had a baby before." Cat was crying. "I know it's dead. Nothing has moved in days. What did I do wrong?"

"Nothing." Cat was crying on her shoulder. "Sometimes it's just not the right time for these things to happen. It's god's way of telling you that you need more time. I don't know—I can't tell you why these things happen."

Both were crying when they reached the emergency room doors. T was there, wearing his pinstripe suit, worry filling his sweet face.

"What is it? Do we know anything?" he asked Maryanne.

"We just got here," she whispered. "But it doesn't look good."

Cat was brought into a room and a fetal monitor was placed on her stomach. Just as they all had guessed, there was no heartbeat. The baby was dead. They put her in a private room where Maryanne and T sat at her side.

"What's wrong with me? I can't even have a baby?" She was crying. "*Everyone* can have a baby—people do it all the time!"

"Oh, Cat," T held her hand. "I wish I knew what to say."

"Could you pull a flower out of my ear?" She smiled.

He did.

"Danny's show should be ending soon," Maryanne noted. "Skipper will tell him where we are. He'll come right over."

"This will kill him." Cat knew he would be a mess.

Danny had wanted the whole marriage and family in the suburbs life from day one. She did too, but like everyone was telling her, this just wasn't the *right* time. Cat found it funny that she helped other people have a baby and now she couldn't have one of her own. Did she really *want* to be pregnant? She had never really thought about the changes a child would make in her life and just accepted it as a fact. Wolf and his wife had sent photos of Mrs. W and her big belly and it made Cat happy to know she had done something good. If she did good things most of the time, then why did bad things always happen? Why was her karma so out of whack?

"Mr. T, you might want to leave before Danny arrives," Maryanne said softly.

Easier said than done. Just as T was getting up to leave, Danny came rushing in, screaming Cat's name and kneeling at her bedside. He buried his head in her blankets and cried. T tried to silently leave the room, but Danny caught him.

"What are you doing here?"

"Cat called and asked for the name of a good hospital," he explained calmly. "I put two and two together and knew you would be doing your show and came to make sure she was treated right."

"Thank you." He hugged him.

"We'll talk later, Cat." T waved and left.

"What happened? What's wrong with the baby?" Danny needed to be told, but Cat couldn't say a word. She looked to Maryanne.

"The baby is dead, Danny." He looked at her. "They think the umbilical cord wrapped around its neck and suffocated it. There was no way Cat would have known and there was nothing she could do."

"What now?" He held Cat's hand and stroked her hair.

"Now Cat has to deliver the baby. They are going to induce labor and she is going to give birth to a stillborn baby. It is a horrible tragedy, but the doctor said this happens to a lot of first time mothers."

"Cat, say something." Danny looked at her.

"Something." She barely smiled. "Danny, I am so sorry."

"It's not your fault," he hugged her. "It's *my* fault for not being around. Let's just finish out my contract here and go back to Chicago. You need to be with your friends and family."

"I *am* with my friends and family." She smiled at Maryanne and Danny.

The next day Cat delivered a baby girl. They decided to name her Maryanne and she was buried in a cemetery outside of Las Vegas. Betty and Rose flew out to offer support and every name on the strip was at the semi-private funeral. Cat was showered with offers of help in the upcoming days and hope for a bright future. Even though she chose not to see the baby, she knew little Maryanne had Danny's big cheeks and her green eyes. And she knew she would have had driven the boys crazy and would have had a great sense of humor.

Everything was a blur. Cat's map of the strip was fuzzy, and no matter how many eye-drops she used or aspirins she took, the road ahead of her covered the windshield with rain and hail and twisters of sand.

And the defroster didn't work.

Rose,

Yoooo! I'm kind of buzzed right now—Danny and I are going to get married tonight!

He's out entertaining clients and I am going to see "the magician" and hang out until he comes home. Then we are going to get a marriage license and go to one of those cheesy Elvis chapels and finally do it!

I think I know now what it is to be in love. When I look at him, I see the future, my future, his future, our future. And for some reason, today I told him I would finally do it!

Is it right for me to have feelings for someone else? Is that wrong?

I wish you could be here, but I'm sure we'll come home and have a big reception or something. I'll make sure they video tape the whole thing so you can watch me, the never-getting-married-girl, get married.

I'm mailing this tonight on my way to the magic show. Maybe I'll grab the man and plant a kiss on him—it is my last night of ever having a chance with anyone except Danny for the rest of my life.

Make sure you tell the gang—J will wet his pants!

I've got to go—I'm wearing the new Marc Jacobs line you sent with some Coach heels—I look hot and maybe he won't be able to keep his hands off of me—is thinking that wrong?

One last night!

Cat

189522E

Learning to drive is the high point in the life of every teenager. The first time they unlock the door and adjust the seat makes any new driver feel like a king on his throne. All of the basics like turn signals, headlights and mirror adjustments are thoroughly explained by the drivers ed teacher, but only a few key points are remembered at first. More often than not, you are taught to drive on an automatic, but Cat had to figure out stick shift.

First they had to find a parking lot or vacant street to practice on. T lived in a gated community with lots of empty streets so Danny decided that would be a good place to start. She wished she could do more than turn the key. Cat couldn't change gears without grinding something or killing the engine. Every time the car died, she started to cry; believing she would never be the master of her own new car; her new piece of freedom.

"Don't worry," Danny was trying to calm her nerves; her hands shaking made her driving worse. "It takes time to figure this out. All we have to do is keep trying."

"I'll get it. I know I will. How hard can it be?" She wiped away her tears. "Let's go back now. You've got to put on a show for those dudes in an hour."

Whales filled the suite as they had paid (or been given) an all-access pass to Danny for the next twelve hours. There were about ten men in shiny suits smoking cigars, enjoying the pinball machines, watching some sport from Japan they found on the satellite television system and ordering Maryanne and Skipper around. Danny was going to be their private tour guide for the day and party with them after the show that night. The only thing Cat knew was that there would be strippers and hookers involved. Would Danny be caught up in the lap dances or the undressing of the lovely ladies who were sent for their pleasure?

She couldn't think about that. She was too busy trying to get around her house filled with these men. All pretended to be polite and each either kissed her hand or cheek when introduced. She helped Maryanne distribute bottles of beer and encouraged them to sit down and play poker while Danny was getting ready. She would even play with them.

"I can't deal," she said giggling. "So, you guys are going to show Danny a good time, right? Just remember you're all married men, but if you forget that little fact, use a condom. Some of the girls get around."

The men laughed and dealt the cards.

"Where did Danny find you?"

"You're a little corker." The chubby one asked.

"Chicago. We've been together since his days at Second City." She smiled and arranged her cards. "He keeps asking me to get married, but you know how it is, I like my freedom."

"The rock you're wearing, that's an engagement ring?" They all looked at her hand.

"Yes, I think it's eight carats, but I *know* it's a pink diamond. Place your bets."

The game went around and around for an hour and Cat won every hand and about five thousand dollars as they were playing with cash.

"Sorry guys, but I live here. Knowing how to play is a

prerequisite." She stood up and was glad she let Danny teach her Texas Hold 'Em. "Who needs a drink? Anyone? OK, I'm going to check on your entertainment for the evening."

Maryanne brought more drinks and Cat went into the bedroom where Danny was fighting with his tie. He looked so handsome in a suit and she remembered why she fell in love with him as he splashed on his Canoe cologne.

"You're not gonna get a lap dance, are you?"

"I will try not to, but I have to do what these guys want. The hotel *needs* them to have a good time, so they will invest to build a new hotel down the street." He kissed her. "I'm not going to kiss or sleep with anyone. My pants are staying on and I will try to not touch breasts."

"Just don't cheat on me."

"Never. What are you doing tonight?" He was sweating.

"I'm going to see T's show. He's got some new trick he wants me to see." She was excited to spend time with T. She still had a crush on the magician. "Then we might try driving my car again."

"Are you going to kiss him?" He smiled.

"*Kiss* him? Are you kidding? I won't be touching any bare flesh." She knew Danny was nervous. "You're going to show them how great you are and keep them laughing and get them to invest. If you want, I won't go to the show. I can stay here and worry all night that you are cheating on your little lady who can't have a baby."

"Cat, we *can* and *will* have a baby when the time is right."

"I have an idea. How about when you get home tonight, we go get a marriage license and go to one of the little chapels and get hitched?"

"Are you serious?" He sat on the bed next to her. "You finally want to do it?"

"I want to keep you and be with you forever." She kissed him. "They're open twenty-four hours so whenever you get back, we can go. Just call my cell when you're home and I'll be back in a flash."

"You're not kidding, are you?"

"*I'm* not the comedian." He kissed her. "I just beat the crap out of those guys playing poker. They've got money to drop and they're not to good at poker, be careful."

"I will."

They went downstairs and Danny greeted the men. They all shook hands and laughed and Danny was given a cigar.

"One more thing, boys," Cat got their attention. "Danny and I are going to be getting married tonight when he gets home, so you better show him a good time. This will be the last night he will be a free man."

Finally the group left and the castaways were left alone.

"They are pigs," Maryanne noted. "I'm sorry, but all they are going to do tonight is get some hookers and go to strip clubs. It disgusts me."

"I'm going to change before T's show. He has got a new trick."

Cat excitedly put on a fresh dress from the Marc Jacobs show Rose had worked a month earlier. She washed her face and primped for T—she still had that crush on him and really loved hanging out with him, which was cool with Danny. Ever since he had been at the hospital with Cat that night, T had earned a prominent place in Danny's book. Danny liked knowing where she was when he was working and felt safe knowing they were together. And Danny still believed him to be gay.

T requested that Cat sit in the house near the front of the stage and wear her hair in a ponytail—it was for the new trick. She was going to be his assistant from the audience that he claimed to have never met before.

When the time came, T asked the audience for a volunteer, someone with a ponytail. Cat raised her hand and was picked. She pretended not to know the way to the stairs to get on stage and then joined him in the spotlight.

"Hi there, what's your name?" He played.

"Cat. Like the animal, you know?" She giggled.

"Where are you from, Cat?" He had started playing with her long ponytail.

"Chicago." A few cheered from the audience.

"Thank you for being so brave and joining me up here." He pulled a pair of scissors from his pocket, held her hair and cut it off at the rubber band. He held her ponytail in front of her and she felt her head to see if it was real. "Does this belong to you?"

"Uh, it did. You better know how to fix it." She didn't have to fake a frightened state.

He waved the hair around and did his slight of hand and presto: her hair was back on her head in the ponytail. He was a genius.

"A round of applause for our guest from Chicago!"

She waved as she went back down to her seat at the table. Everyone around her was touching her hair to see how he did it. He probably had no idea, but she was honestly freaked out when he handed her the hair—she had always had long hair and to suddenly loose her security blanket would have been a nightmare.

"You are so lucky you know what you are doing!" She laughed in his dressing room after the show. She was drinking vodka and cola and could not stop running her fingers through her hair, which was now down. "How *do* you *do* this shit?"

"Slight of hand."

"Slight of hand, my ass." They sat next to each other on the couch with their feet on the table. "You know, tonight may be your last chance."

"Last chance at what?"

"Last chance at me." He looked at her. "Danny and I are going to the Little White Wedding Chapel when he gets back tonight. So that means if you ever want anything to happen between us, it has to be tonight."

"You know how to put a man on the spot, don't you?" He kissed her quickly and sat up. "Why don't we start with some strip poker?"

"Danny is the one who taught me how to play and I'll kick your ass." She moved to a chair across the table from him. "Do you *want* to be naked first?"

"I'll take my chances." He smiled. "Do you think getting married is going to stop this tension between us? He thinks I'm gay and lets you have sleepovers at my house when he is on the road. This just makes our tension a little more fashionable."

"I *do* like the tension." She took a drink.

"So where is Prince Charming tonight?" He dealt the cards.

"Entertaining, I told you. They want to build a new casino and hired Danny to show investors around town. Just try and tell me he's not getting jerked off by a hooker."

"I love your dress. Are you ready to take it off?"

"Nope, your pants first."

They played a few rounds and both were in their underwear; Cat had on a slip and he wore boxers. The stage manager came in and sat in for a few rounds. After losing too much, he left.

"OK, truce." He put down the cards. "Come over here and kiss me."

"I feel guilty, but I don't because I know they are all getting their rocks off, especially now that they know Danny and I are getting married when they are done with him."

"Why don't *we* get married?" He gazed as she slipped back into her dress.

"You and me?" Where was this going?

"*Yes*, you and me." She sat on the couch next to him. "We are *practically* best friends and have everything in common and the only thing we haven't done together is have sex. I think we'd make a great married couple."

"What is your definition of a married couple?"

"Waking up next to you every morning, cooking you breakfast, teaching you how to drive that car of yours, maybe having a couple kids and then growing old together in this wonderful desert that brought us together."

"*Magic* brought us together," she reminded him. "Do you want me to believe you think magic is more powerful than comedy?"

"Comedians come and go." He kissed her cheek. "But magicians never loose their tricks."

They kissed on the couch and T began to unzip the dress she had just put on. She stopped him and pulled herself together.

"You've got tricks?" Cat smiled and kissed him. "Like with a magic wand or are you going to marry me in a straight jacket?"

"That's good! You're funnier than he is." They stopped and looked at each other.

"Yes, I make good press releases." She looked into his eyes and felt guilty. "I think we should get back to the cards. Unless you can use your slight of hand to produce a diamond ring I won't take you seriously."

"A diamond ring?" He smiled as she sat back on the over-stuffed chair. "Is that all?"

"Yup."

He put his right hand behind her left ear and came out with a casino chip. She laughed and tossed it on the table with her cards.

"There's a lot of stuff back there—give me a minute. Have a drink."

Again his hand went behind her left ear and instead of handing her another trick flower, he softly pulled her face to his for a kiss.

"Come on," she stopped him with her words, but she wanted more. "You're stalling."

"OK, one more try."

From behind her ear came a beautiful princess cut diamond ring.

"How did you—"

"Slight of hand. Loss of heart." He smiled and held it in front of her. "Will you?"

"Ohmigod, did you plan this?"

"Months ago. When he was sleeping with that groupie I thought about it."

"He never *slept* with her. He told me he never even kissed her."

"The boys in the union accidentally saw them making out his dressing room."

"*I've* never been in his dressing room." She looked at the ring in his hand.

Her cell phone began to buzz. Cat jumped up and hit the button.

"Hello? You're back already? It's four o'clock? Man, I had no idea it was getting that late. No. I'm at the theater. We're playing cards. No, when I told him about the driving today, I started to cry and I didn't want to get all red and blotchy from another horrible attempt at driving. Are you OK? You sound funny. Yea, T says hello. OK, I'll come back and change and we can do the deed. You still want to? Are you sure? T says if *you* don't, then *he* will. Yea, he asked me to marry him and I want to. But you are totally lucky. I'm on my way. I'm just going to finish this hand. I love you, too. Bye."

"He's back?"

"Yea, but he sounds really strange. Like on acid or something fucked up," she explained. "You don't think those investor guys would be into acid or x, would they?"

"It wouldn't surprise me. X is everywhere." He put down the ring. "You have a choice here, Cat."

"I know and I am totally shocked." She was bewildered. "He lied to me and I've never done anything but give you a kiss or two and now something that I fantasized about is in front of me in a double mirror."

"If he did take something, they won't let you get a license." T drew her to him again for a kiss that went longer than it should have. Minutes later, they stopped and stared at one other. "I don't think you're getting married tonight, but it *is* my last chance."

"You make a great argument." She kissed him again. "I'll see you tomorrow."

"Take this with you. *Think* about it. Think about me, about *us*."

Cat left through the employee exit and grabbed a taxi to take her to Danny. It felt like years as she walked through the lobby, waving at the various employees. The valet guys asked her how the driving lessons were going and a girl at the front desk said she had seen Danny's group leave about twenty minutes earlier. She stopped at the gift shop and bought a dozen postcards and stamps to announce the news of her wedding to the gang back home. She skipped past the public elevators, smiling at the waiting patrons and finally made her way to their private elevator. So much had happened that week and suddenly there were piles of questions to mull over.

"Danny? I'm back!" Skipper and Maryanne had gone to sleep hours earlier and Cat took off her shoes and walked up the stairs to the bedroom. "Are you in here? I have the most perfect dress to wear tonight. Remember when Rose did the Vivienne Tam show and sent me that cream dress with the flowers? I think it's just right."

He didn't answer. As she walked toward the bathroom, she saw him lying on the floor. His tie was loosened and there were lipstick stains on his white shirt, but he was lifeless— probably wiped out from the long day.

"Danny? Are you asleep?" She knelt down and nudged him. He did not move. She put her ear on his chest to listen for a heartbeat; there was none. She started screaming,

"Maryanne! Maryanne! Somebody get in here! I need help!"

Skipper was on the phone calling for the paramedics while Cat and Maryanne did CPR. He was gone, but they would not stop trying.

"Why did this happen?" She began looking around the bathroom and found a couple little white pills. It was ecstasy and he had apparently overdosed. She instinctively hid the pills and any other drug paraphernalia that was lying about while still screaming, and finally began to cry. "How could it be that I was on the phone with him not ten minutes ago and now this happens? Maryanne! What am I going to do? Why weren't you watching him? Why weren't you awake? Why wasn't I here?"

Maryanne held her tight and rocked her until the doctors arrived and pronounced him dead at the scene. Cat was inconsolable and nothing could be done this time. It wasn't something he could sleep off or get over with a bloody Mary in the morning. This was final. Her wedding plans were destroyed and now she must pull into the gas station for help with a problem she never imagined she would have to face again, funeral arrangements.

The medical examiner took his body to the morgue to determine a cause of death and slowly they began to gather details regarding the wake and funeral. Cat's hands shook as she picked up the phone and before she could call Danny's mom, she called T.

"You have to come over."

"Cat, what is it?" He was half asleep. "Are you all right?"

"Danny's dead."

"Oh my god, I'll be right there."

Minutes later, T was at her side on the bed holding her.

"I've got to call his mom. What am I going to say? I can't tell someone something like this? I can't tell her that he overdosed and fell dead seconds after I talked to him. I can't tell *anyone* this. I just can't. I don't even believe it myself."

"I will." T took the phone and Cat dialed Betty. "Hello, Betty? This is T and I am sitting with Catrin right now. She doesn't have the strength to speak at the moment. Danny has had an accident and I am sorry to have to tell you this, but he died this evening. Yes, I'm sure. Cat found him. Yes. Yes. Sure, hold on."

He gave the phone to Cat who was sobbing. "Betty? It's true. I would never play a joke like this. We were going to get married tonight and I just found him lying on the bathroom floor. I don't know for sure, but he was out all night with some investors and must have gotten into something over his head. No, I had just talked to him. They are going to run some tests to see what it was, I'm sure. Yes, I'll have the jet sent to Midway. OK. Bye."

"OK, that was done. Who else?" He asked warmly, stroking her hair.

"Rose. Tell Rose to go to Midway and find the Palace jet."

"No problem." He gave her a kiss.

She dialed the number and handed him the phone. She could hear a rumble of people downstairs. All of the hotel's bigwig's were gathered and discussing how to handle the press and the months of already sold-out shows. Wanting to know their plans, Cat went down and joined them. Each tried to console her, but were unable as she had taken her mind and placed it in a jar to be opened after the money mongers left. Eventually, the suite was empty and she was lying on the bed. T was still stroking her hair.

"You can cry now, they're gone," T said.

"So is Danny." She was suddenly filled with anger. "How could he be so stupid?"

"He didn't do it on purpose—he never wanted to hurt you. He didn't mean for this to happen." He lay down beside her and held her in a spoon. "This is the last thing he would ever have wanted to happen in the world. All he wanted was you. Everything he did was for you."

"I wish I was with him." She got up and pulled the pills from her make-up case. "Here they are. Why don't we just take them and see what they do? These were next to him. I'm going to take both."

"Stop that!" He fought for the pills in her hand and threw them in the toilet before flushing. "Get back in bed and cool down. You're talking crazy."

The hotel doctor came and gave her a shot to "help her rest" and she fell asleep in T's arms.

Not only was there no more map, but the compass had been broken as well.

There was no direction to take and no suggestions were offered.

She was lost in the middle of the neon universe.

Out in the woods
Or in the city
It's all the same to me
When I'm drivin' free, the world's my home
When I'm mobile

Going Mobile
—Pete Townsend

KITTEN

Cat jackknifed in Vegas for a few weeks following the memorial. Major players paid their respects to Cat and Betty whose engines were blown. Rose and Tim flew out and had the task of cleaning up the bottleneck Cat and Betty were stuck in as they continually reflected on the insane waste of a life. After the service, the body was shipped to Chicago for another wake and burial. Danny was laid to rest in his favorite jeans and button-up that he wore during the show, the mirror from Driver's cage, a casino chip and the bobber that lit up the night from their first date. None of the photographer flashes, spotlights or neon signs could define him—it was the little yellow bobber that would indefinitely identify his eternal flame; their night inspired by the Nitty Gritty Dirt Band.

The general manager of the hotel—although he would never publicly admit it—felt partially at fault for allowing Danny to slide into the embankment without better quality brake pads. He had known Danny was headed for a fender bender and partying harder as the days passed—the autopsy report was filled with cocaine, alcohol, Xanax and ecstasy—but did nothing to help. As long as Danny kept the seats packed and the waitresses busy night after night, he was satisfied—at any cost. Because of this, he gave the green light for Cat to remain in the suite with Maryanne and Skipper until she was ready to unlock the doors and hit the road for whatever life she would begin fresh.

It seemed that every member of the hotel staff had stopped on her one-way street and sought out Cat to pay respects. For Cat, their few words or hugs would never fill the pothole his death left in her heart, and in all honesty, hearing the same "I'm so sorry" over and over was getting old.

The crew from his show took the blow personally and some blamed Cat for not stepping into traffic and cleaning up his reckless driving—even though they were the ones supplying his dope and looking the other way when he did it. The finger-pointing stage manager did not know how persistent she had been in trying to get him to ride shotgun in her drug-free car. But as everyone knew, Danny was strong-willed and sneaky; if he wanted something, he got it. He had no problem quitting temporarily when she told him about the baby and promised to be sober to support her when she had to shake her lifestyle. But by then he was a functioning user able to hide any mind-altering substance. Many pondered the subject, but no one would ever know the truth.

Not even Cat.

The day before she planned to leave, Cat took a final lethargic stroll down the strip to personally say her good-byes to all the places she had grown to love and knew she would miss. She remembered the night Danny blew off his show to take her to a Wayne Newton concert at the Stardust. It was everything she expected an old-time Vegas show to be and Wayne was fantastic—seeing all the older ladies crammed into seats close to the stage in hopes of getting a wink from the one and only was a trip. As she reached Treasure Island, she was just in time to gaze in amazement as the pirate ship sank. For a year she had been trying to figure out how they managed to pull it off every hour, but her mind now thought of nothing but her brownstone and the chance of flurries. A quick stop at the

Mirage brought her up close and personal to a few tigers—
there are a couple of casinos that offer a lion view, but this was
her favorite. She wished she had time to enjoy another night of
Siegfried and Roy—she would even sit through the Monte
Carlo's magic act, Lance Burton, if she could stay just one
more night.

But she could not.

Excalibur seemed brighter and larger than ever and in New
York New York, she rode the roller coaster one final time and
made a quick stop at the oxygen bar. Following no route in
particular, she had a drink at each of the casinos and gathered
souvenir chips from all to add to her collection that Danny had
started when they first arrived. Farewell, Monte Carlo. Adios,
Mirage. Toodles, Flamingo. Bye-bye, Bally's. See you soon,
Sahara. Miss you already, MGM.

The final stop on her walk was her favorite casino, Circus
Circus. The sight of the neon clown in the distance brought a
smile to face and she momentarily forgot she had parked in a
tow-away zone. Cat played some carnival games and won a
handful of stuffed toys, had a couple of drinks on the spinning
merry-go-round bar and watched the bizarre circus acts
performing a few feet away. For the money, there was nothing
better than cocktails while watching trained housecats and
clowns parading around the family-friendly casino. She was
thrilled to catch each for one final bow.

Saying goodbye to her regular haunts was easier said than
done; she felt a sort of melancholy with each stop. Cat would
never find a place like this again; a town that thrived on
amnesia, quickie weddings, and good times is hard to find.
She also guessed she would never again live in a city filled
with people like her who survived on overnight shifts, costume
compliments, friendly faces and free booze. She wondered if
leaving was the right thing to do and toyed with the notion of
taking the job with R's local office to keep her new friends
within reach.

But, with every glance, came a memory of Danny. She saw him on street corners, in shops and lobbies everywhere in town.

Finally, Cat knew in her heart that a special farewell needed to be paid to her magician friend, T, the man who had sparked her interest enough to question her devotion to Danny. As soon as she entered the empty theater she was noticed by a member of the lighting crew and received a greeting.

"Well, if it isn't little Kitten!" he yelled.

"Is the magic man around?"

"Backstage—check his dressing room," he responded from above.

She knew the route all too well from her late night visits and the occasional daytime rehearsals she had been invited to view. Stage right, up the stairs, take a left at the straight jacket, down the hall covered with celebrity photos and presto, the dressing room. Cat knocked, but was hesitant to enter when he yelled to come in.

"Hey, there," she smiled at him and stayed by the door. "I was just making my rounds and couldn't leave without saying goodbye."

"Leaving? Back to Chicago?" He faced her and took her hands in his. She had his ring in her hand. "Don't give this back to me. You know you don't have to go. There are plenty of things for you to do here. If nothing else, I'm here and you'll miss me. I'll miss you. I know that for sure, but if you don't believe it for some reason, I'll say it again—I'll miss you."

"I'll miss you, too." She kissed his cheek. "And I will miss the dancing waters and the ability to have dinner with nutty people who keep pet tigers at their feet and the whales hitting on me and all the wedding chapels and pawn shops and the copper mines and the porn lit and every monkey I lost at blackjack tables in almost every casino on the strip. Did I use enough slang?"

"Perfect vocabulary." He kissed her lips softly. "If you're ever in Vegas, you know where to find me. I'll be waiting for you."

"You're fairly smart. I think you can find Chicago on a map and I am positive this joint will let you use the jet. It's one of the better planes I've been in around here."

He pulled a daisy from behind her ear.

"Slight of hand." He smiled. "I hid it when I kissed you."

"Slight of hand." She took the flower. "I'll miss that."

"What if we never see each other again?"

"I'll see you again." Cat kissed him and left.

Game over.

She had fallen for the magician months earlier and the two acknowledged a mutual attraction, but nothing had ever happened because Cat was true to Danny. In spite of his drug use, excessive drinking, overeating, over-reacting and insignificant infidelities, Cat still accepted him with open arms. There wasn't a foolish thing he did that she could not forgive—even the time spent with Ms. Blondie Blonde was trivial in the big picture. He was human and prone to mistakes—mistakes Cat blamed on herself for not being as involved with his life as he desired or deserved. She knew Danny needed positive feedback every night after every show or appearance and she wasn't the great cheerleader and grew tired of watching his show. All the applause and sold-out crowds and screaming fans didn't give him an ounce of the confidence he required. When Cat wasn't waiting backstage night after night, he found someone who was and that someone just happened to have a perfect body, beautiful blonde hair and the ability to muster adoration on a regular basis, never missing a beat.

She thought again about the magician and considered returning to his dressing room for an evening of forbidden passion. For just one night, she could have the man she had dreamed about on the nights Danny didn't return to the penthouse before dawn. Weeks of sleeping alone and not knowing Danny's whereabouts gave her the right to play the game on his terms, but she never did. Now, at this moment, on a silver platter, was the opportunity to fulfill her fantasies without the mess of strings attached or remorse for her actions that were fueled by desire. She was never described as a good girl back in Chicago, but in Las Vegas, those were the most common words people said when speaking of her. Sleeping with T would not be the "good girl" thing to do.

If they only knew.

She turned around and walked back through the casino to the stage and finally his dressing room. Instead of knocking, she walked in to find him polishing a black and white Doc Marten. No words were spoken as she knelt to his level and began to kiss him the way a man like him deserved to be kissed. Already dressed for the show, she pulled off his suit jacket and unbuttoned his white shirt, tugging it out of his pants and tossing it to the floor. He took her in his arms and carried her to the couch.

"I couldn't leave without—"He put his hand over her mouth. "No talking."

They were naked within minutes and every move made surpassed her imagination. She had been faithful and slept with no one since meeting Danny and this was turning out to be a satisfying decision that would forever be remembered on the pages of her journal—many pages would be filled with every detail of the magnificent sex that afternoon. She had forgotten what all the fuss was about and questioned herself for not doing this sooner. The magic man had moves designed for her pleasure and he didn't hold anything back or pull flowers from behind her ears. There was a knock on the dressing room door and a shout from the stage manager that the show was starting in ten minutes.

"Can't you skip a show?" Cat wanted to keep him to herself.

Susan Kathleen

"No, I'm not Danny." She looked down and he touched her chin. "I'm sorry, I didn't mean that."

He began to don his trademark suit and matching shoes. Cat also started the dressing process. It was not uncomfortable or awkward as they searched for items thrown about in their moments of lust. By the time the manager called for the five-minute countdown, both were presentable. Nothing more needed to be said. She kissed him one last time and left.

"Another drink, Cat?" W, the day bartender asked.

"Huh?" She was in dreamland. "Oh yea, I'll take another, if you don't mind."

"You must be thinking about something good—you're blushing."

"Thinking, yea, that's all it was."

Their minutes of lovemaking were nothing more than a daydream, but it felt authentic and wonderful. Maybe next time.

The open road begged for the trusty Beetle to begin their journey. Memories filled the car and they were all she cared to take from her year living the good life in Sin City. In reality, she packed all her make-up, a couple suitcases and a few miscellaneous items that she could fit in the tiny car. Everything else was loaded into the Bentley and driven to the Windy City by a casino employee. Although petite, the little yellow car held a lifetime of happy times, sadness, joy, honesty and love. She had finally found and actually believed in love and just as she trusted this emotion, it was stolen as easily as it had sprung into her life years ago. Love was a real thing and the beautiful Beetle was tangible proof it could be found in this messy world. No longer did she need a map or knowledge of the detour ahead; she took the turns as they came, obeyed speed limits and occasionally stopped for a roadside attraction.

Being clueless when reading a map, Cat thought the trip home would be around 1800 miles and take her through five or six states; she wasn't sure. She never trusted directions from

Map Quest and no single map could illustrate the full route from Nevada to Chicago. She plotted a rough draft, starting in Vegas and then hitting Utah, Colorado, Nebraska, Iowa and finally Illinois and her sweet home in Chicago.

"So that's the story." Cat looked up at Mick and drank from her pint glass. "You glad you heard it?"

"It's not what I expected." Mick was honest. "I'm sorry about your baby and Danny and all that other shit that went down."

"It's not for you to be sorry about. I'm the one who wakes up with the memories and I'm the one who carries the grief and I'm not sorry. I took chances. I lived." She smiled. "And I look pretty good for what it's worth."

"You look wonderful." He was astonished at her strength. "Never better."

She picked up her old Versace wallet and pulled out another fifty and laid it on the table.

"I've still got the wallet—it's my good luck charm. Oh, I do have that Bentley here. They had a Palace employee bring it here that's parked in my garage. It'll come in handy in the winter, I think. You are welcome to it in case you ever need to borrow a car to impress a chick." Cat stood up from the booth, put her shoes on and grabbed her book before kissing his forehead. "I'll see you around."

"You're not going to stay? Talk to the gang?"

"For a few minutes, I guess." She walked over to the table of friends and Mick returned to his place behind the bar. "Hey, guys. What's up?"

"We are all wondering where Danny is?" Q said. "Did you break up?"

"No, we didn't." Cat looked at the floor. "Danny died a couple of weeks ago. Don't any of you watch the news or read the papers?"

"Jesus, Cat, I am so sorry," J lied; happy Cat was back on the market. "That must have been terrible for you. How are you handling it? Do you have someone to talk to?"

"I've still got my bird and he's all I need. But thanks."

"Sit down with us for a while and have a drink." R offered a chair.

"Did you gain weight?" The always-bitchy Q got down and dirty.

"Yes, I was pregnant. Thanks for noticing." Cat was giving a quick outline of her life to people she didn't need to rely on anymore. "Not that long ago, I was pregnant and then I wasn't. Let's just say I've had a rough year. But I'm home now, me and Driver."

"Sit down, Cat." J pleaded. "Just have one drink."

"Are you kidding?" She looked at her watch. "It's almost time for Leno."

"Can I walk you home?" J asked.

She stopped and put her hand behind his ear and pulled out a casino chip that had Danny's smiling mug on it and handed it to him. "Slight of hand."

"You know magic now?" J asked.

"I know a lot of things. Thanks for the offer, Jackson, but I can walk myself. I'm pretty sure I still know the way."

Cat didn't feel their daggers bouncing off her back as she began the emotionally long walk toward the front door. A table of old friends was left in her wake and she did not care to or have the time to start a conversation. The only constant in her life at this point was her regular date with Jay Leno and that wasn't going to change tonight.

"I'll see you around," she waved as she left the bar.

CPSIA information can be obtained
at www.ICGtesting.com
Printed in the USA
LVHW091309310521
688947LV00003B/36